VASHTI HARDY

D0189819

WILDSPARK

A ghost machine adventure

SCHOLASTIC

Scholastic Children's Books
An imprint of Scholastic Ltd
Euston House, 24 Eversholt Street, London, NW1 1DB, UK
Registered office: Westfield Road, Southam, Warwickshire, CV47 0RA
SCHOLASTIC and associated logos are trademarks and/or
registered trademarks of Scholastic Inc.

First published in the UK by Scholastic Ltd, 2019

Text copyright © Vashti Hardy, 2019
Cover illustration by George Ermos
Map illustration by Jamie Gregory

The right of Vashti Hardy to be identified as
the author of this work has been asserted.

ISBN 978 1407 19155 3

A CIP catalogue record for this book
is available from the British Library.

Printed by CPI Group (UK) Ltd, Croydon, CR0 4YY
Papers used by Scholastic Children's Books are made
from wood grown in sustainable forests.

1 3 5 7 9 10 8 6 4 2

www.scholastic.co.uk

To *my mum*, Erica
– a belated birthday pressie!

The world of
WILDSPARK

Chapter 1

THE STRANGER

On the bright side of the valley, ten furrows from Lane End and some twenty furlongs from the village of North Owlcot, in a place where the great metal city of Medlock was just a dream, there was a small farm. The farmhouse was a time-worn cottage nestled in barley-swathed fields divided by drystone walls. Wayward geese busied themselves near the pond and sheep grazed around single-standing oak trees. Automaton farmers sowed seeds, while scarebots kept the crows at bay.

Prue watched from the upper field, her elbows perched on the back of a broken mechanimal plough horse, oily hands clasped together, as a speck of a figure wound his way up the lane. Even from this distance, Prue could see there was a smart uprightness to the stranger's walk unlike anyone she knew from the surrounding farms. As he neared, he paused and looked into the lower field where the automated potato digger ambled through the furrows, and Bess, one of the mechanimal dogs, patrolled, waiting to be called for evening herding. After a few moments, the stranger continued onwards and took the path towards the farm. When he turned, he looked up in Prue's direction. She ducked behind the mechanimal horse, which in retrospect was pointless because she was certain he'd already seen her.

A sudden ping, followed by the squeak of metal, drew Prue's attention to the ground in front of her.

"Darn it!" she said as the hoppity wrench sprang merrily down the hill. Barley whipped her calves as she chased after it, its little steel jaws bobbing up above the golden tops before disappearing again. "Come back here, you little metallic monster!" She dived and wrestled with it for a moment, as it battled to jump away. This particular hoppity wrench not only seemed to have a loose restrainer, but a faulty homing device; it should've been able to make its own way back to the tool shed, but she had often found it hopping its way down the lane towards North Owlcot. Francis had tried to fix it last year, but he said some things just didn't want to be fixed.

She breathed out heavily and clipped the loose restrainer back in. "There." It bobbed its legs for a few moments, then gave up trying. When she peered above the barley, the stranger was nearly at the farm doorstep. Prue hurried downhill, through the tracks towards the house, keeping out of sight by stooping low, the hoppity wrench clamped firmly under her arm. She slowed her pace as she approached, then, after another quick peek to make sure the stranger wasn't looking, she hurried behind the water butt which was beside the farmhouse, close to the door. There was a sharp knock. After a few moments the door creaked open.

"Hello," said Mrs Haywood, an edge of suspicion in her voice.

"Hello. My name is Charles Primrose, Craftsman Primrose," he said brightly.

"And how can I help you, sir? Are you looking for produce?" Mrs Haywood asked doubtfully.

"I hope you don't mind me arriving out of the blue, but I was in Staplefield and someone mentioned that you have an extremely proficient young mechanic." He looked down at a note in his hand. "By the name of Francis Haywood?"

Prue's stomach lurched at the sound of her brother's name. Mrs Haywood didn't answer.

"Do beg my pardon. I'm from the Imperial Personifate Guild of Medlock – I expect you've heard of the innovations in bringing ghosts back into the world of the living."

Prue's heart gave a little jump.

"Yes, we do have newspapers in the country."

"Of course."

There was another awkward pause.

Prue peered from behind the water butt. Craftsman Primrose had a friendly, youthful face, with hair that was floppy on top and neatly trimmed at the sides. He wore wire-rimmed spectacles and was dressed in practical, but well-cut, expensive cloth – a fitted jacket in earthy brown tweed and matching trousers. A watch chain looped from his waistcoat button to pocket. He looked exactly how Prue would imagine one of the city inventors to look. Craftsman Primrose's eyes flicked in Prue's direction and found hers. He gave a quick smile. The sun lit a flash of silver writing as he took a midnight-blue card from his pocket and held it towards Mrs Haywood.

"We're looking for apprentices at the Guild. Developments are happening all the time and we need the very best young minds to learn our craft and carry on the great work. We're searching far and wide; in fact, I'm looking for my own apprentice to take on."

"If things are moving fast that's a sure sign to slow down, don't you think?" said Mrs Haywood. "Just because you can do something, it doesn't always mean you should."

Prue huffed to herself.

Craftsman Primrose lowered the card. "Not keen on the personifate technology, Mrs…?"

"Haywood."

There was an awkward pause.

"Perhaps you'd like to keep this and think it through. It really is a wonderful opportunity for a young person: the chance of an apprenticeship with a craftsman at the very forefront of technology. There would be an initial trial period, of course; nothing is guaranteed."

Prue admired his polite persistence, but Mum was like an immoveable boulder when she wanted to be. It was where Dad said Prue got her determination from.

The man gestured out towards the farm. "The machines in the fields are quite fascinating, and very unusual for a remote farm like this, if you don't mind my saying – and I'm certain the engineer who made those," he glanced down at the note again, "Francis, would be very keen to find out more about my offer."

Hearing his name again sent Prue's mind into overdrive, the thoughts of what had happened closing in, the lights turning out in her head. She forced it away.

"I'm afraid there is no one here who would be interested."

Prue desperately wanted to jump out and say that she'd made the machines too, but it was as though she suddenly had her own restraining lock on.

"Oh, that is a shame," said Craftsman Primrose.

Mrs Haywood didn't answer him. Dad would maybe have invited him in at least.

"It's getting rather late. I'm looking for bed and board. Do you happen to have…?"

"I'm afraid we don't take in strangers."

"Perhaps you know of a local establishment?"

"There's an inn back in Staplefield."

"There's nowhere closer?"

"It's the nearest there is."

Apart from the bed and breakfast lodge in North Owlcot, Prue thought.

Craftsman Primrose put the card back in his pocket. "You really do have some impressive machinery on the farm. It would be a pity for young inventing talent to—"

"Good day to you, sir. I'm sorry I couldn't be of help."

Craftsman Primrose dipped his head respectfully, turned, and began walking back down the path. Mrs Haywood watched him until he was out of sight, then she exhaled a long breath. Prue pushed herself deeper into the shadows as her mum took a few steps outside of the doorway and turned in her direction, towards the west field.

"Proo-ue!" she called, in a sing-song voice. "Tea's on the table!" Then she sighed and said under her breath, "It's for the best."

There was the soft click of the latch closing and the waft of warm sourdough loaf. Prue counted to twenty, making sure her mum was well out of hearing range, then she ran down the path. Craftsman Primrose had already disappeared around the bend in the lane. Prue began jogging after him, but a flicker of silver caught her eye in the wall. She slowed to a stop, then pulled out the card and a rolled-up piece of paper that was beside it.

The card was a beautiful shade of midnight, embossed with a silver symbol: three interlaced arcs enclosed in a circle. She flipped it over – in silver print it stated:

Charles Primrose
Craftsman of the
Imperial Personifate Guild of Medlock
By appointment of the Sovereign Chancellery

Prue unrolled the note. In neat handwriting it

simply said: *I leave for Medlock tomorrow morning.*

Her heart thumped in her chest. It was understandable that her mum hadn't told the man; it had only been a year since Francis's illness. She sighed. Convincing her parents would be impossible – what was she thinking? And anyway, he'd been looking for Francis, not her. She threw the card and note into the weeds and stomped back towards the farm.

But after a furrow, she found herself running back, picking them up and stuffing them into the front of her patched dungarees.

Chapter 2

MECHANICART

At teatime, the card weighed heavily in Prue's pocket. "Did I see someone in the lane earlier?"

"Just a traveller," said Mrs Haywood, placing a jug on the table. She didn't make eye contact.

"They looked like they were dressed in city clothes."

Prue caught her dad throwing a quizzical glance at her mum before he sat down.

"Just someone from out of town passing through," she said.

Prue poured a glass of milk.

"How's that old mechanimal horse doing?" Mr Haywood asked.

Prue had forgotten all about it and had left it half-finished in the top field. If it rained that night, it would seize. "The moto-heart's broken. I've taken one from the scarebot that rusted up last year and just need to finish connecting it. I'll go up before it gets dark."

"Good thinking." Mr Haywood grinned. "That sort of creative recycling will keep the farm on track. Didn't I always tell you she would be smart! Now invent me a machine that makes the sun shine brighter than all the worldly jewels and grow me some sweet island plums, and I really will be in heaven."

Mum always said he had a smile and a twinkle in his big browns that could light up the darkest room, but Prue couldn't help but see the shadow of sadness in the edges that hadn't left this past year.

"One day," Prue said, but her mind wasn't on the farm, it was imagining what the Imperial Personifate Guild of Medlock was like; perhaps a great building similar to the mills of Batterthwaite, but grander, with important-looking inventors, modern whirring machinery, churning smoke, and mysterious sparks lighting up the sky at night.

Mrs Haywood took a pin and secured one of

Prue's wayward springs of hair, then sat down opposite. "I said tuck in, Dolly Daydream – you look like you were a thousand furrows away then." Mum's honey hair was always pinned so neatly, her blouses without a crease, even after a day working the field.

After tea, Prue took a chaos lamp and went up to the field, where she got to work connecting the new moto-heart in the mechanimal horse. The farm had been in Mrs Haywood's family for years. Mr Haywood had been travelling and researching new technology for his home island's farms when he'd met Mrs Haywood. He never went back. He said he'd found home.

But nothing felt like home any more. Not to Prue. Not without Francis.

Prue sat in the barley, took the card from her pocket and turned it over. Since the visit that afternoon, something had changed and her mind wouldn't be still.

What she'd read about had seemed like such a remote dream; that in Medlock they'd found a way to bring ghosts back, held inside animal-like machines. Yet there had been a craftsman on their very doorstep. She looked at the metal horse in front of her. "Imagine if you could talk?" she said. She knew from reports that the ghosts in Medlock had no memory, that there was no way to know who was who when they came into this world ... but she couldn't help but think: what if she could find a way? What would it mean to her parents, to bring Francis back? A band tightened around her heart. She missed him more than she'd ever thought possible. Surely Craftsman Primrose's visit was a sign.

The light was fading, and Prue quickly finished the last of the connectors, inserted an ion battery plate and shut the side panel. With a *whirr* and *clunk*, the mechanimal horse's metal legs shuddered. She pressed the homing button. It lifted a foreleg, took a step, then was off, heading back towards the storage shed for the night.

"Come on, Prue! I give up," he pleaded. "Where are you?"

She stubbornly ignored Francis's calls to surrender.

"It's so late now! Mum's going to be mad if we're much later for tea!"

He eventually stumbled across her in the storage shed, inside the belly of a half-made mechanimal horse.

"Prue, I can't believe you didn't submit. It's been two hours!" He helped her out. "Honestly, you can be an annoying lubberwort sometimes!" He was so agitated in his urgency to leave the shed, that he slipped and landed on broken glass – a chaos lamp Prue had dropped earlier; she'd honestly meant to clear it up. It cut deep into his cheek. It was entirely her fault, yet as Dad patched him up, Francis had told Mum that he was to blame, that it was his idea to play out late. Even when Prue tried to contradict him, he insisted.

But that was Francis; he always had her back.

Prue stood on the hilltop watching the silhouette of the mechanimal horse until it was safely inside the shed.

Then she looked back to the lane. And sighed.

*

That night Prue couldn't sleep. She went to the window and watched the stillness of the farm under the grey-blue spell of evening. The silver symbol on the front of the card glistened in her hand. She imagined the city of Medlock in the south and the mechanical ghosts roaming the streets there. It was natural for Mum to keep her daughter from going off to the city; she'd already lost one child. But if there was some way to bring Francis back, for all of them, shouldn't Prue grab it with both hands? Shouldn't she at least try to lift the cloud of gloom that had seeped into every inch of the farm? Craftsman Primrose was leaving in the morning – it wasn't as though she had time for a debate with her parents, which would undoubtedly end in a no anyway.

She picked up the frame bedside her bed which contained a photograph of Francis. Her brother's dense, coiled mane of hair, like her own, framed his infectious grin, just like Dad's, his hazel eyes like Mum's, dimples in his cheeks like Prue's. He was leaning against a mechanimal plough horse – they'd just finished adding a turbo to it that morning, then they'd raced it around the farm together for the afternoon and been told off by their parents for not getting the bales made like they were meant to. She put a finger to the scar on his cheek, too faint to see in the picture, but she knew it was there. He had been only one year older than her – the photograph had been taken just a few moon cycles before he became ill. That meant the age he was in the picture wasn't far off what she was now. The void inside of her tugged terribly.

Again, she looked out the window at the farm and imagined she was sitting with Francis under Haywood's Oak, the tree Granny Haywood had planted as a girl. In the quiet of night, everything seemed possible. It was like stepping out of time.

Somewhere, not far away, an owl hooed; she knew it was stupid, but it felt as though it was calling to her.

In less than a minute, Prue had put on her best shirt (the one with daisies on, which Francis had mended the pocket of), a woollen jumper and long dungarees, bundled her hair into a messy bun on the top of her head, and gathered a few other items on to her bed: comb, toothbrush, Dad's home-made rosin soap, underclothes, and her best mini-hand-tool set. She grabbed her bag and stuffed it all in, then remembered the sixpence under her pillow, which she put in her front pocket along with the photograph from the frame and the card. Then she crept downstairs and took the notepad from the dresser.

I'm going to the Imperial Personifate Guild. I

need to do this. Sorry. Please don't be angry or worry. I'll write.

She scribbled instructions for fitting the restrainer on the hoppity wrench, put the note on the breakfast table beside the butter dish, crammed some oat cakes, a chunk of bread and some apples into her bag and quietly stepped outside.

Moonlight caught the edges of the stone walls and mist clung to the fields. Trees cast dramatic silhouettes against the ashen sky, and the lane to Staplefield trailed between the valleys like a silver ribbon. Prue took a breath, pushed all the doubt down into the pit of her stomach, and started walking. The night air held the last breath of summer warmth – the seasons were shifting. Mum always said time flowed like a river and there's not a thing you can change about it, but Prue couldn't help but think: what if you swam against it? She walked swiftly down Lane End. Perhaps she should've taken a mechanimal horse, but she'd have had to leave it at North Owlcot and trust that from there it would make its way back to the farm, and it would've been far too noisy. Besides, she'd walked this lane many times and would easily be in Staplefield just after sunrise. She crossed the split in the road that led to North Owlcot, and hurried onwards.

Dawn was arriving in milky hues on the horizon by the time she reached the sign: *Staplefield fifty furrows to go*. Prue paused there; she was exhausted to the bone, but she brushed herself down, snatched up her pack and ran along the path. When she rounded the next corner, Staplefield was nestled into the hollow of the valley. One lane coming in and one going out, like connecting wires to a moto-heart. She jogged towards it.

Staplefield was a market town and was already bustling with street stalls. As she hurried between the stands, she tried not to think about Mum and Dad waking up and finding her note. Her stomach groaned at the smell of rye rolls and fruit buns as she passed the baker's stall, but there was no time for breakfast. She ran into Driffold Lane and knocked on the door of the Hawk's Head.

A red-faced man holding a broom opened the door.

"Excuse me. I'm looking for a Craftsman Charles Primrose."

"Ah, from Medlock, yes."

"Yes, I'm here to see him," Prue said eagerly. She took a breath; this was it.

"He left at daybreak."

"Daybreak?"

"Said he was catching a morning mechanicart to Batterthwaite in time for the Gigantrak."

"Batterthwaite?"

"I've got no time for you repeating what I say. Now on your way unless you're wanting lodgings." The man narrowed his eyes. "Wait, aren't you Rosamund and Fayard's girl from Haywood Farm?

"Yes, I'm just delivering a special order to Craftsman Primrose. When's the next cart to Batterthwaite?"

"On the hour dot, every hour dot, outside Flocking's Yard."

"Thank you!" Prue called over her shoulder.

As she reached Flocking's Yard it was almost on the hour. An old man sat with his feet up on the wheel of a mechanicart. It was a standard cart, much like you'd see pulled by a horse in times past, but with a metal automaton man attached to the front, about the height of a normal person plus a third again. He was dressed in steel plates made to look like formal clothes; a long coat, a bit like those worn by wealthy city people, and a metal top hat.

"How much to Batterthwaite?" Prue asked the old man.

"Sixpence."

Prue looked at the solitary silver sixpence in her hand. She had no idea it would be so much. "But I'm not exactly a full fare."

"You wouldn't be travelling alone if that were the case, and it looks like you're the only one; it won't be worth sending out a mechanicart with only one passenger if I take less. Sixpence, or on your way." The conductor waved his hand dismissively.

Prue approached him and pressed the sixpence begrudgingly into his palm.

"Busy this morning. There was a city man, wanting a mechanicart early – heading for the Gigantrak." The conductor shrugged. "Great gobbling hulk of metal if you ask me, don't see what the fuss is about. See, the real elegance is in these mechanicarts."

Prue glanced towards the clock tower. "Yes, but is it fast?"

"Why is everyone obsessed with speed these days? Things get there when they get there. On you hop, then."

Prue stepped into the enclosed cart while the conductor adjusted some settings on the automaton. Smoke started pouring out of its hat.

"All set for Batterthwaite," the conductor said. Prue coughed and shut the window.

With a jolt, the automaton started jogging out of Flocking's Yard, pulling the cart behind it. It turned left into the main street then out of the town on the lane south to Batterthwaite.

The mechanicart was hardly the cutting edge of technology and after an hour of bone-shaking bumps and knocks as it rattled along the road south, Prue had a feeling that she'd been well and truly rooked out of her sixpence. She was certain she could run faster. After another half an hour, they began heading up a steep hill and the mechanicart slowed to a walking pace. Prue leaned out of the window. The wind suddenly changed, and thick black smoke chugged into her face. She coughed and went to the other side. Mechanicarts usually had some basic reciprocal technology where the mechanism could register basic instruction – stop, go, that sort of thing. She opened the door, leaned out and called, "Speed up!"

"The mechanical cart requests you stay inside the vehicle."

She tutted. "Go faster!"

"The mechanical cart requests…"

Then, above the crunch of wheels grinding on gravel, a low deep horn came from the east. It was a proud noise that declared itself unapologetically across the land.

"Can't you go up a gear?" she called.

"Gear change activated."

There was a *whirr* and *clunk*. The legs moved faster for three seconds, then it slowed back down again. Prue huffed.

"Engage turbo!" she ordered, hoping it had a similar mechanism to the mechanimal farm dogs.

"The turbo drive is deactivated during inter-town leisure travel for your safety."

As the distant horn sounded once more, Prue couldn't help herself. She opened the door and climbed on to the step, then edged along the rim of the cart. Reaching out, she flipped back the main cavity door of the automaton's torso and peered across as best as she could. The internal mechanism was similar to the mechanimal horses. A restrainer had been fitted to save on fuel. She unclipped it then twisted two disconnected wires together. With a sudden grind and *whirr*, the legs of the automaton suddenly doubled in speed. "There, who's deactivated now!" she said.

They hurtled upwards and were soon at the brow of the hill where the ground levelled. A great town spread in the valley below – large brickwork buildings with orderly windows, mills with tall smoking chimneys, the dome of a town hall. To the east, an inconceivably large steam locomotive chugged great clouds, leaving a storm-grey streak melding into the air as far as the eye could see. It was the Gigantrak arriving in town. Right on schedule.

With a bolt to her chest, Prue realized that the gradient of the landscape had suddenly changed – they were pointing down at an alarming angle, with the turbo now in full motion. Wind rushed through her hair as her hands clutched the edges of the mechanicart with all her strength.

They zoomed down the path, her teeth rattling in her jaw. At this rate, there was no way she could risk climbing back in; all she could do was grip as tightly as she could. The Gigantrak was slowing as it approached Batterthwaite, but the mechanicart kept gaining speed and was out of control. Trees whizzed past as it reached the bridge that crossed the river to the north of the town. The mechanicart clanked and battered across the wooden planks.

Prue yelped and pressed her body against the side of the cart as they narrowly missed another cart travelling in the opposite direction.

As they neared the first buildings, Prue shouted to a group of people to get out of the way, but they were facing the other direction, unaware. She had to stop this thing before it rammed straight into them, but if she let go, she was bound to fall, and the cart would hit them anyway. Before she could act, there was a sudden jerk, and the cart took a turn where the main road into town intersected. It wobbled horribly and for a heart-stopping moment veered on to two wheels, so that Prue soared into the air, holding on for dear life with one hand. It crashed back to four wheels – a man carrying a bundle of fabric yelped and leapt out of the way, sending plumes of material into the air. She fumbled to open the flap again, but she was rattling around so much her eyes couldn't focus. She began yanking at anything she could as they bolted onwards.

Then she spotted a stack of hay beside a house. With all her strength she pitched back so that her weight pulled the cart to the right, then with a sudden pop and whoosh of air, the automaton's legs froze mid run, and the cart lurched into a spin, sending everything plummeting. Prue was thrown into the hay as the cart crashed beside her in a tumult of clattering metal.

She lay there for a moment, bumped and bruised but unbroken, looking sideways into the face of the automaton, smoke from the top of its crumpled metal hat wafting upwards.

"The turbo drive is deactivated on all mechanicarts for your safe—"

"Oh, shut up!" she said.

A crowd of people rushed towards her.

"Are you all right, Miss?"

After a moment, she pushed herself up and slowly brushed as much hay and dust from her dungarees as possible. "Must've been a faulty combustor." She coughed.

"You ought to have words with the owner. It could've killed you!"

"Honestly, I'm fine." Out of the corner of her eye, she became aware of something enormous casting a huge shadow. The Gigantrak locomotive had come to a standstill not far away.

"All aboard for Medlock!" someone called.

Chapter 3

GIGANTRAK

Prue retrieved her bag from the battered innards of the twisted mechanicart and ran towards the locomotive. The Gigantrak was an enormous metal hulk as tall as three houses, its great pipes, cylinders and panels were like a huge insect's exoskeleton. Steam poured from the frontal spout while mechanics busily checked wheels as high as an oak tree. Passengers were boarding midway on a metal stairway; perhaps she could blend in and pass along with one of the groups? She adapted her run to a nonchalant amble, trying to look invisible, but as she approached, her smoke-smudged face and dishevelled appearance after the crash drew stares from the crowd. She turned as if walking northwards, then did her best to tuck everything in and tame her hair, her dad's voice in her head telling her it was no use trying to fight those curls into place; they had a will of their own.

Her parents would have found her note and would probably have gone after her to North Owlcot by now, although she doubted they would go further than Batterthwaite; they had barely been beyond the farm since Francis … she pushed the thought away and swallowed. She had to get on the Gigantrak. When she got to Medlock, she would send another note to tell them she was all right, and that they shouldn't worry.

She saw a large family with five children joining the back of the line.

"Yes, I've got the tickets, you all concentrate on not getting lost!" said a man, who she presumed was the dad. He was brown-skinned with a round, smiley face like her own dad's, and the children's hair was deep brown with dense curls similar to hers – she might pass as one of them.

She slotted in behind them. The smallest turned

and looked at her for a moment, but when Prue made no eye contact, he started twisting in his sister's skirt again. It wasn't long before there were others behind her in the queue and she began to feel more invisible. The line was moving fast.

"All aboard, hurry along now, we depart in five minutes. Gigantrak is never late!" the conductor called. She had ink-black, shiny hair and a neat green uniform; her appearance matching the efficiency with which she was whizzing people onto the locomotive.

The family Prue was behind started up the metal steps.

"Tickets, please," the woman said, and with a practised snippety snip of her marking tool, she'd checked the man's tickets and was hurrying them inside. Prue tucked in tight so that the youngest was hidden and six children would look to be five.

Then, the young child suddenly yelled, "My boot!"

Prue had been trying so hard to keep close that she'd caught the child's boot with hers and it had been pulled off. She crouched and hurried to find it for him, but as the child had not been heard by the dad the first time, he exploded with tears, repeatedly sobbing, "My boot!"

All eyes were suddenly in their direction, including the conductor's.

"*She* did it!" the boy shouted, pointing at Prue.

Prue had found the boot and was holding it out to the dad, with pleading eyes. He frowned. But it was too late.

"Hey! There were five children on your ticket, you've got six there, sir."

"No, five it is, Madame, you can count them again."

"If you're trying to get away with—"

He began patting his children on the head and counting as though to illustrate the point. Prue was frozen, hemmed in by people on either side, her heart rushing like a rotavator.

The youngest had stopped crying. He was still pointing at Prue.

Everyone within ten deep of the queue stared. The conductor's lips tightened, and her eyes narrowed. She held out her hand to Prue. "Ticket, please."

"I … I lost it."

"No ticket, no ride." The conductor pulled Prue back to the steps.

"What's all the commotion about?" came a voice.

The conductor paused, and Prue looked up at the kind face of the man who had visited the farm and left the card: Craftsman Primrose. She took a swift deep breath; in that moment she knew what she had to do. "I'm Frances Haywood," she said to him.

Craftsman Primrose tilted his head, then his face broke into a smile. "This young lady is with me." He presented two tickets to the conductor.

"Seems mighty strange that she was trying to..." The conductor's eyes flicked to a pin which Primrose wore on his lapel. It was the same silver symbol as the card: three interlaced arcs enclosed in a circle. "Do pardon me, sir. I didn't realize."

With a congenial nod, Craftsman Primrose indicated to Prue to follow him on to the Gigantrak. "Come along, let's find our compartment; it says thirty-two on my ticket."

Prue tried to say thank you, but it was as though her jaw had seized. She'd just told the biggest lie of her life, and she could hear her mum's voice in her head telling her how dishonesty shows on your face, like a big smudge of oil. But was it really a lie if it was necessary to achieve something so important?

They hurried back through the locomotive, past booths bustling with excited passengers stowing luggage above and beneath their seats, until they reached a large compartment with plush fringed armchairs, patterned rugs, red velvet curtains and, to Prue's astonishment, a crystal chandelier.

"Here we are," Craftsman Primrose said. "Do take a seat."

Prue put her bag beneath one of the armchairs.

"I must admit you threw me for a moment there. I wasn't expecting a girl. I was told there was a talented *boy* on the farm called Francis Haywood, so I didn't realize."

"I'm afraid you must have been told incorrect information," Prue stammered, crossing her fingers by her side.

"Well, Frances, I'm so glad you decided to join me. Clever new apprentices are hard to come by. But you do seem to have attracted rather a lot of attention already."

"Oh, I'm so sorry about that."

Craftsman Primrose smiled. "There is one thing I do need to confirm before we proceed. Do your parents know you've left?"

Her cheeks burned. "Yes."

He tilted his head. "How old are you?"

"Twelve."

Craftsman Primrose frowned. "By Medlock law you are old enough to enroll without permission, but perhaps if you send them a note the moment we reach Medlock, they'll know you're quite safe and we can take it from there. How does that sound?"

She nodded. "Thank you."

A loud *clunk* reverberated around them. Prue clutched the sides of her chair.

"Did you know that the Gigantrak can get you to all the great cities of the country in just one day?"

"Really?" Prue said.

"Have you ever been on the Gigantrak before?"

Prue shook her head. She looked up at the curved iron ceiling and felt like she'd shrunk and been placed in the belly of metal giant. There was another great clunk, then a shudder. The crystal lights clinked, the table vibrated, the seat juddered, and everything outside began moving. They travelled slowly at first and then, with an abrupt pull that glued Prue back in her seat, they were propelled forwards like a stone from a catapult. A yelp escaped from Prue's mouth.

Craftsman Primrose laughed. "Don't worry, it soon smooths out."

After the initial rush, a calm settled inside and although the landscape was flashing past at an alarming rate, Prue felt as though she was suddenly enclosed within a serene bubble.

Craftsman Primrose leaned forward and held out his hand. "I believe proper introductions are in order. I'm Charles Primrose, craftsman by appointment of Master Hannah Woolstenbury of the Imperial Personifate Guild of Medlock."

It sounded so grand. Prue shook his hand, suddenly hoping her hand wasn't covered in grease from the mechanicart.

"And you, I already know, are Frances Haywood."

Prue nodded and bit the inside of her lip to contain the truth.

"I'm very pleased to meet you. To be honest, I was giving up hope of finding an apprentice, then I heard about your farm. Your mother seemed rather resistant. Does your being here leave them awfully short-handed on the farm? I could send a personifate to help, you see? Although strictly speaking, the personifates are owned by the Sovereign Chancellery of Medlock so they stay within the city, but I'm sure we could bend the rules just a little, between you and me."

"The farm pretty much runs itself and my parents are good enough with the machinery. They've just been through a lot in the last year." A rush of guilt hit Prue. Had she really left her parents? She knew they could manage the farm work – they did when she was at school – but she was their last child; she didn't want to cause them more pain.

But it would all be made better when she found a way to bring Francis back to them.

"I just had a feeling that I shouldn't go without leaving the card, so you at least had a choice. Tell me more about what you do on the farm – its machinery is the best I've seen north of Medlock."

"Really?" Her cheeks flushed with pride. "The farm has been in the family for years. Grandma Haywood was great at inventing machines to make the farm work easier and Mum built from there. My first working machine was the mechanimal sheep dog." Prue had to stop herself mentioning her brother; it seemed wrong to talk about these things when they had developed them together.

"Fascinating. I always say the best way to learn is by getting stuck in. You clearly have a natural talent."

A gentleman in the same green uniform as the conductor entered their carriage with a bronze trolley.

"You must be hungry," said Craftsman Primrose. "I ate a large breakfast, but I don't expect you've had time."

Prue was about to say she was fine with the apple and bread in her bag, then she saw the shiny pastries and buns and her stomach rumbled hungrily. Craftsman Primrose chose a variety for her and poured her a steaming cocoa.

They talked some more about the machines on the farm, and after she'd eaten, Craftsman Primrose gave her some notepaper to write to her parents as he settled to read the *Medlock News*. She wrote that she really was sorry for leaving without saying goodbye, but she had needed to see if she could take Francis's place at the Guild, and Craftsman Primrose had agreed. She just couldn't miss this opportunity, and she reassured them that she was quite safe. After she'd finished the note, she gave a quick glance to ensure he wasn't watching, swiftly signed her note "*Love from Prue*", then popped it in the envelope and sealed it. She sat back and watched the distant roving hills. Her eyes were heavy and with the smooth rush of the locomotive she was soon asleep.

She had no idea how long it had been when a gentle hand on her shoulder awoke her.

"Frances, look out of the window."

She opened her bleary eyes and was amazed to see buildings merging together in the distance – a great thrum with smoke rising from chimneys, and piercing spires, domes and rooftops, one on top of another as far as the eye could see. She stared in wonder.

Soon, they were part of it. The chandelier clinked and the silver cutlery on the table clattered with the vibration as they swiftly decelerated and within moments came to a stop.

"Welcome to Medlock," said Craftsman Primrose.

Chapter 4

MEDLOCK

As Prue stepped from the Gigantrak into the enormous station, she looked in awe at the expansive glass vaulted ceilings. Hundreds of people busied along the platform, and as Craftsman Primrose stepped forwards, she hurried behind for fear of losing him. The marbled walls and floor led to grand steps and a wide, arched exit, above which hung a huge clock. It was late afternoon.

Tingles ran the length of Prue's spine as they reached the top of the stairs and stepped into the heart of Medlock. Before them was a great square with buildings packing the perimeter: iron pipes trailed the walls like ivy, and amber lights pricked through the brickwork with figures busying behind. The peaks and points of the rooftops rose confidently into the sky, with great bridges crisscrossing between structures. Creation and invention were everywhere. She had never seen so many people in one place, but she suddenly realized there weren't only people – there were many animals too: dogs, cats, several foxes, and two owls who seemed to be racing above the square.

She did a double take as her attention was drawn by a golden spaniel and a fluffy grey cat close by; their mouths were moving, almost in a human-like way – they were having a conversation! Could it be that they were personifates?

She looked at Craftsman Primrose. "Are they...?"

He nodded and smiled.

She'd read about personifates, but she couldn't believe how convincingly life-like they appeared, yet shifted a little. Seeing them walk along the street and talk was extraordinary, like spotting a tree with pink leaves, or if the moon suddenly became square.

A rabbit hopped between their feet.

"Do excuse me," he said in a low voice.

Prue spun around to watch it leap away, but her muscles froze, and she gave a little gasp – a lynx prowled metres from her.

"Don't be alarmed," said Craftsman Primrose. "I do rather take it for granted living here, but personifates come in many forms for a variety of reasons. It's quite usual, nothing to worry about."

Prue couldn't help but take a quick step back.

"Good afternoon, Craftsman Primrose. Successful trip, I see," said the lynx personifate, looking Prue up and down. "There *is* talent to be found outside of the city after all."

"Indeed." Craftsman Primrose smiled.

The lynx dipped her head amiably and carried on through the crowd.

"They're voices are so … *human*. There's no hint of machine," Prue said, amazed.

"We've developed high-tech voice boxes which seem to replicate how they sounded in the first life."

Prue couldn't wait to learn more.

Craftsman Primrose looked up and called to several birds perched on a chaos lamp above. "Messenger, please!"

He put his arm out just in time for a kestrel to

land on it.

"Ah yes, perfect." He glanced at Prue. "Only personifates that can pass as wildlife are allowed to deliver messages outside of Medlock. They are restricted from interacting with any humans on their journeys to prevent any panic or unease. We don't want to frighten your parents, do we?" He smiled at Prue, who suddenly noticed that not only birds flew above, but there were some more unusual-looking creatures in the distance, including what appeared to be a flying hare – and a wolf with wings!

"Have you got the note you wrote to your parents?" he asked.

Prue held it out.

"Good. Tie it to the leather rope around her neck."

She carefully attached the rope to the kestrel, her hands suddenly shaky as she accidentally brushed its feathers. They felt so real.

Craftsman Primrose addressed the bird. "If you could deliver this to Mrs and Mr Haywood; you'll find them in a little farm in a valley just north of a village called North Owlcot, which is north of Staplefield, which is north of Batterthwaite. Thank you for your service." Craftsman Primrose dipped his head respectfully.

"Of course, Craftsman Primrose," said the kestrel in what sounded entirely like the voice of an old woman. The kestrel took flight and swiftly disappeared from sight.

"Is everything all right, Frances?"

She realized her mouth was wide open. "It's just I didn't expect them to be quite so real; I imagined them to be more machine-like. Perhaps upgraded versions of what we have on the farm."

"More like the automatons and mechanimals? Technology has come on leaps and bounds in Medlock. All these creatures − well, apart from a few of the pigeons you see roosting above − are personifates, or ghost machines, if you like.

"They're incredible! Utterly lifelike."

Craftsman Primrose smiled proudly. "I'm delighted you think so, although it's best not to use the term 'lifelike'. Some personifates and first lifers can be rather sensitive to the word, you know, with the whole philosophy on what defines the term 'life'."

"Oh, sorry. And they're all … ghosts?"

"They certainly are − well, they were alive before,

as far as we can tell. We like to think of their current situation as something different – a second life."

"Oh, I see."

"It's very important to be respectful to them in the words we choose."

Prue took in the square: roads branched off all around and there were all manner of shops and grand-looking buildings: Acton Chaos Lamps, Bard's Precision Tailoring, Cogs & Co. In the centre of the square, rising above the people, was a sculpture. It looked to Prue like a huge mechanimal bee, great metal components whirring as a clockwork mechanism lifted and lowered the wings in a recurring pattern, as though the insect was captured in a perpetual moment of slow-motion flight.

"It's a symbol of Medlock as a hive of industrious invention," said Craftsman Primrose proudly.

"It's incredible."

Craftsman Primrose looked at his pocket watch. "Now, I'm afraid I have other business to attend to, so you'll be on your own for a while. You need to head to Deakins Entire on Smithy Door first for your uniform and supplies." He pointed across the square. "Keep along this side then cross at the sculpture. Take Burlington West and walk right to the end, then take a left into Pickwick and halfway along is Smithy Door. Have you got that?"

Prue nodded. "Statue, Burlington West, Pickwick, Smithy Door."

"Good. Here's a note for you to hand in from me."

Prue took the note, but panic was rising; she would soon be alone in this enormous city. Craftsman Primrose must have read her expression because he put a hand on Prue's shoulder and said, "Don't look so worried, Frances. The shopkeeper at Deakins will tell you the way to the Guild from there and I'll meet up with you later."

Hearing him call her Frances made her stomach twist, but she smiled and nodded. Craftsman Primrose turned and disappeared into the crowd.

Beneath her feet, metal cobbles mixed with stone. Prue watched the flurry of activity. Everyone was dressed so smartly: tailored jackets, straight trousers, big skirts, puffed shoulders, satin bows, patterned velvet, high collars, silk cravats pinned with jewelled brooches, tall hats, flat hats, nipped waists, shiny buttons and polished shoes. It made her head spin. She looked down at her patched-up dungarees. But like Francis had told her before her very first tree climb: *do one brave thing and the next one will be easier, and before you know it, you're climbing mountains.* He was right, of course, and she'd never looked back, scaling the highest oaks she could find in all of North Owlcot – being rather a nuisance to all manner of birds and squirrels. Now she was with the city people, and she had to act like a city girl: be confident and blend in.

Bells clanged in a distant street as she marched on through the crowd. She passed a store called Everade Easylife – Makers of Steam-Driven Pantry Appliances and paused for a moment to marvel at the strange contraptions in the window – there was some kind of self-mixing pudding bowl whirring and a belt circulating bubbling pots. She carried on towards the sculpture. *Cross at the statue, Burlington West, left into Pickwick then Smithy Door,* she repeated to herself. She hurried across the road past the sculpture and towards the other side. Opposite was a sign – *Burlington West.* She smiled; she could do this. Then a bell rang again, but this time it was loud and jarring. She frowned to herself. At that moment she realized she was the only person standing in the middle of the street. Glancing over her shoulder she saw a towering mechanical tram heading straight for her!

Suddenly, there was a cry, and her body was thrust forward. She tumbled on to the pavement on the other side. There was a rush of air and a loud clatter as the tram whizzed by, metal sparks nipping through the air. Prue lay stunned on the cobbles. Beside her was a girl, about her own age, with bright blonde hair and thick, dark eyebrows. The girl stood and brushed down her smart trousers and neat violet jacket. Prue felt too stunned to move.

The girl stared down at Prue with large, wide eyes. "Have you got a death wish? You'd be flatter than sheet metal if I hadn't just pushed you out of the way. Are you all right?"

Prue stared back, still trying to figure out what had happened.

"I said, are you all right?" the girl said more slowly.

"Err, I think I am."

A small crowd had gathered. "That was a close call!" said a young gentleman.

"Lucky the girl acted fast!" said a lady.

"Are you injured?" said a personifate goshawk, swooping to land beside Prue and peering into her face.

"I'm fine," said Prue quietly, trying to take in that she was now being addressed by a second lifer while lying on the ground. She sat upright and rubbed the side of her head. "Thank you," she said to the girl.

"You're welcome. But you might need to watch your step a bit more."

"Really, I'm fine," Prue said, hoping the gaping crowd would stop staring.

The girl helped Prue to her feet and turned to the small group. "She's not injured, you can all move along."

The goshawk personifate took flight and the people scattered.

"You're not from the city, are you?" said the girl.

"How did you know?"

"Your lack of tramtrax awareness. This isn't the country, you know. Things happen fast here."

"I can see that."

"And your clothes, they're not exactly *city*." The girl looked her up and down and re-buttoned her own jacket.

"I usually live on a farm."

The girl tilted her head a little. "How quaint. My name is Cora Duval."

"I'm Pru—" she quickly stopped herself, thinking fast, "—prudent, when I cross the road … usually … that is." She gave a little cough and Cora frowned her dark eyebrows at her. "I mean to say that my name is Frances, I've only just arrived in Medlock."

Cora shook Prue's hand politely then absently brushed it on her jacket. "Well, if you're fine, I'll let you get on with your city tour, or whatever it is you were doing. I need to get going; I'm picking up my uniform for the Imperial Personifate Guild. I'm going to be an apprentice," Cora said, flicking her hair behind her shoulder. She turned on her heels.

"Wait!" Prue called. "I'm going there too." She felt a rush of relief at the thought she'd now know someone in the same position as her.

Cora turned back. "Pardon?"

"To Deakins Entire to pick up my uniform; I'm going to be an apprentice too."

"Really?" Cora said, wrinkling her nose.

Her tone instantly made Prue straighten her frame. "Yes."

"Are you sure? Didn't you say you were from a farm?"

Prue nodded trying not to scowl. The girl had just saved her life after all.

Cora looked like she had tasted neat lemon cordial. "Well, I suppose I can show you the way."

Chapter 5

DEAKINS ENTIRE

Prue followed Cora into Burlington West.

"Have you been to Smithy Door before?" Prue asked, feeling like a lost puppy following in her shadow.

"I know every inch of this city," said Cora, striding on.

They passed more shops and grand buildings in Burlington West. Prue's eye was caught by Aloysius Pye's Pastries. The windows were heaped with shiny buns and fruit rolls. The next store was Bletchley Steam Peddlers with all manner of steam-enhanced bicycles. Dad would've loved them.

"Are you from Medlock, then?" Prue asked.

"I'm a Duval," Cora said, smiling patronizingly as if to say *poor little country girl doesn't know anything.* "Generations of Duvals have lived in Medlock. My family has always worked within the elite of the Sovereign Chancellery."

It didn't mean much to Prue, who swerved out of the way as a toad jumped from a small outlet pipe in front of her.

"Mind out, lady!" the toad personifate said, glaring up at her and folding his arms grumpily.

"Sorry!" Prue said.

The toad was closely followed by an aqua green lizard with a crested head and back. "Is that all the pipe inspections completed for the day, Felix?"

"There's one at the Sovereign Chancellery we'd better do," the toad replied as he jumped away.

"Wow, they really do come in all shapes and sizes," Prue said, but Cora was charging ahead.

At the end of Burlington West, they took a left into Pickwick, another grand street with many red-bricked houses. About halfway along was a small cobbled street called Smithy Door. They carried on past smaller, quaint-looking shops, Medlock Fudge

& Co, Swifty Second-hand Books, Penelope Parker's Portraits. After that was a double-fronted shop with a bronze swinging sign reflecting the afternoon sun:

Deakins Entire
Proud suppliers to the Imperial
Personifate Guild of Medlock
by appointment of the Governor

Cora pushed the door open. A bell clattered. Prue followed her inside and the door thumped closed. The floor was warm walnut, and the numerous shelves were filled with sumptuous midnight-blue, mustard-gold and deep ruby-red fabric. Ladders on wheels rested on each side. The dusty, warm smell of books and wood lingered in the air. A girl standing in front of the counter spun around to face them. She was about the same age as them and had short russet hair, a pointed chin and face that looked as though it had never seen the sun, and she wore a plain but smart brown dress.

"Hello," Prue said brightly.

"The shopkeeper is just out the back," the girl said. She looked at them with wide, amber eyes;

Prue thought that the phrase her mother used, "rabbit caught in the mechanicart lights", summed up her expression perfectly.

"Are you a new apprentice too?" Cora asked.

The girl nodded, then smiled in a kind but awkward way, as though her face wasn't used to it.

"Great. I'm Cora and this is Frances." She reduced her voice to something near a whisper and added, "She's a farm girl."

"Oh ... I'm Agapantha." The girl's mouth warped as though embarrassed by her name, or was it that she was judging Prue too?

"Weird name, don't your parents like you?" said Cora. Then she laughed to herself while Agapantha looked down at the floor. "No, really, I'm just kidding. But I don't think I recognize you. What's your family name?"

"Young."

A door at the back of the store banged and there was the sound of scratching on floorboards behind the counter. A bundle of clothes was heaved above, then, after clumsy scurrying, a creature about the size of a badger pulled himself up. He was the most curious thing Prue had ever seen: long toes and fingers, string-thin arms and legs, whiskers on a bent snout and a course-haired body – like an exceptionally large rat. Two mustard-yellow, pop-out eyes stared at them.

They hesitantly passed him the notes from their mentors.

"Great, two more," he said, in a voice that was spiky, rolling his eyes and sounding like it was the least thrilling prospect in the world. "It's very late in the day for a fitting," he snapped.

"Well, that can't be helped," said Cora. "What's your name?"

The rat personifate looked at her suspiciously. "Finblewick."

"Best get started then, Finblewick."

He scowled at her, then sent Agapantha to the changing rooms out the back to put on her uniform. Finblewick's tail drooped unhappily across the floorboards as he scurried around the shop gathering piles of books and equipment. Prue moved to the nearest shelf, where all sorts of tools were placed in neat boxes with green velvet lining: tiny clamps, snippers, needle pliers, miniature vices, magnifiers, wire strippers, solder, wick, and the tiniest precision screwdrivers Prue had ever seen.

Cora joined her. "What an ugly personifate," she whispered.

A notebook flew past their heads. "I have excellent hearing," Finblewick said, scampering towards a stepladder in the middle of the store, trailing a tape measure.

"He's right, you shouldn't say such things, Frances." Cora laughed.

Prue opened her mouth to protest, but Cora just pushed past towards Finblewick. "I'm next," she said.

Prue shook her head and wandered to the counter and leaned over to view an intricate contraption that had caught her eye; it looked like some sort of spectacle machine. She reached out to pick it up.

"Don't touch!" Finblewick shrieked.

She retracted her hand and muttered an apology.

When Finblewick had finished measuring Cora and had gathered her uniform, he sent her off to get changed and called to Prue. "You, the nosy one with bushy hair, come here. Well, come on, I don't have all day."

Prue could already see that although personifates

had no memory of their lives before, it was quite clear that their personalities were very much there. It was so strange to think that this curious rat had once been alive as a person. He was probably a mean shopkeeper then, like the one in Peck's Supplies in North Owlcot. She'd always pushed Francis ahead of her to go in there.

Finblewick instructed her to lift her arms and turn this way and that while he hurried up and down a ladder beside her. Agapantha appeared wearing a long, blue jacket that reached her knees and was sharply cut, neatly buttoned with silver, showing a glimpse of a crisp white shirt. A thin line of silver embroidery ran the length of the arm. Her brown shoes had been replaced by long, black boots with shiny buckles. Prue couldn't believe she'd soon get to wear a uniform as nice as this.

Finblewick began collecting various items of clothing from the shelves and bundled them on to the counter for Prue. She ran her hand over the blue velvet of the Guild jacket placed before her – it was as soft as the feather-top grass on the farm.

"What are the other colours for?" she asked.

"Blue for apprentice, gold for craftsman, ruby for

master." Finblewick looked her up and down. "Not likely you'll make it out of blue, though."

Prue ignored his snipe and took herself to the changing room. She carefully folded up her farm clothes. Her new uniform smelt of the same pleasant book scent that permeated Deakins. There was no mirror in the changing room, so she had no idea how she looked, but had to admit that Finblewick had done a great job of getting the sizes precisely right. Before she left the room, she tied her hair back into a plait, then put her hand to the silver symbol on her lapel and closed her eyes. Her heart was thudding in her chest. She wondered how long it would take for her note to reach her parents. She ached for home, but she ached more for Francis.

When she whipped back the curtains, Agapantha's eyes flicked in her direction and she smiled. Cora was busy spinning and looking at her own reflection in one of the glass cabinets, and Finblewick was still gathering equipment into three groups on the counter. Then he disappeared out the back, while strange whirring and grinding sounds came from the unseen room. Eventually, Finblewick returned and put leather toolbelts and rosewood cases on the counter. On the front of the cases in silver was etched *Apprentice Haywood, Apprentice Young* and *Apprentice Duval*. Prue ran her fingers over her name. It looked so fancy.

"Did you just engrave that?" Prue said. She was amazed at how skillful a personifate machine could be.

Finblewick nodded. "Well, it didn't just etch itself! Your tools go into your cases. You'll need a set of day clothes, judging by what some of you arrived in." He stared unashamedly at Prue. "You are apprentices; your appearance needs to reflect the privileged role you now have." Finblewick then went to the shelves for navy woollen jumpers and plain trousers.

They started sorting the tools into their cases.

Finally, Finblewick dragged three tan leather suitcases from the back. They had rounded brass corners, extendable wheels and the Guild symbol in silver in the top left corner.

"Right, that's everything. Now, pack up and be out of my sight," said Finblewick, disappearing out the back and slamming the door.

"Wait, we need to know how to get to the Guild," Prue called after him.

Cora laughed. "Silly, I know the way. I see that I'm going to have to take on the responsibility of guiding your naïve farm feet around the city, or you're likely be flattened by a tram. Honestly, Agapantha, you should've seen her bewildered little face!" Cora pulled an exaggerated shocked expression while Agapantha flashed Prue an apologetic smile.

Agapantha didn't say much, but Prue warmed to her much more than Cora.

By the time they stepped back out into Smithy Door, the sun was halfway behind the metal spires in the west. They made their way to the main square, where people and personifates were still hurrying about. In their smart new apprentice uniforms, the three girls drew glances and people stepped out of their way. Prue spotted a couple of mustard gold jackets in the crowds, and a ruby one – craftsmen and a master.

As they crossed the square, Prue noticed a large group had gathered down one of the roads.

"What's going on?" she asked.

"The Sovereign Chancellery is down there," said Cora.

"Really! Oh, I'd love to see it. Could we go and

have a look? Have we got time?" said Prue.

Cora sighed. "Well, I suppose, as it's all such a novelty to you, Frances."

They hurried over to where people gathered around an expensive-looking mechanicart that had come to rest outside a great white building.

A personifate fox unhitched the steps of the carriage.

"Governor Watson-Wentworth is very popular with the people, and the personifates," Cora said. "He's the one who introduced the Personifates for All, and All for the Personifates bill."

"That's the Governor's cart?" asked Prue.

"You really do live in the middle of nowhere, don't you?"

A middle-aged man stepped from the carriage. He wore a sky-blue jacket with matching shawl, cravat, and a golden waistcoat. He glanced at his reflection in the carriage window and ran a hand through his wavy, brown hair. The crowd pressed in, pushing the apprentices closer.

Governor Watson-Wentworth must have noticed the girls' Guild uniforms because he came straight over to them. He took a bundle of cards from his jacket and proceeded to sign and tuck one in each of their pockets. "What fine new apprentices, working to help keep our wondrous city at the forefront of technology. I look forward to seeing you all in action soon! There are busy times ahead." He paused at Cora. "Ah, Miss Duval! Your parents said you were starting at the Guild. I know we'll see great things from you, if your brother is anything to go by!"

Cora smiled politely but Prue couldn't help but notice the way she straightened up and gave a little sniff.

Then Governor Watson-Wentworth breezed away towards the golden gates of the Sovereign Chancellery.

As the crowd dispersed, Prue saw a commotion by a building opposite. A man and two personifates – a brown bear and a huge cat with a spotted tawny coat and enormous ears – stood by the wall. The bear personifate held the arm of the man and was talking sternly to him.

"What's going on?" Prue asked.

"They're likely personifate guards," said Cora.

They stood before a large poster that clung crookedly to the facade. It had a white circle enclosing three black letters: *ASL*.

"What's ASL?" Prue asked

"Anti-Second Lifers – they're first lifers against the new tech," said Cora.

The personifate big cat swiftly pulled down the poster, but as it was removed, another poster was revealed: a white hand with a green paw print in the palm – it read *Rights for Personifates*. The big cat paused, then pulled it down too. Then they escorted the man responsible for the ASL poster towards the Sovereign Chancellery.

"He'll get put away for a day or two, which is too lenient if you ask me," said Cora.

"The sun's nearly down," said Agapantha quietly. Prue realized Agapantha had hardly spoken two words since they'd met her. She imagined if Agapantha was a personifate, she would perhaps be a little russet field mouse. Cora would possibly be a bird of prey.

"Then we'd better get to the Guild," said Prue.

Chapter 6

THE GUILD

The peach warmth of sunset brushed the rooftops of Medlock as Prue, Cora and Agapantha crossed the square and arrived in Sovereign Row. They stopped outside a city mansion that both dwarfed and outshone the buildings to each side. Warm ginger brickwork rose five-storeys tall, and the front was ornate with balustrades and a variety of arched and rectangular windows. At the top were triangular, cone and bell-shaped roofs. In the centre of the building, marble steps led to a dark blue door. Prue and Agapantha followed Cora, who strode confidently up to the entrance and knocked loudly.

Beside the door was a plaque with the encircled silver arcs which stated: *Imperial Personifate Guild of Medlock, Founded by Master Hannah Woolstenbury.*

She had read about Master Woolstenbury, the greatest technician and inventor that the world had ever known. Hannah Woolstenbury had been ridiculed by other inventors for most of her life for believing in ghosts, let alone her lifelong ambition to connect with them; people had said her methods were unscientific. But she ultimately found a way to bring them back into this world.

As they waited, Prue's eye was caught by a brightly coloured peacock and lemur making their way along the pavement. She marvelled at how their movements had an edge of human characteristics in their relaxed chatter and gesturing. How Hannah Woolstenbury had proved everyone wrong.

Footsteps sounded beyond, and the door swung open. A woman with grey-brown streaked hair flowing over her shoulders stood there. She wore an apron covered in flour over a voluminous skirt with some flour smudged on her nose. Was this Master Woolstenbury? After surveying them for a moment, the woman clapped her hands together, a large smile broadening on her face.

"Well, here you all are – and what fine young apprentices!" She brushed her floury hands on her apron. "I must say, I was expecting two girls and a boy, but there you have it!" Before Prue knew it, they were engulfed by warm embraces. Cora stiffened, but when it was Prue's turn, she welcomed the scent of roses and yeast, which instantly reminded her of home.

"I'm sorry, I should introduce myself. I'm Lavender Luckhurst, head of boarding. Well, half of the head, that is."

"I'm Cora Duval, this is Agapantha Young, and this is Frances..." she turned to Prue. "I'm sorry, what even *is* your family name?"

"Haywood," Prue said.

"Oh, I see, hay, as in farm!" said Cora. Then she lowered her voice just a touch, as though somehow Prue wouldn't hear it. "She's from the country."

"Well, that's just lovely," said Lavender. "I'm from Bimbledown, a small village north of Gawthorpe myself. A warm welcome, my darlings. Now come along and I'll show you what's what." She ushered them inside.

Prue stepped into an enormous hallway. It had a chequered blue-and-white floor, mahogany paneled walls and a great staircase that climbed the walls in a squared spiral, leading to door upon door. Prue couldn't help but turn and look up as she walked inside, taking in the intricately carved posts, candy-twisted spindles, and the walls filled with gold-framed paintings. Were the secrets of creating personifates behind these doors – her way back to Francis?

Footsteps sounded beyond a door at the back of the hallway. It started to open.

"One hundred? Are you quite sure, Amelia?"

"Indeed. It's certainly going to be the most challenging few moons we've ever had."

Craftsman Primrose entered, now wearing the mustard-gold jacket of a craftsman, along with a woman wearing a long red skirt with a silk trim matching her ruby Guild jacket. They noticed the girls and smiled warmly.

"Ah, here you are!" said Craftsman Primrose. "Good to see you've met some other apprentices, Frances. May I introduce Master Amelia White."

The young woman had a relaxed look about

her – blonde hair half tied back with strands loose around her face, cheeks pinched with pink, jacket unbuttoned.

She smiled and approached them, shaking Prue's hand first.

"You have an excellent mentor. Craftsman Primrose is an absolute marvel at design and construction." She spoke briskly.

"I'm apprenticed to Master Sollentude," said Cora, stepping forward. "I'm Cora Duval."

"Ah, of course, you must be Larkin's sister," said Master White. "A tough act to follow."

"I think I'll manage," said Cora with a tightened smile.

"Fighting talk, Apprentice Duval," said Master White. "Excellent." She turned to Craftsman Primrose. "Now you must meet my new apprentice. I found Agapantha in your home city, Gawthorpe, although she's originally from Medlock. I persuaded her parents that with her remarkable mathematical flair I just had to give her a try at the Guild."

Master White smiled at Agapatha, and Craftsman Primrose shook Cora and Agapantha's hands and said he was very pleased to meet them.

"Right, let's get you settled in," said Craftsman Primrose. "We can get all the paperwork signed in the morning. We must stick to the protocol. The Sovereign Chancellery is very particular about form-filling and secrecy, that's why the Guild is—" he stopped himself. "Best you find out for yourselves tomorrow. Over to you, Mrs Luckhurst."

Lavender clapped her hands together. "Leave your cases there and we'll get you fed, then I'll show you to your rooms. The other apprentices have all eaten, I'm afraid, but I've set some food aside for you. Will you be staying, Craftsman Primrose? Master White?" She threw them a knowing glance.

"We'll be off, thank you, Mrs Luckhurst. We have lots to prepare for our first day of teaching tomorrow."

Master White turned to the apprentices. "Meet us here at eight a.m. sharp and we'll show you to the Guild. Then the hard work begins."

"But..." said Prue.

"Yes, Apprentice Haywood?"

"But I thought we *were* at the Guild?"

Craftsman Primrose exchanged a grin with Master White. "You'll see soon enough."

Craftsman Primrose and Master White left through the front door, and the three new apprentices followed Lavender towards one of the rooms coming off the hallway. "That Primrose and White have such a flame for each other – warms my heart, it does," she said.

The group paused as a spritely lady walked down the stairs towards them, about the same age as Lavender but with short grey hair and a more serious expression. "Don't be daft, Lavender, I've never known a pair as committed to their work. Master Woolstenbury would never allow romance between her craftsmen."

She stopped before them. "My name's Liddy Luckhurst. Welcome to your new lodgings." She frowned. "Lav, weren't we expecting two girls and a boy?"

"Oh, I think it's my fault," said Prue hurriedly. "I'm Frances, with an *e*, and Craftsman Primrose assumed it was an *i* and that I was a boy."

"Ah, easy mistake. Well, I'm sure I can make a quick rearrangement with the beds," said Liddy.

"We could take one of the doubles from the girls' room and replace it with two singles from the empty boys' room?" suggested Lavender.

Liddy nodded. "I can ask a couple of the older apprentices to help. I'll take your cases to your room while you tuck in." She picked up a couple of cases and started up the stairs.

"Right, then," said Lavender. "The room to the right is the parlour; you're welcome to use it anytime. It's a good place to mix with the other apprentices and get to know them." A cosy glow shone from underneath the closed door and laughter sounded inside. "We'll not overwhelm you by introducing you to them just yet – all in good time. The kitchen is down the hall there, and ahead through this door is the dining room."

Lavender led them into the dining room. The walls were set with shelves bending from the weight of ancient-looking books and various objects: glass orbs, beads, dangling crystals, lamps, goblets, jars of dried herbs and flowers, claws, and a stuffed crow. Prue looked around in wonder at the many chaos lamps hanging from hooks; they were different here, producing a sunnier, more orange light than the lamps at home – perhaps they used a different oil?

There was a large rectangular table surrounded

by at least twenty chairs. It was laden with bowls filled with peas, carrots, marrow, corn, potatoes, golden-brown pies and steaming jugs of gravy. It smelled like Sunday at the farm.

"Do sit down," said Lavender.

Prue pulled out a gold painted seat nearest to her.

"Best not sit there, dear," said Lavender swiftly.

"Oh, sorry," Prue said, wondering if it was perhaps a very precious antique chair. She sat in the next empty chair and the others all took seats.

A delicate cough came from under the table. Lavender stood up. Prue looked to Agapantha who shrugged. Lavender gestured to them to stand too.

Something furry brushed past Prue's legs, making her jolt.

The gold chair beside Prue creaked back slightly, then a cat jumped into it. The cat was grey and white, wearing a lace-trimmed red velvet dress with a gold piccadill collar, jewelled tiara and ruby necklace. The cat observed the table with piercing blue eyes, then waved her paw and said, "You may be seated."

Prue marveled at the way the cat's face moved

with such precise detail, her voice graceful and polished.

"I trust you had a good rest, Queen Adelaide?" Lavender asked.

"One did," the cat said.

Prue couldn't help but let out a snigger. *Queen Adelaide?*

The cat glared at her.

"This is Frances, Agapantha and Cora – new apprentices," said Lavender.

Queen Adelaide gave a nod.

Lavender instructed them to fill their plates as high as they liked, and Prue jumped at the chance, feeling famished from the journey and events of the day.

Cora proceeded to tell everyone all about her many talents in design, invention, mathematics, precision mechanics, how she had travelled far and wide – Prue thought it impossible that one person could really have done so much.

Lavender, who was sitting the other side of Prue, leant across and whispered. "Adelaide thinks she was a queen in her past life. Poor dear, we think there may have been a problem with her harnessing, addling her mind a bit. But she's harmless, really, and it's a bit of fun for the house. She was brought back as a companion a year ago but proved too demanding for the home she was assigned to."

"Like a pet?" Prue whispered.

"Dear no, don't let the personifates hear you say that. The term *companion* is much more acceptable."

"Oh, sorry."

"And you're Larkin's sister?" said Queen Adelaide to Cora. "Also, apparently a multi-talented apprentice. I daresay you will both be in the gold of a craftsman in record time."

"Why don't you tell Queen Adelaide about yourself, Agapantha?" said Lavender, looking across at her, but Agapantha's face turned red and she pushed a piece of carrot around her plate. "Come on, dear, we're all the best of friends here. No need to be shy."

Prue took the opportunity to pile her plate with more buttery potatoes.

Agapantha spoke quietly. "My parents are from Medlock originally, but we moved to Gawthorpe. They tech-travel all over the world and they were at a meeting in Medlock when they met Master White, and they got talking about me. Master White visited me in Gawthorpe and the next thing I knew, here I am."

"And your parents don't mind leaving you here while they travel?"

"No, they're just happy for the opportunity for me."

"It's not the same for those apprentices with family in Medlock who can pop back on a weekend." Lavender gave Agapantha a little pat on her arm. "You and Frances are a long way from home."

Prue thought of how she'd left her parents so suddenly – and hardened her heart.

"Where are you from?" Queen Adelaide said, turning to Prue.

"I'm from a farm north of Medlock."

Queen Adelaide looked Prue up and down. "A farm girl as an Imperial Personifate Guild Apprentice?" She blinked several times in quick succession.

Cora smiled snidely.

"Don't be such a snob, Queen Adelaide!" said Liddy as she walked into the room. She sat down next to Agapantha. "I've swapped the beds between rooms and put your cases on the beds. It was completely random, so the bed your case landed on is the bed you'll get."

Shortly, a boy walked in quite as though he owned the place, chin high, and firm strides. His hair was dark at the sides and roots, with bright blonde spikes, his eyebrows dark as night – the same as Cora.

"Heard you were here," he said, nodding at Cora.

"Larkin has scored one hundred percent in all the tasks he's ever been given," Queen Adelaide said proudly.

"That's impressive," said Prue, trying her best to sound like it really was, when actually her initial thought of Larkin was that he seemed a bit stuck-up, like his sister.

Larkin turned to Prue and Agapantha. "I'm with Master Sollentude. If you ever need expert advice you should come to me." And with that, Larkin left.

"There must be so many masters and craftsmen, but does anyone apprentice for Master Woolstenbury?" Prue said quietly to Lavender.

"Oh, Master Woolstenbury doesn't take on apprentices, dearie. She's far too busy."

Once the apprentices had finished, Liddy showed them upstairs. Their bedroom was on the fourth floor at the very top of the house. It had dark wood-panelled walls and three beds with posts. There was an enormous tapestry on the wall depicting a forest with woodland animals including rabbits and squirrels, but some unrecognizable creatures too, like fairy-tale pixies.

"Here we are. The bed by the tapestry is bigger, but as I said, the first case to land there is the lucky recipient."

It was Agapantha's case. Prue's bed was by the window with Cora's beside her. They were small beds, but she didn't care.

"The washroom is on the third floor. Just shout if you need anything. Breakfast is laid out from seven until nine, so come down when you like. I'll leave you to it."

Cora commandeered the wardrobe, insisting she needed to hang everything in her suitcase and it needed space to breathe, so Agapantha and Prue decided to share the chest of drawers.

"It's exciting, isn't it?" Prue said, starting to unpack her few possessions.

Agapantha nodded.

"Do you miss home?"

"A little," said Agapantha.

"Me too, but it's just so thrilling to be here, isn't it?"

"Yes, it is," Agapantha said.

Prue noticed that Agapantha didn't make eye contact very often, preferring to look at an invisible point about forty-five degrees towards the floor.

Prue carefully kept the photograph of Francis hidden by folding it inside her jumper in the drawer. She allowed herself a quick peek when she was sure the others weren't looking.

Prue shut the drawer. "I still find it amazing that Queen Adelaide, or Finblewick, or any other of the personifates we've seen today, aren't real. Well, they're real, but you know what I mean? How do you think they actually work?"

"I expect we'll find out soon," said Agapantha.

Cora cleared her throat loudly. She was sitting on her bed smiling.

Prue sat down on her own bed facing her. "Come on, spit it out."

Agapantha sat on the end of Prue's bed.

"I can't possibly tell you. Larkin swore me to secrecy."

"Oh, that's a pity," said Prue. She turned away and rested back on her pillows.

There was a slight pause, then Cora said, "Well, if you insist." She leant in towards them. "He told me that it's all down to a material called qwortzite."

Prue let the word run through her mind: qwortzite – she'd never heard of such a substance, but it sounded almost magical.

"It's incredibly rare and hugely valuable – only the wealthiest families in Medlock can afford it, so I'm afraid you'd stand no chance to buy it, Frances."

Prue scowled at Cora but she didn't seem to notice.

"Not that it's available to buy freely, anyway," said Cora.

"What does the qwortzite actually do?" Prue asked.

Cora widened her already moon-like eyes. "It can hold the soul of a spirit."

"How does it do it?" Prue persisted.

"I think I've told you more than enough."

"Oh, you mean you don't know," Prue said.

"No, I just don't want to say," Cora said haughtily.

Prue noticed a small grin on the edge of Agapantha's lips.

They changed into their night clothes and Prue went to the window. It was now dark, and stars specked the sky. As she looked at the ash-grey twists of chimney smoke, spires and rooftops of the city reflecting the ivory light of the three-quarter moon as far as the eye could see, she thought of how much Francis would have loved it here. The summer before the illness, they'd snuck out late one evening and climbed Haywood's Oak. It had been a three-quarter moon that day too, and they stood in the uppermost branches looking over the pearl-brushed fields under a cloudless sky. If she closed her eyes, she could still see it just as it was.

"Look, sis, it's the lights of Medlock."

"Where, Francis? I can't see them."

"There – just within reach." He held his hand out and grabbed the air.

Prue laughed and copied him. "I've got them too."

"One day, sis, we'll go to the big city, and we'll show them what we can do."

Francis would have jumped at the chance of

going with Craftsman Primrose. He should be here. Prue tried to close the chasm opening in her chest again. It felt as though she was plunging off the edge of a precipice, being dragged in.

She pulled the curtain shut.

As she climbed into bed, she focused on the thought that she would soon be at the Guild – the place where she could find a way back to her brother.

If she didn't get found out as an imposter first.

Chapter 7

THE IMPERIAL PERSONIFATE GUILD OF MEDLOCK

Prue, Agapantha and Cora arrived promptly for breakfast at seven the next morning. A couple of apprentices also came down early: Sira, who had long, shiny black hair and was sixteen, about to be made a craftsman; and Wil, a second-year apprentice who told them about all the best books to read first.

After breakfast, Craftsman Primrose was waiting for them in the hallway.

He observed them through his thin-rimmed glasses then looked at his pocket-watch. "Right on time. Don't worry, you two, Masters White and Sollentude will meet us later. We're a little ahead of the other apprentices today, as I thought it would be nice to avoid the morning rush on your first day. Now, if you could sign the papers laid out for you on the table."

They approached the table where three forms titled *Secrecy Statement* were placed, the Guild Symbol stamped in silver in the corner. Prue started reading it:

I hereby declare that anything I see within the walls of the Guild from this day forwards until such time as my first life comes to an end, will remain secret and not be passed beyond those walls.

It seemed straightforward enough. Prue picked up a pen and began signing.

Like a bolt of lightning to her chest, she realized she'd started writing *Prue*. Craftsman Primrose was standing not far away, while Agapantha and Cora were busy signing their own names. Quickly, Prue tried to turn the P into an F. She looked at the signature and decided it was passable, if a little scruffy.

"All finished?" Craftsman Primrose asked. "Excellent. Follow me."

Prue had no idea where they were going or what to expect, and excited butterflies were dancing inside her. This was what she had come here for – the Guild was her way back to Francis; it was really happening!

Craftsman Primrose came to a stop by a stretch of wall covered in paintings, then pulled one edge of a small picture of a mouse back, revealing a keyhole behind.

"Something about secrets being quiet as mice," he said.

He took a key from around his neck – it was silver with the end shaped into the symbol of the Guild. With a soft click, a hidden doorway in the wall paneling opened and there was a rush of air. The apprentices looked at each other in wonder.

"Exciting, isn't it?" said Craftsman Primrose. He pulled three keys on chains from his bag and passed them one each.

They followed him down a dimly lit spiral staircase. The curved brick walls had chaos lamps set into recesses that gave off a warm glow. At the bottom, rather than finding themselves in a basement room, the space opened up and they found themselves on a platform in an underground tunnel. Around the height of two people, the tunnel's arched brickwork was illuminated by many flickering chaos lamps, and it was warm and smelt earthy. Beside them, running the length of the tunnel, was a metal tube that half-filled the space.

"This is your daily transport – the pneumerator!" said Craftsman Primrose proudly. "Developed by the masters using the old Medlock sewage system."

"Gross," said Cora.

"No, perfectly spotless, and it'll get us to the Guild in under a minute. Of course, you can walk above ground if you'd prefer, but that'd take you around an hour, and you'd have to pass through security at the outer gate," said Craftsman Primrose. "There's a pneumatic station at the other end of this tunnel, and it works to either push or pull us. It's a wonderful invention."

Prue marvelled at the sound of it, and instantly imagined one back home to get you from the far field back to the farmhouse.

"Now, if the pod is at this end, the lever on this control panel will be up; if it's at the other it'll be down." He pulled the lever up. "It can get rather busy at peak times, which is why I've brought you along early."

In hardly any time at all, there was a whooshing sound and the glass panel in the tube illuminated.

"It has a built-in braking system. It used to be manual, but it was … *problematic*. Come along, everyone!" Craftsman Primrose reached for a handle and slid open a door in the tube. One by one, they stepped inside the pod, which was just big enough to stand up in with dozens of red leather seats facing forward.

"You can sit with me, Agapantha," said Cora, grabbing her arm.

Prue didn't mind sitting with Craftsman Primrose; at least she would be able to ask him questions.

"This silver lever is to close the pod. Then, in about five seconds, we're off."

After a moment, the pod shot forward, pinning them to their seats. The trajectory was straight at first, then the whole pod seemed to rotate to the side and tilt, rolling this way and that as they navigated the tunnel.

"How does it work?" Prue asked.

"It's all about air pressure. We pull air from one end, creating a vacuum that propels the pod between each terminus. There's a slight rise soon."

The pod abruptly tilted upwards and slowed as they hit the uphill section.

"We're out of the old sewer tunnels now and into the purpose-built uphill section. It's all automated, no intervention needed," said Craftsman Primrose as the pod came to a sudden standstill. He pulled the lever and they stepped out into a large metallic room. They followed Craftsman Primrose towards the doorway.

He paused, his hand grasping the handle. He smiled. "Now, a true welcome to the Imperial Personifate Guild of Medlock – the factorium!"

They stepped through the door into the fresh air of outside. They had been in a hut of some sort, but before them was a great lawn leading like an emerald carpet to an enormous building. Prue couldn't speak because her breath had completely been taken away by the size and magnificence of the factorium before her. It rose proudly from the ground, something like a chaos factorium but much more stylish and grand: warm clay brickwork; row upon row of neat, gleaming windows; pipes running in orderly patterns from the main building to enormous cylinder-shaped sub-buildings; huge, polished steel chimneys that seemed to almost reach the clouds; and a fountain, the likes of which would usually be seen at a fancy country home, shimmering in the morning sun. Prue could feel there was something about this whole place, a prickle in the air, like the expectation of lightning – everything was alert. Prue had so many questions bursting inside of her, she couldn't wait to get started.

"It's magnificent," Prue whispered, looking up at the white smoke chugging into the sky.

"That exhaust you see is not harmful in any way. We do it to keep up the illusion that this is just another Medlock factorium, but really it's perfectly safe artificial vapour," said Craftsman Primrose. "Come on, I wanted to show you all a little of the grounds before everyone else arrives."

A central pathway led from the main factorium building to great gates; the transport hut they'd arrived in was about halfway along.

Craftsman Primrose walked them up the long path to what he called the "official entrance". He used the same key he'd used back at the house to activate the huge gates to the outside where there was a big sign that stated "Medlock & Co Chaos Production".

Craftsman Primrose tapped his nose. "Our little cover story."

Beside the gate, on the factorium side, was a small building like a tiny brick house with one door and windows on all aspects. A girl in regular trousers and jumper came to the door when she saw them.

"Good morning, Grace. All quiet this morning?" said Craftsman Primrose.

"Yes, Craftsman Primrose. New apprentices?" she said looking at the girls and smiling.

"Indeed – I'm just showing them around." He turned to Prue, Agapantha and Cora. "We like to keep someone on security duty out here, either personifate or a plain-clothed older apprentice.

There were a few large buildings some distance away, other factoria, but the Guild factorium was in quite a secluded position nestled on an arm of land with forest arcing around them. Prue guessed they were on the furthest outskirts of Medlock.

"What happens if strangers stumble upon it?" Prue asked.

"Master Woolstenbury likes to keep everything as secret as possible, although it's not easy. Usually people just walk on past without a thought, or whoever is on duty will ensure people move on. Many of the factoria in Medlock employ personifates, so it's not unusual to see them in such places. The biggest threat comes from other cities that would dearly love to get their hands on our technology. The perimeter fence helps, of course, but it only goes as far as the forest." Craftsman Primrose pointed to a tall, narrow building close to the main factorium. "Our messenger tower over there doubles as a look-out. There are personifates on duty twenty-four hours – not needing to sleep certainly has its advantages. Plus, our personifate guards keep an eye on the surrounding forest, although it spreads back for twenty miles south, so it's unlikely we'd find anyone spying on us from in there!"

A rabbit hopped across the road before them.

"Morning!" Prue called brightly.

It froze and stared at them, startled for a moment, then took flight into the bushes.

"What was the matter with her? Or him."

"I do believe it was a just a wild rabbit, Frances," said Craftsman Primrose.

Cora burst out laughing. Agapantha turned red on Prue's behalf.

Craftsman Primrose rocked back on his heels. "It's actually a very easy mistake to make. We do, after all, pride ourselves on our ability to create realistic forms. Most wildlife never show any interest in the personifates – indeed, they seem to be scared off by them – we believe they detect something in the high-pitched sounds of the mechanics. Some animals have become used to it in Medlock, so you may have noticed that pigeons seem to coexist quite happily these days." He looked at his pocket-watch. "Right, almost time for a special morning meeting that Master Woolstenbury has called, then we'll get straight to showing you around inside."

"Special meeting?" Prue said.

"Indeed. You've all arrived at the Guild at a rather exciting time," he said.

Craftsman Primrose led the apprentices back

from the perimeter gate towards the main factorium building, past the crowds of people swiftly emerging from the pneumatic transport hut behind them. As they neared the factorium, a slender man approached. He wore the ruby-red cloak of a master. He swept a hand back through silver-white hair, cropped short at the sides. His face had a crooked angle to it, with white eyebrows closely guarding pin-sharp eyes; his mouth was tight and purposeful.

"Glad you made it, Apprentice Duval," the man said to Cora. "Primrose, you're taking my new apprentice for the morning. Master Woolstenbury has planned urgent discussions with the masters about the hundred after the meeting this morning."

Prue didn't like the way he'd told Craftsman Primrose rather than asked.

"Of course, Master Sollentude."

"Didn't Master White say something about one-hundred back in Medlock?" she whispered to Agapantha.

She nodded in reply. "I wonder what it means?"

Cora opened her mouth to say something to Master Sollentude, but he had already turned to walk away. He called loudly to a mole personifate not far ahead. "The lawns are overgrown, tidy them up."

The mole dropped the basket of potatoes he was carrying and they bounced across the ground. "Of course, Master Sollentude."

Master Sollentude just breezed on past. Craftsman Primrose tutted quietly and rushed to help the mole. Prue and Agapantha hurried to help too.

"A please from Sollentude wouldn't go amiss," Craftsman Primrose said, shaking his head. "Honestly, sometimes I wonder if he's any better than the ASL. Here you go, Abel."

"Much obliged, Craftsman Primrose," said Abel, carrying on his way. "Best get on with tidying the lawns."

"You have as much right to be at this meeting as Master Sollentude. I'm sure some of the other personifates can help you later," Craftsman Primrose called after him.

Prue felt glad she was apprenticed to Craftsman Primrose – he had a kind heart.

"Right, we'd better all get inside," he said.

Chapter 8

THE NEW APPRENTICE

Prue felt like a mouse beneath a great oak as they approached the entrance to the enormous factorium. The doorway was huge, leading into a central atrium lined with flight upon flight of ornate ironwork stairs around the edges and access walkways. There were two lift systems on either side, cogs and pulleys left in the open for all to see. Autumn sunlight streamed in from a glass ceiling, casting shadowed web patterns on the wall from the intricate metal latticework above.

Apprentices, craftsmen, masters and personifates mingled in the atrium. Prue saw a golden lynx, just like the one she'd seen when she first arrived in Medlock, and there was also a rabbit personifate who darted through the people to join a winged wolf, a large brown bear and a golden eagle who was perched on the railings. Many more joined them. Prue noticed that the personifates stayed together on one side of the atrium.

"Do all those personifates work here?" Prue asked.

"Yes, we have many allocated to the factorium: messengers, technicians, gardeners, cooks, assistants and whatnot," said Craftsman Primrose.

Prue spotted five masters in red, including Masters White and Sollentude. There were many more craftsmen in the mustard-gold jackets, around thirty to forty in total, Prue guessed, and about thirty apprentices in blue.

"And do the craftsmen and masters live here?" Prue asked.

"No, most live in Medlock, or nearby villages, but we all travel here daily to work. Come along, we'll stand here, and I'll stay with you rather than join the craftsmen, as it's your first day."

Chatter stopped as the golden lynx took the

platform, followed by an older woman dressed in a cropped ruby-red jacket. Her hair was white, and immaculately styled short on the sides with a chic, brushed-back quiff. Her face had an arresting stillness and strength. Even if Prue hadn't known who she was, it was obvious that this woman wielded power. Next on the platform was a face Prue recognized from Medlock – it was Governor Watson-Wentworth. Master Woolstenbury looked to her colleagues, who all dipped their heads to her. She gestured to the governor to take a seat on the platform. Even though the governor had more formal power as head of the Sovereign Chancellery, Master Woolstenbury's authority here was evident. It was as though an entirely different atmosphere had taken over the room. Everyone seemed to be standing straighter and every single eye was on her. The lynx personifate went on to the side of the platform where several other personifates were lined up.

Master Woolstenbury's gaze took in the room. "Good morning, everybody. We have some important announcements, but firstly, I would like to welcome three new trainees: Apprentices

Haywood, Young and Duval." She gestured her hand towards Prue, Agapantha and Cora, and all heads turned to face them.

For a horrible moment, Prue felt as though everyone could see deep inside of her to the truth. She glanced to her side and saw Agapantha's cheeks instantly flush, while Cora beamed confidently. Master Woolstenbury's eyes met Prue's directly for a few seconds, which felt like a lifetime.

Master Woolstenbury addressed the girls. "As you will have discovered from your first journey here, we like to keep our location away from prying eyes where possible. I remind you that what you see, hear and learn during your time here stays strictly between these walls."

The three new apprentices nodded keenly.

"At the Guild there are numerous facets and specialisms. You will learn all the many areas, but just because you excel in one, it doesn't mean you will earn yourself a place as a craftsman of the Guild. An understanding of *all* aspects is crucial to achievement."

There were murmurs of confirmation from the other masters and craftsmen. Craftsman Primrose looked down and gave Prue a reassuring smile.

A flood of panic hit Prue. She figured she could find her way round the mechanical side of things, but didn't have the first idea about anything else. But she reminded herself she just had to stay long enough to find a way to Francis without getting found out.

"But, if there is one thing I want you to take away from your time here it is this: a personifate is not property; they are friends, companions, vital parts of the working community of Medlock, and first and foremost they are individuals. My personal assistant, Zareen, is not only a colleague, but a good friend." Master Woolstenbury nodded respectfully at the lynx, who returned the gesture.

"On that note, I would like to continue with a special announcement. We live in an era of great progress and change, and today is a momentous occasion for us at the Guild." She gestured to a white personifate stoat who was standing not far from Zareen. "I would like to extend a warm welcome to former personifate technician Edwin Snow-Moon, who has been taken on as the *first personifate apprentice.*"

A flurry of looks exchanged – a range of shock, uncertainty and excitement. Chatter rippled throughout the atrium.

Prue noticed Cora roll her eyes.

"Edwin has shown an exceptional aptitude for design and creative thought, and will be joining Craftsman Primrose. Please take your place with the others, Apprentice Snow-Moon."

Prue felt a pang of disappointment; she wasn't sure she wanted to share her apprenticeship with anyone else.

Craftsman Primrose placed a hand gently on her shoulder. "Sorry, Frances. I couldn't mention it before – Master Woolstenbury wanted to keep it a secret until today."

A ripple of polite applause went around the atrium as the personifate stoat scampered nervously down the steps towards them and stood beside Craftsman Primrose.

Master Woolstenbury put her hand up for silence, which was almost instant. "We work together for a better, more understanding world for us all. If you work hard and remain at the factorium, you will all be privileged to be at the forefront of a bright future.

"Now, I would like to invite Governor Watson-Wentworth to say a few words. He has kindly joined us this morning, to officially share some more ... exciting news."

The Governor stood up. He wore a silk red cravat and shimmering gold jacket. He took a few moments, clearly enjoying all the eyes on him.

"Demand for personifates is at its highest, therefore keeping up with the social need is one of the greatest challenges we have to meet. In just a few moon cycles we will experience a blood moon – harnessing new signals will be at optimum possibility. Therefore I have commissioned the Imperial Personifate Guild of Medlock to create..." He looked around the room then broke into a big grin, spread his hands wide and said, "*One hundred personifates*, to be awoken on the night of the blood moon!"

The apprentices in the room all gave an excited gasp, but the masters and craftsmen looked unsurprised. Prue noticed several cynical looks being exchanged between them.

"I have no doubt you will all rise splendidly to the challenge! Not only that, but I should like to remind all of you that it's only two weekends until the Inventors Parade of Medlock, a wonderful celebration of our city. I hope to see you all there!"

Prue didn't know what the Inventors Parade was, but it sounded thrilling.

Master Woolstenbury left the platform along with the Governor, and the masters, craftsmen and other apprentices hurried off in all directions. Craftsman Primrose remained talking with Master White close by. Prue looked down at Edwin, whose black, bead-like eyes were flitting around the room. He looked nervous.

"Hello, I'm Frances," Prue said, crouching down and holding out her hand. Every time she said the name out loud, it felt easier, despite how it threatened to bring the bad memories back.

He shook a finger with his paw. "I'm Edwin."

"You must be pretty excited to be the first personifate apprentice?"

He smiled awkwardly. "It's a bit nerve-wracking, to tell you the truth. But I'm glad to be with another apprentice."

His voice was young; she guessed he must have been about her age when he'd left his first life. Like

Francis. Despite her earlier misgivings, she realized it could be very useful to know a personifate in her mission to find a way back to him.

Agapantha joined them. "Master White says I'm with you this morning; the masters have a meeting about the hundred with Master Woolstenbury."

"This is Edwin," Prue said.

Agapantha offered her hand to Edwin. "I'm Agapantha. I think it's great they've got a personifate apprentice," she said quietly.

Edwin's shoulders relaxed, and he smiled and shook her hand.

Cora came over, and said in a loud whisper to Agapantha, "I must say, I'm not sure if I've been apprenticed to a factorium or a farm."

Edwin stepped forward and extended his paw, but Cora looked over his head as though he wasn't even there.

"Cora, this is Edwin," Prue said loudly.

"I know," she said forcefully.

"Ah, glad to see you all getting acquainted," said Craftsman Primrose, approaching them and clapping his hands together. "Let's get straight to it – we will begin with the design lab."

Chapter 9

DESIGN LAB

"Ah! Charles, my good friend!" An older gentleman with grey balding hair and portly belly looked up from a nearby table as the four apprentices followed Craftsman Primrose through the large metal doors of the design lab. He straightened a tweed bow tie before putting his hand on his hips and observing them.

"Apprentices, I'd like you to meet the great Craftsman Rami Shad." Craftsman Primrose patted Craftsman Shad on the shoulder. "You won't find a finer designer in Medlock."

Craftsman Shad chuckled. "Flattery will get you

everywhere!"

"We have several design labs, but this has become known as Design Central," Craftsman Primrose said, gesturing to the hive of activity.

It was a cavernous space, and craftsmen in their mustard-gold jackets stood working around large tables with drawing boards. At the far end were numerous personifate bodies at various stages of development: Prue could make out an eagle and a border terrier, but there were also many metalwork skeletons of different sizes, and something huge at the back that was covered by a sheet.

"Delighted to meet you all!" said Craftsman Shad. "Although Edwin and I of course have run into each other once or twice in the labs," he said, shaking the girls' hands in turn.

"This was always my favourite place to run errands." Edwin beamed.

Craftsman Shad looked to Craftsman Primrose. "Brave choice going for a personifate apprentice. Don't get me wrong," he said, turning to Edwin, "I'm all for equality." Then he brought his voice down a little. "Some of the craftsmen are a little more old-fashioned in their views, but don't you mind them. I hear you're quite the talented artist. Primrose should be careful I don't poach you for my own apprentice! Master Woolstenbury tells me I should take on more, uses it as a carrot to the red robe, but in truth I'm far too busy with my latest creations to deal in politics." He quivered his head and shoulders as though politics was rather odious. "Why don't you all come and see my most recent project!" He lifted an arm on to Craftsman Primrose's shoulders and hurried to the far end of the room.

They passed numerous personifate shells: cats, dogs, birds and some even more weird and more surprising creatures. There was what appeared to be a giant butterfly, a dragon the size of a small dog, and a creature with the head, shoulders and front legs of an eagle and the back end of a horse.

Craftsman Shad paused by it. "Impressive, eh?"

"Yes," Prue said keenly. It was amazing. Prue wondered what new body would be best to bring Francis back in. Then a thought struck her. "Craftsman Primrose, why does the Guild use animal forms?"

"A very good question, Frances. We call it the Biomorphic Principle."

"Biomorphic?"

"Yes; initially, more human, robotic-like bodies were tried, something like your farm creations, but the spirits, or ghost frequencies, didn't latch on to the qwortzite very easily. Qwortzite is the substance that makes it all possible, but you'll find out more about that soon. One of Hannah Woolstenbury's great innovations was realizing that realistic animal-like forms have a much higher success rate. The supernatural view says that there's something deep about human souls that connects with animals – many cultures have animal spirits in their folklore and customs for this very reason. Also, nature is the best designer, so, at the factorium, we've melded technology with the wild."

Craftsman Primrose patted the back of the eagle-horse. "I hope we get a good match for this one, Rami. Are you thinking guard material?"

"Indeed."

Prue wondered what he meant by a good match, but she couldn't ask because Craftsman Shad was already urging them on towards the back of the lab and the huge covered object. Craftsman Shad hauled the sheet from it.

Beneath was an enormous pure-white lion, twice the size of a real lion, with ivory-coloured, feathered wings. "What do you think?" Craftsman Shad asked, chuckling to himself.

"It's certainly something, Rami." Craftsman Primrose pushed his glasses up the bridge of his nose.

"Of course, the darned Sovereign Chancellery won't license it, some bish-bosh about limits and necessity, and I can't even get Woolstenbury on my side; she said something about a craftsman's humility. It'll likely never see a personifate life." He sighed. Then with a twinkle in his eye he nudged Craftsman Primrose and said, "We can but try! Well, that's for the future, when it's not a blood moon." He winked. "Let's just say I'm predicting that some of the more creative projects will be put on hold and we'll be sticking to the Sovereign Chancellery specification until then. It'll mostly be a commission for companions, guards and messengers from what I've heard behind the scenes so far."

"Do you think we'll manage it?" asked Craftsman Primrose.

Craftsman Shad pulled in a long breath. "It's going to be tight. Not sure if the Sahwen celebration will happen this year. But I'm certain Master Woolstenbury will pull all resources to get ahead."

Craftsman Primrose looked to the apprentices. "You'll certainly be in at the deep end!"

"What have you got planned for the young whippersnappers this morning?" Craftsman Shad asked.

"Well, I thought—"

"Think no more! I have the perfect task to get them started. A little project I've been dabbling with for a while. Some fresh eyes might be just what it needs."

Craftsman Shad led them back to the art boards and faced the apprentices. "This is a task with practical implications. Let's test your ability to design a new personifate with a specific purpose. Imagine that there are huge mineral supplies to be found under the oceans at a secret location. The mining of such material would be problematic, unless we had some personifates designed for underwater use. I'd like you to get working on the problem. Let's see what animal forms you can come up with. Use what you know, but be creative!"

They were all assigned to a design board. The

others got straight to work. Prue stared at her paper for a full minute. She picked up a pencil. Put it down again. Picked up another. Suddenly her mind was as blank as the page before her. She became aware of Craftsman Primrose moving around the group. He spent the next minute with Edwin, who was behind Prue, and had already got to work on something detailed. Glancing over her shoulder, she marvelled at how his small paws moved with precision.

Panic was setting in. Francis would've been able to manage it; he was always much better at drawing the plans for machinery than she was. What if she was about to be found out? She tapped her pencil rapidly on the paper. What could she do? A fish? Too boring. A whale? Not practical. Then she thought of a book Francis used to read her when she was tiny. It was a myth from their father's homeland called *The Merman*.

She drew a circle for the face and then attempted a body with a fish tail.

Cora, who was beside her, was drawing a perfect tentacled creature. She sniggered. "Seriously. What is that? Is that some country bumpkin folklore?"

Prue scowled and put down her pencil.

Craftsman Primrose walked over. "Is everything all right, Frances?"

She nodded, "I'm just thinking."

"Why don't you try something simple first, perhaps like Agapantha's drawing – a sea serpent?"

"I wanted to come up with my own idea."

"Sometimes the best ideas are well-executed copies of existing things which you bring your own flair to. Besides, human forms are strictly forbidden for personifates."

"Even those with a fish tail?"

He laughed. "Look, we can't all excel in every area at the factorium, but if you can't draw your ideas, you won't be able to share them as easily."

Prue glanced across at Cora's perfect drawing. "Master Woolstenbury said we need to be able to turn our hands to all aspects if we're to be successful."

"As long as you are willing to work on your weak areas. If I'm correct, your strengths will lie primarily in mechanics, but it doesn't mean you can't improve in other areas."

Prue nodded.

"Let's see if I can help you on your way a little

with this design."

Craftsman Primrose clipped a fresh piece of paper to the board and started helping Prue design a sea serpent, giving her instructions of shape and where to shade.

After a while he smiled reassuringly. "Now you're off to a better start. I'll go and see how the others are doing."

Prue noticed that Cora not only kept looking across at her work and throwing sneering looks, but she kept glancing at Edwin's, her lips tight.

At the end of the task Prue had produced a design that, while not as good as the other drawings, was something that she wasn't wholly embarrassed of.

Craftsman Shad congratulated them all on their first foray into personifate design and smiled warmly as he observed each finished artwork in turn. "Lovely serpent there, Apprentice Young; I like the way you've labelled the internal workings of the fins, and you've included calculations, I see … yes, extremely thorough and advanced mathematics." He nodded in approval, then moved on to Cora. "Apprentice Duval, I can see you're going to have no issues in design. Such a clever idea to go with a small octopus with easily manipulated tentacles – sure to reach places other personifates may fail to reach! Now, Apprentice Snow-Moon, this is what I'm looking for. Oh yes indeed, a sea monkey with gills and webbed opposable thumbs! An ingenious idea!" When he observed Prue's, there was an uncomfortable pause. Prue saw the glint of pity when he turned to look at her and said, "Valiant attempt, Apprentice Haywood."

Chapter 10

PLACE AND TIME

After the Design Lab, to Prue's relief, Cora went with her brother Larkin to meet Master Sollentude. Prue, Edwin and Agapantha had been instructed to meet Master White by the front entrance. She was waiting for them standing hand on hip, her blonde hair blowing messily in the soft breeze and a large backpack by her feet.

"Good afternoon!" she said brightly. "I'm sorry I wasn't with you this morning, but I trust Craftsmen Primrose and Shad gave you an excellent introduction to the Design Lab."

They all nodded.

"Good. Craftsman Primrose and I have decided to pool our mentoring skills where possible – we each have specific expertise which we feel you'll benefit from, plus it helps us to have two perspectives on our apprentices." Master White began walking and they all followed.

"Additionally, as you discovered this morning, we have the small matter of preparing one hundred personifates by the blood moon, so the start of your apprenticeship is going to require fast learning. We've decided to give you introductions to as much as we can manage over the coming week, then it will be all-hands-on-deck for the next few moons. You won't see as much of us as you should, but we'll do our best. We'll need all the help we can get with the hundred, although your tasks will of course be limited due to your inexperience.

"You may wonder why I have chosen to take your lesson outside," said Master White.

The three exchanged questioning glances. She smiled. "Curiosity is a great motivator, so I will tell you the answer lies at the top of that chimney."

The three apprentices gazed up at the soaring structure.

"How do you all feel about heights?"

For once, Agapantha's cheeks didn't fill with red, but her face became alabaster white.

"No objections? Excellent. I've turned off the artificial smoke for us. Let's get climbing!" said Master White, striding towards the highest chimney of the factorium. Edwin leapt behind, but Agapantha didn't move.

Prue put her arm around Agapantha's shoulder. "Someone once told me that if you do one brave thing, the next one will be easier and before you know it, you're climbing mountains. Sometimes you've just got to go for it – come on."

Agapantha smiled weakly and let Prue grab her hand, pulling her along after the others.

They began climbing the exterior metal staircase spiraling up to the top. It had a sturdy railing, although Prue went behind Agapantha to help her feel safer. Agapantha moved rigidly and she kept a firm grip on the handrail.

As they climbed higher and the staircase twisted around the back, Prue looked down to see an orchard and great vegetable patches behind the factorium with what appeared to be the mole personifate, Abel, busying around, although Prue couldn't be sure from this distance.

"We pride ourselves on being self-sufficient and grow all manner of things at the factorium," Master White called.

By the time they reached the top rim, they were hot and thirsty. Although the rim had high-bricked edges almost to their shoulders, Agapantha stayed equally distant from either side. Master White laid out a picnic blanket and passed Prue and Agapantha cups of elder water. Prue leant her elbows on the wall. The views were breathtaking: Medlock's great towers and spires glimmered like crystals and to the sides were lush green hills and sun-soaked valleys.

"Who can tell me what lies in a straight line eastward?" asked Master White.

Edwin tapped Prue's leg. "May I?"

She smiled and nodded, and he jumped up on to her shoulder to see over the walls.

"The city of Gawthorpe," he said.

"Indeed. How about in the west?"

"Doric Wells?" Prue suggested. She'd never been there, but Mum had told her it was a traditional city, resistant to technology. Grandpa Haywood had come from there.

"Correct. And to the south?" Master White moved her arms as though conducting the landscape.

Prue looked behind her where trees stretched into the distance. "The forest?" said Prue.

"Yes, but far beyond where the eye can see?"

"The city of Augustine," said Agapantha.

"Yes, good. And to the north, we have not only Batterthwaite, but Scar Pike."

Prue knew that place; her parents had taken her and Francis there when they were little. They called it the haunted mountain because it was so tall and bleak.

Master White took a rolled-up piece of paper from her pack then spread it out on the floor. It was a map detailing the cities and the landmarks she'd mentioned.

"For your first lesson with me, let's get down to basics. Master Woolstenbury discovered that there are locations where the walls between our world and the spirit world are weaker –intersections which we as humans gravitate naturally towards but are usually unaware of."

Prue frowned. It all sounded rather unscientific.

"Bear with me, Apprentice Haywood." Master White smiled. She drew neat lines joining the sites and sat back. "What do you see?"

"The lines all cross right where we are," said Edwin, jumping down from Prue's shoulder for a closer look.

"Indeed, this factorium is situated in an intersecting weak spot between worlds. When Hannah Woolstenbury, then a promising young scientist, first started ghost hunting, as it was called several decades ago, she explored all the existing methods of spirit searching, practices which were generally ridiculed by the scientific community. It alienated her from many colleagues, and she was targeted by the Medlock press as a sham. She lost her position in society."

Master White carefully took some papers from her bag; they were old newspaper cuttings with headlines such as: *Ghost Sham Brings Shame to City*; *Give up the Ghost, Woolstenbury*; and *Once Eminent Scientist Laughing Stock of Medlock*.

"A lesser person would have given in, but Hannah knew that although many were false leads and superstitions, there was something big waiting to be discovered. Through persistence, determination, a lot of trial and error, and a sharp scientific brain, she found a way."

Master White took a book from her backpack and opened it before them. There were images of the different stages of the moon.

"One of the biggest breakthroughs came when Hannah discovered that not only were there physical intersections where the walls between worlds were weakest, but there were also time intersections."

"When it's a full moon?" said Prue.

"Yes, the full moon phase is seen as a most favourable time to harness spirit frequencies, or as we usually refer to it, the wildspark – so named on account of how hard it is to capture. But there is also the new moon phase; that's when the moon rises at the same time as the sun and the sun's bright rays mean you can't see the moon. The nights are darkest then, and spirits are also near."

Prue tried to remember which moon phase they were in at the moment; approaching a full moon, she guessed.

"Now, this connection between the moon stages, locations and the ghost world weren't necessarily new thinking – for centuries people have associated the full moon with the supernatural, and been drawn to certain sites, but what Hannah Woolstenbury did was to pin down the details, and most importantly she found the practical connection with science."

Master White reached inside her jacket pocket, then held out her hand, clenched fist downwards. Slowly, she turned it over and opened her fingers.

There, in the centre of her palm, about the size of a plum, was something crystal-like – but this was no ordinary mineral. It glowed with kaleidoscopic light in a myriad of colours: gleaming silver, lightning blue, blazing pink, blistering gold, searing red. It radiated shimmering light on to Master White's hand.

Master White spoke in a hushed tone. "This, young apprentices, is qwortzite." She let the moment sit with them while they all huddled in, transfixed. "When Hannah Woolstenbury discovered there was a wildspark beyond, she looked for a way of luring it back into our world. She suspected it could be trapped or harnessed inside a material, so she travelled the world searching, never giving up, following every lead, until she discovered qwortzite. Thanks to this, some twenty years ago, the Imperial Personifate Guild of Medlock was formed, or the Ghost Guild as you may have heard it referred to informally."

Prue couldn't take her eyes from this amazing crystalline substance. "Where does qwortzite come from?" she asked.

Master White smiled. "Deep in the ground, but that's all I can reveal. I'm afraid that part is highly secret to both apprentices and craftsmen."

After a few moments, Master White put the qwortzite back in her pocket.

Prue sat back on her heels but kept looking at the pocket. That material was the key to getting back to Francis. Everything she did with the machines on the farm was so mechanical – she understood the workings, the connections, it all came naturally to her – but here there was a new mystical element which made her feel dizzy to think about.

"Right, time for some lunch. This was prepared by Lavender," said Master White, placing neatly wrapped parcels of brown paper tied with string on top of the picnic blanket. Inside was a rye loaf, cheeses, red apples and a sweet berry pie.

"Sorry, Edwin, I do feel quite rude eating when

you can't. Do you mind?" said Master White.

"Not at all, I'll do some sketching," he said, taking a small notebook and pencil from the bag around his body.

"Do you ever miss eating?" asked Prue.

Edwin thought for a moment. "I don't miss hunger, but I do miss what I think is a memory of what it felt like to enjoy food."

"Our gardener personifate always said he gets great pleasure out of working the vegetable garden even though he doesn't get to enjoy the spoils," said Master White. "Frances, what about the farm your family have – what does it grow?"

Prue told them about the vegetables and fruit they produced, and about the machines she'd built. She felt bad taking all the credit for them when really it was always her and Francis together.

The sweet-berry pie was delicious, almost as good as Dad's island plum pie. Prue helped herself to a second slice and thought how extraordinary the day had been so far. She was still unsure about the moons and thin wall between worlds, but seeing a bit of qwortzite made the prospect of finding a way to Francis feel closer.

Just as they were starting to pack up, a scream echoed below. They all hurried to the edge to look, apart from Agapantha. Movement attracted Prue's eye at the forest edge; a personifate hawk swept over from the tower towards a cat who was standing stock-still, pointing to something.

Master White ran towards the steps and the apprentices hurried after her.

They made it down twice as quickly as it had taken them to climb up. By the time they reached the bottom, a master who Prue recognized from the morning was already there, along with several other personifates.

They jolted to a halt as they reached the scene. Prue put her hand to her mouth.

"Oh no," said Edwin.

"Poor thing," Agapantha said quietly.

A pearl coloured personifate that looked like a winged rabbit was lying limp and lifeless in the ferns. Its belly was ripped open, revealing the inner wires, synthetic muscles and mechanical workings. It was distressing to see the complex components hanging out and ripped apart, but also to think this poor personifate had died again.

"What happened, Master Tinubu?" Master

White said, her voice hoarse.

"Go ahead," Master Tinubu said to the personifate cat.

"I was taking a walk about the grounds, when the white fur of this poor jackalope caught my eye," the cat said sadly.

Edwin slumped against Prue's leg.

The personifate cat shook her head. "I think she was called Rayana. She had just joined the messengers. She'd not even been in her second life for a full moon cycle."

"I know her," said Master White. She swallowed hard, her eyes filming. "I harnessed her."

Zareen the lynx came bounding across the field. She looked more closely at the body of the dead personifate hare, then at Master White and Tinubu. "The qwortzite has been ripped right out."

"It's like what happened at the beginning," said the personifate cat.

"What do you mean?" asked Prue.

"It was before my time, but early on there were incidents of people catching and dissecting personifates to learn their secrets." The personifate cat shivered. "It all stopped when people came to accept that the qwortzite was useless without knowledge of the technologies used to capture the spirits."

"Indeed, but I doubt that would be the cause here. It's likely a confused wild animal," said Master White. "Nevertheless, say nothing to anyone until we've spoken with Master Woolstenbury." Master White glanced at Prue, Agapantha and Edwin. "That means you too. We don't want panic breaking out – Master Woolstenbury will want to handle it directly."

They nodded obediently.

Master Tinubu went to alert Master Woolstenbury, while Master White sent the hawk up to the top of the chimney to fetch the picnic blanket, then they carefully wrapped the body before Zareen took it in her mouth and hurried back to the main factorium building.

The three exchanged a wide-eyed look as the personifate crowd swiftly dispersed.

Master White turned to them. "I think we'll call it a day, apprentices. You can go back to the house. Craftsman Primrose will be conducting your lessons tomorrow."

*

Back at the house, they were greeted by Lavender and Liddy, who were dusting the pictures in the hallway.

"You're back early," Lavender remarked, then she noticed Edwin. "Ah, Edwin. Master Woolstenbury said we should expect you!"

"We're delighted to have you at the house," said Liddy. "We've put you in with an apprentice called Samir who's been here six moon cycles. I'll show you up."

"Before you go, there are some letters on the mantelpiece in the parlour, girls," said Lavender. "I haven't had a chance to sort through them yet."

Prue's stomach lurched with a sudden realization; if her parents had written to her, they would address it to Prue Hayward, not Frances! She'd be found out. "I'll have a quick look for us," she said hastily, then looked to Agapantha and Edwin. "I'll meet you both upstairs in a minute."

Liddy, Edwin and Agapantha climbed the stairs, while Lavender continued with her dusting. Prue hurried to the parlour and looked through the letters. Sure enough, there was one for "Miss P Haywood". She ripped it open and drew in a long breath.

The handwriting was her dad's. They were

angry and exasperated with her, he wrote, for leaving without even discussing it with them. But, he continued, they understood she was safe, and cross as they were, they had decided after a long debate not to come after her. He finished by saying they hoped to hear from her soon. Prue exhaled the breath she'd held while reading. She would give it a day's space and write back tomorrow.

She tucked the letter in her pocket and headed upstairs to join Agapantha and Edwin who were in the girls' room. They sat on Agapantha's bed.

"I'm glad Cora's not back yet," said Prue.

Edwin looked over his shoulder as though to check Cora wasn't about to walk in. "She's not the friendliest person, is she?"

"If by *not friendly* you mean *totally stuck up*, then you've already got the measure of her," said Prue.

They laughed.

"It's been an interesting first day as an apprentice," said Edwin.

"You must've felt right in the spotlight at the meeting this morning," said Agapantha shrinking back a little at the idea.

He nodded. "It was a bit daunting, but not too bad."

"Craftsman Primrose and Master White are nice, aren't they?" said Prue. "I think we got the best mentors. I definitely wouldn't want Sollentude. Master White was so fascinating with all that knowledge of the moons and the qwortzite."

Agapantha turned pale. "I actually found it hard to concentrate, you know, what with the height."

Edwin nudged her with his paw. "You'd better hope she doesn't take all her lessons up there."

"Oh no! She wouldn't, would she?" Agapantha said, wide-eyed.

There was a pause then they all giggled.

The jollity soon faded to silent thought, their minds now on what had occured afterwards.

"What do you think happened back at the factorium with that poor personifate?" asked Prue.

"I think Master White was right and it had been attacked by a wild animal," said Edwin.

"Sorry, Edwin. It must've been pretty distressing to see that," said Prue.

Edwin gave a small nod.

"It was probably a wolf or something that thought the jackalope would be real food," said Agapantha.

"But didn't Craftsman Primrose tell us that

wildlife stayed away from personifates?" said Prue.

Agapantha nodded. "Yes, that did cross my mind."

"Whatever it was, it ripped the qwortzite right out," said Edwin. "It's quite scary to see that. I know this is a second life, that it's almost a bit greedy to have two, but I don't remember being alive before. Seeing what I just saw makes it, well, it makes it feel like it could be snatched away again so easily, and then what? I go back to being a frequency lost in some dark world beyond? And even if I happen to become a personifate again, I probably won't remember any of this life. But I like my second life. I don't want to die."

"Don't talk like that," Agapantha said gently.

Cora burst into the room. "You'll never guess what happened by the forest today!"

"We're meant to keep quiet until Master Woolstenbury handles it," said Prue.

Cora's shoulders slumped. "You already know?"

"We were with Master White just after it happened," said Prue.

"Larkin overheard Master Sollentude talking to Master Ashby. Apparently, there were bits of internal mechanism all over the place," said Cora, spreading her arms wide.

"Cora!" Prue snapped, glancing at Edwin whose muscles were rigid.

"Look, it was probably a confused fox. Things happen," said Cora matter-of-factly. Then she sniggered. "Imagine expecting food and getting a mouthful of wires."

"Let's hope others are as compassionate if *things* happen to you," Prue snapped.

Edwin jumped off the bed and left the room.

Prue scowled at Cora.

Cora shrugged. "What?"

*

Smoke trailed from the factorium chimney, gently rising to be captured by the breeze and sent twisting above the neighbouring forest. The dense trees stretched for many miles to the south, unbroken, apart from an abandoned and forgotten cluster of buildings deep in the forest's heart, with crumbling brickwork, tiles hanging, and shutters unhinged. In the dusk, a single light shone.

Chapter 11

THE HALL OF LOST PERSONIFATES

That night, Prue slept fitfully. She dreamt Francis was in the forest all alone, calling to her.

She sat up in bed and took the photograph of her brother from beneath her pillow. It was too dark to see anything except the vague outline of his wild hair.

"Hurry up and take the picture, Prue. Let's race to the post."

"Only if I can pick my horse."

"All right, but not Lucky. I've just fitted a turbo to his front legs!"

"Well, that just leaves Pippi and Admiral. Dibs on Admiral."

"I knew you'd choose Admiral." He smiled. "But I'm still going to win!"

Click.

She drifted off again, then woke as the first hint of light edged around the curtains. Agapantha and Cora were still in what looked like a deep sleep, so Prue dressed silently in her white shirt and trousers and crept downstairs. The comforting, yeasty smell of proving loaves wafted up from the kitchen. If she closed her eyes, she could almost be back on the farm.

To her surprise, Edwin was already in the dining room with Queen Adelaide.

"You're up early," Prue said. "Couldn't you sleep?" She wondered if he was still bothered about the personifate attack.

Edwin shook his head. "No need – qwortzite keeps going."

"Oh, of course. I can't imagine what it's like, not even needing to sleep. So, it runs for ever?"

There was an awkward silence as Edwin and Queen Adelaide exchanged a glance, then Edwin said, "Not quite for ever – it varies. They say ten to fifteen years is the average life of a fully charged unit of qwortzite. With a spirit in it, the material degrades over time."

Prue hadn't realized the personifates had a time limit, and that it was such a short lifespan. She thought it must be hard to live with the knowledge that there was probably only ten years to do all the things you wanted to in life.

But she would give anything for one more week with Francis, let alone ten years.

"But the craftsmen advise resting our bodies," Edwin added. "Some say it may prolong second-life a bit. But my thoughts are usually too active."

Lavender came into the room carrying a tray full of pastries. Prue grabbed one as she passed, like she used to at home.

"Hey, they're not even on the table yet, Missy!" said Lavender.

"Manners," Queen Adelaide said, shaking her head.

Prue felt a little embarrassed, but she took a bite anyway.

"How are you, Queen Adelaide?" said Lavender.

132

She turned to Prue. "Master Woolstenbury sent a note over explaining what happened in the forest yesterday. She said you all saw it. A terrible business, to be sure, but Master Woolstenbury says there's likely nothing to worry about."

"That's easy for her to say – she's not knee-high to a human," Queen Adelaide scoffed.

"Oh, Queen Adelaide, you barely leave the house!" said Lavender.

"Well, I have my subjects to think about."

"They've searched the area and found nothing. She thinks it's likely a wolf or fox passing through, hungry with autumn setting in. Nevertheless, they are assigning more guards and telling the personifates to be careful of the forest."

"I'm not certain that I feel reassured," said Queen Adelaide haughtily.

Liddy walked briskly into the dining room and put a jug of juice on the table. "Stop fretting, Queen Adelaide. I'm sure it's nothing to get overly panicky about."

"That's what I said, Liddy." Lavender gave a "told you so" nod.

*

"Good morning, all!" said Craftsman Primrose, who was waiting for them outside the factorium. He was holding a bundle, which he passed to Edwin.

Edwin unwrapped it; inside was a small version of the Guild uniform coat. "I asked Finblewick at Deakins to make it specially."

"Wow, thank you," said Edwin as he put it on, blinking in amazement.

Prue caught Cora rolling her eyes.

"It fits you perfectly," said Prue.

Craftsman Primrose clapped his hands together. "Right, time for one of the most important lessons you'll have."

They followed him into the atrium, to the back of the factorium, where a long corridor ended in a cast iron doorway marked with the Guild symbol.

"Welcome to the Hall of Lost Personifates," said Craftsman Primrose, pushing open the door.

They entered an enormous space; it was something like a gallery, with long benches and framed works of art. The paintings were all portraits of animals. Glass cabinets dotted throughout the room contained what looked to be various inanimate personifate bodies.

Craftsman Primrose took a seat beside a painting of a hawk and gestured to them to sit on the bench opposite. "Now, who can tell me where we are?"

"The Hall of Lost Personifates," Prue said, suddenly realizing it was an utterly daft thing to say because he'd just told them that. She didn't need to look at Cora to know she would be smirking.

"Continue, Frances. Look around. What do you see?"

She stared at the various canvases. "Are they designs for new personifates?"

"Not quite," said Craftsman Primrose.

Cora coughed. "Sir, they are the painted records and bodies of personifates who have lost their second life. The room is a shrine to their service. Every uninhabited machine here was once a ghost brought back from beyond, a second life personifate. The esteemed Hannah Woolstenbury believes it's important to recognize the commitment and contribution that the personifates make to modern community in Medlock. Without respect we lose our humanity."

It was as though she was reciting a passage from a textbook, Prue thought. No doubt something she'd pre-learned from Larkin.

Prue glanced at Agapantha and raised an eyebrow. Agapantha gave a quick smile. On the other side of Agapantha, Edwin seemed a little on edge and quiet. The room was, Prue supposed, the ghost machine equivalent of a tomb and must've been yet another reminder to Edwin of his own limited time as a personifate. She thought about what Edwin had told her at breakfast about qwortzite having a limited lifespan of ten to fifteen years. She swallowed... Francis had only been twelve.

"Indeed," said Craftsman Primrose. "Of course we don't keep all of the machine bodies in here, some are archived in the factorium, but all previous personifates have a painting displayed."

"Would the Guild use the bodies again for another spirit?" asked Prue.

"A very good point, Frances – these machine bodies are expensive to create. It was tried, but Master Woolstenbury found that newly harnessed

136

qwortzite does not take to a machine body which has been inhabited previously." Craftsman Primrose stood up. "Now, I'd like you all to choose a painting and I want you to spend some time looking at it. Read the plaque, think about the words, and then choose another."

The paintings depicted many different animal types: for some, you wouldn't know they were machines, but others looked more experimental and robotic with part-visible metal frames and cog work, perhaps the early models. Prue looked around and found herself gravitating towards a painting of a hound. She'd always liked the dogs on the farm, before money became tight after Francis and they'd had to give the last away. Mechanimal sheep dogs weren't the same, but they didn't need feeding. Prue imagined how wonderful it would be to have a personifate sheep dog that could talk. She smiled to herself and read the plaque:

Wilhelmina Blue-Moon
Companion
Capax Infiniti

She looked around. There were numerous other dogs, many cats too, which also read *companion* – they seemed a popular choice – and there were gardeners and messengers, and shop workers too. Then she noticed a painting of a storm-grey hare with intelligent eyes.

Carl Cold-Moon
Technician
Capax Infiniti

A technician was different to anything she'd seen so far. Technician of what? It certainly had paws that looked like they could manipulate machinery, almost person-like, rather like Edwin.

"Ah, one of my favourites," said Craftsman Primrose, approaching Prue. "From before my time at the Guild, but I believe he was the first technician to be created." Craftsman Primrose addressed the group. "What do you notice that the paintings have in common?"

They were all animals, of course, but Prue wasn't sure that was what Craftsman Primrose meant. She read the hare's plaque again and was about to speak when Cora said, "Capax infiniti."

"Which means?" said Craftsman Primrose.

"Capax infiniti means 'holding the infinite' in the old language."

"Correct. Thank you, Apprentice Duval."

"And the names," Prue jumped in. "They're all something-moon."

"Quite right. Do you know why?"

Cora's hand shot up, but Craftsman Primrose ignored her and turned to Edwin. "Perhaps Edwin could tell us."

"We take on the name of the moon under which we were brought into our second life."

Prue thought that was nice, and quite poetic. Perhaps Francis could be Francis Harvest-Moon.

"Now, going back to the words below, *Capax Infiniti*; I would like you to think – and without giving me a textbook answer – tell me why we choose these words?" Craftsman Primrose looked at all of them in turn.

The meaning of *Capax Infiniti* rolled through Prue's mind: *holding the infinite*.

Edwin raised a paw. "Is it a reminder that the thing that makes us who we are is not the outer body, but something deep inside, and that our bodies, whether flesh or ghost machine, are just a shell. It's a stage in our history and future; which is, you know, infinite? Or something."

The silence became enormous for a moment.

Then Cora said, "That was a bit deep!"

Craftsman Primrose smiled to himself. "Edwin is correct in his line of thought – truly only an insight that a personifate perspective can bring. Although none of us truly understands the nature of what Master Woolstenbury discovered by harnessing the wildspark in qwortzite, this certainly opened a new chapter in the infinite story of life." He let it sit with them for a while, then added, "Your journey as an apprentice is about so much more than the mechanics we achieve here."

Prue's cheeks blushed with warmth and the word *imposter*, unbidden, echoed in her ears.

"But understanding the greater picture is entirely something else." He observed each one of them carefully with his knowing eyes, staying a moment longer with Edwin and Prue. Prue could tell it was so much more than a job to Craftsman Primrose. He was part of something that made history.

"Take some time to look around. I want you to pay specific attention to the different types of machinery in the early personifates, make sketches and take notes in your journal. This will all form part of your ongoing research into the evolution of personifates."

They spent two hours drawing and recording their observations. Prue's depictions were dreadful; she thought a baby would've drawn better. Agapantha's were good, and Cora Duval's drawings were annoyingly neat and exact again, but it was Edwin who was in his element. He drew not only with precision, but with flair; his sketches seemed to bring the inert paintings before him to life, as though inhabited once more.

Cora sidled up to Agapantha and smiled sweetly. "These are impressive, but I'd expect no less from a Young."

"Yes, but I'm not sure being skilled at art is to do with—"

"Don't be modest. I can spot good breeding and talent from a hundred furrows." She glanced at Prue. "Perhaps Edwin was from a respected family in his first life too."

Prue was just about to rise to the bait when Craftsman Primrose approached.

"Excellent work, apprentices. Now, you may break for lunch. Cora, you will meet Master Sollentude afterwards; Frances, Agapantha and Edwin, I will meet you in the atrium at one o'clock sharp. You have had your most important *lesson*, and after lunch I will take you to the most important *place*."

Chapter 12

THE MOST
IMPORTANT PLACE

There was a lounge room on the ground floor where apprentices could gather at lunch and break times. Cora bounded off to meet Larkin, while Prue, Edwin and Agapantha decided to go outside. The sun was unusually warm for autumn, and they sat on a bench in the gardens with the lunch packs Lavender had made. To her surprise, Prue discovered there were two packs in her bag. She opened the first and inside was what appeared to be a pretend sandwich knitted from wool.

"Do you think Lavender is a bit bonkers?" she

said, holding it up.

"Look, there's a label," said Agapantha.

Prue read it. *"For Edwin – so he doesn't feel left out, L&L x."*

Edwin frowned. "It's a nice thought, but I'm not sure what I'm supposed to do with it?"

They all giggled and shrugged and Prue and Agapantha ate their vegetable pies while watching a rabbit personifate busily digging up potatoes several furrows away. Along the perimeter wall, a large black bear personifate was on patrol.

"It's all right for that guard personifate," said Edwin, nodding in the bear's direction.

Queen Adelaide did have a point this morning: the smaller personifates were more vulnerable if there was a rogue wolf in the forest. Prue wondered whether she could do something to help. It wouldn't be difficult to go into the woods and set a trap and try and catch the wolf or whatever it was. Prue used to love creating traps on the farm with Francis. Catching the perpetrator would be an excellent way to prove herself as being the capable young apprentice they expected from Frances Haywood, and it would also show that being from the country had its benefits. And at least Edwin and the other personifates would all feel safer too.

"I was thinking: we should catch the beast of the forest."

"Us?" Edwin asked doubtfully. "And how do you propose we do that?"

"I mean it. It wouldn't be that difficult; I know how to set traps. And if it doesn't work, no one will ever know."

"Shouldn't we keep away from the forest?" said Agapantha.

"It'll be fine – nothing will attack us if we're together. Now, look at all that netting on the pumpkin patch. There's bound to be more of it lying about. We can use that! Let's set it at the weekend, when less people are around. Come on, it might even be fun," she added.

"It's not a bad idea," said Edwin. "I would actually rather do something than sit here moaning."

They both looked at Agapantha, who frowned uncomfortably.

"We'll need someone to work out the mathematics of the counterweight…" said Prue.

"Come on, Ag, live a little…" said Edwin.

Agapantha sighed. "All right."

"That's settled then," said Prue. "Let's think on it this afternoon and start working on it tonight."

*

They met Craftsman Primrose immediately after lunch and followed him to a large oak door on the first floor different to all the other doors.

"Welcome to the most important place at the factorium: the library," said Craftsman Primrose. He pushed the door and it swung wide.

Warmth radiated from the room in the auburn and umber tones of book spines and dark wood shelving that ran the length and height of the room in two layers. Enormous world globes, illuminated within by chaos lamps, were set in tables down the centre of the room. Close by, sitting at a desk, was a huge brown bear. Prue's muscles tensed, such was his size. When he saw them, he stood up suddenly, which made the desk screech forward and his chair tip backwards noisily.

"New visitors!" he exclaimed, rather over-excitedly. He rushed from behind the desk,

146

accidently sending a pile of books flying. "Whoops-a-daisy!" he said, carrying on towards them. He towered above them and would have been utterly terrifying, were it not for the fact he was wearing a garish red bow tie with bright yellow spots, and an enormous grin.

"Apprentice Haywood and Young, this is our librarian, Phineas. Apprentice Snow-Moon, you already know Phineas, of course."

Edwin nodded and smiled.

"Never was there a more bookish personifate!" Phineas declared. "When Edwin was a technician, he would be in here every break time, always learning."

"Indeed, it's where I first noticed your interest and talents," said Craftsman Primrose.

"You'll find many of the personifates like to come here whenever they can. It's open to all, even those working within Medlock occasionally pop back." Phineas reduced his voice to a whisper. "The Municipal Medlock Library isn't always the friendliest of places for them. Don't get me wrong, the librarians there are lovely, and they have several second-lifers. Indeed, I work very closely on new fiction stock with Milly, a delightful ferret personifate." Phineas reduced his voice even more, so that they were all leaning right in to listen. "It's the ASL. They target it as a place to spin their propaganda and hate for second lifers."

Prue remembered the poster she'd seen the day she arrived.

"Anyway!" Phineas said suddenly in a voice so loud that they all jumped back. "Anything you need at any time for your studies, just come and ask. If you can't find it, I'll locate it in the blink of an eye," he said, waving his arm to the side and knocking another pile of books over. "Oops! Come along, no need to hover by the door!"

"Do you mind if I show them around, then let them choose some books?" Craftsman Primrose asked.

"Be my guest. Perhaps start with the history section – that's my favourite – then mechanics, art and design; oh, the joys you have ahead of you! Now, you may borrow as many as you can carry out of the library, aside from those with the Guild stamp on the spine; those must stay within these walls. It helps protect the secrets." He winked.

"Thank you, Phineas," said Craftsman Primrose, and he led them deeper into the great room. "This is the history section, where you'll find anything from ancient times right up until the mechanical revolution. It's so important to have an understanding of where we are in time and place. There's a fantastic shelf dedicated to the history of pre-personifate ghost theories and studies – absolutely fascinating stuff."

Prue made a note to have a good look in that section.

"Over here is a section on art and design, where you will find both practical and aesthetic guides. This section here is mathematics – one for you, I hear, Agapantha – and personifate mechanics is above; the whole section there is devoted to the various aspects of synthetic muscle and internal mechanisms. Indeed, there are one-hundred and ninety-one books on internal mechanisms alone, I believe."

"One-hundred and ninety-two," said Phineas, flying along the rolling ladder above them and popping a book into a vacant slot. "And opposite is our fiction section, somewhere to truly lose yourself, or find yourself, in fact. It's rather bursting at the seams. I've had to ask Master Woolstenbury's permission to extend into the old storeroom next door, but it won't be ready for a while. If there's anything you can't see on the shelf, then I may have it tucked in a box somewhere – just ask." And with that he scooted his foot along the floor and flew back the other way, holding the ladder with one paw and waving the other.

Craftsman Primrose clapped his hands together. "I think the best way to learn is to explore. Find your own interests and spend some time discovering. I have some research to do myself, so just ask me or Phineas if there's anything you can't find."

They began browsing, and Prue went straight up the ladder to the mechanics section. A book titled *Early Personifate Technology* by Grenvil Ashby caught her eye. She had a quick flick through – it was utterly fascinating, seeing how simply constructed the very first ghost machines had been and to see how far they'd come in just eighteen years. But it wouldn't help in her search for Francis. She needed to work out how to find him, and how to make sure that when she did, she could bring his memory back.

She carried on browsing the shelves and found

a subsection labelled *The Art of Harnessing*, which sounded promising, and within that, a book titled *Unlocking the Secrets: How Hannah Woolstenbury Broke Through to the Other Side'*, which looked like an excellent place to begin. She also grabbed one called *Constructing Lifelike Mechanimals: A Study of Basic Framework Principles* on her way back down the ladder; she didn't want her real interests in being at the Guild to become obvious.

Prue paused as her eye was caught by some ancient-looking books. She gently ran her fingertips across their old fabric spines. They were just like her mum's old fairytale books back at the farmhouse. She and Francis used to take them on free afternoons and he'd read her stories under Haywood's Oak. The thoughts made her ache for carefree summer days on the farm and what had been. She pulled one out a little way – *The Talking Sparrow and Other Tales*. It was the exact same book they had at home. Francis had loved the talking sparrow.

"Francis," someone said in a hushed voice.

Prue looked up suddenly, searching the room for her brother.

"Frances, over here, come and sit with us." Edwin beckoned.

"Oh, right, sorry," she mumbled, her heart sinking back down into a black pool. She took her books over to the table where Edwin and Agapantha were sitting.

"It was like you'd forgotten who you were for a moment!" Edwin laughed.

"Ha, I know, sorry," Prue said, her face filling with warmth.

Edwin was reading something about art and Agapantha had a book called *Mathematical Principles of the Wildspark*. As Prue read, there was so much she wanted to take notes on, but it would look too obvious perhaps, so she decided to simply mark down the page numbers and come back another time to start a new journal, just for making notes related to her mission to find Francis.

Shortly, Craftsman Primrose joined them, putting a large book on the table called *The Variant Power of the Moon Cycles*. "Thought I'd brush up on the blood moon," he smiled. "Ah, I see you're reading about harnessing, Frances. Straight in at the deep end!"

The sound of books tumbling made them

all look up to the other end of the library, where Phineas had knocked a great pile over. "Sorry!" he called, pointing at his rear. "It's so much smaller in my mind."

Craftsman Primrose hushed his voice. "You're probably thinking he's an odd choice for a librarian. We were hoping for a guard, but Phineas turned out to be quite the peace-loving book fanatic and so took the library under his wing."

"Couldn't the craftsmen have just moved him to a new body, maybe something less … bulky?" Prue asked.

"A good question, Frances, but transferring spirits is against the regulations set by the Guild and the Sovereign Chancellery. It was briefly tried before the Guild realized the risks. It's a delicate enough procedure to harness a ghost in the first place. There would be a chance of disrupting the wildspark signal held within the qwortzite if we moved it to a new body."

"Oh, I see."

"Obviously it's good when we get a serendipitous match. We've been experimenting with different forms for many years," said Craftsman Primrose.

"Sometimes it works out and sometimes there is disparity, so we try a wide variety and celebrate when they do match well."

"Are most personifates happy with their new bodies?" Prue asked.

"Usually they are. The biomorphic principle means there is usually a connection formed, but our sense of self is quite fragile and rooted in our physicality. But perhaps Edwin would like to provide us with his unique insight, from a personifate perspective?"

Edwin shrugged his small furry shoulders. "I guess I was lucky to be brought back as a stoat technician. My paws are nimble and I like drawing and working with machines, so it seems like a good fit. But also, I am who I am, I don't know otherwise. But if you think about it, isn't that the case for first and second lifers? None of us can help what we are born into."

Craftsman Primrose nodded. "Exactly, Edwin. An excellent point. It is what you make of what you have that means something. What you choose to do with your time here, whether second or first life."

"But there's really no way of knowing who Edwin was before?" asked Prue.

Craftsman Primrose shook his head. "I'm afraid not."

Silence fell for a moment and then Edwin, Agapantha and Craftsman Primrose went back to their reading.

But Prue's mind was still turning over. After a while she said, "Could there be a way of making sure of a suitable match by locating the right ghost? Some way of making it less random?"

Craftsman Primrose looked at her over his wire-rimmed spectacles. "I'm afraid not, but our experience over the years has given us some clues. For example, we know the ghosts harnessed at the factorium are from a certain geographical radius because we can safely assume the voices and languages originated in their first life. We have occasionally harnessed a second lifer with the ability to speak in two languages, meaning they were likely living in this land but were originally from another."

"Do you know how far the radius is?" Prue crossed her fingers under the table.

Craftsman Primrose's eyes narrowed slightly, and she hoped she hadn't been too inquisitive.

"We estimate somewhere in the region of two hundred miles."

Prue contained a smile; that meant there was definitely a chance she could bring back Francis at the Guild.

Craftsman Primrose looked at his pocket watch. "Ah, time for me to get along. You three finish up here and check out any allowed books with Phineas. I'll see you all soon."

Agapantha was suddenly scribbling furiously in her notebook.

"What are you doing?" Prue asked after a while.

"Calculations; the current population of Medlock and the surrounding area, and the population history of the city. What Craftsman Primrose said got me thinking about the probability of being brought back. And this equation should work it out. It's not accurate by any means, without precise statistics, but it would give a rough idea."

Prue wasn't sure she wanted to know. Edwin peered over at Agapantha's calculations.

"I mean, these are approximate guesses at

numbers, but I would say P, that stands for probability, equals something in the region of 1 in 859,746."

"Oh, that's low," Prue said, suddenly deflated.

Agapantha thought for a moment. "True, but what are the chances of you being born into a first life?"

"The odds of that are probably off the scale!" said Edwin.

"And there may be other factors at play that are not in my calculation. For example, I was reading that based on a predominance of modern languages and dialects, some believe that it's easier to bring back someone who has recently passed on from their first life."

Prue felt a surge of hope knowing that.

Edwin nodded thoughtfully. "And maybe if a spirit wants it badly enough there's more of a chance too."

Prue thought back to a time she'd been out with Francis at the river near North Owlcot. They'd made a rope swing to get across; Francis had gone first and just made it to the other side, teetering on the edge for a while, flailing his arms before gaining his balance. He called back to her to join him.

"I won't make it!" she'd shouted.

"You will if you want to! It depends how much you really want it."

"I'll fall."

He folded his arms. "Then you stay that side and go on back to the farm, and I'll stay here and eat all Dad's apple tart to myself." He grinned, took it out of his backpack and held it to his mouth.

"You wouldn't dare!" she shouted.

"I did dare, and now I'm this side of the river. It's you who won't dare!" He laughed, and Prue tightened her lips and scowled at him.

"But the chances of me falling in the river are higher than reaching the other side. If I stay here the odds are one hundred percent certain I'll stay dry." She sat on the bank.

"Oh, come on, Prue; the odds are better if you believe it's possible! Just believe."

She'd stood up, closed her eyes for a second, then took an almighty run up and grabbed the rope. For a moment she'd felt like she was flying.

"Let go!" Francis called, and she released the rope and hurtled into her brother on the other side, knocking the wind out of his chest and sending the apple tart flying into the grass.

"Are you all right, Frances?" Edwin said. "You looked like you were miles away for a second."

"Err, yes – I was just thinking about the wolf trap," she said quickly. "Come on. Let's get back to the house and sketch some plans before Cora gets back."

Chapter 13

LUELLA

In the parlour, Prue and Edwin used Edwin's sketchpad to draw a plan for their trap. Prue instructed him on the design, until at one point, Agapantha gave a little cough and asked them if they minded, and she made a few adjustments to the calculations for the counter balance and rope lengths.

"That's brilliant, Ag. Yes, I think that will work better," said Prue, impressed.

They decided the quietest day at the Guild would be Sunday, so it would be easiest to sneak around and get equipment to set the trap then.

When they finished planning, Prue put the drawing in her bag and they went into the dining room for tea.

Afterwards, Agapantha and Edwin went upstairs and Prue sought out Liddy in the parlour to ask for some notepaper and an envelope to write to her parents.

"When you're done, you can go to the messenger tower at the factorium, and one of the personifates will deliver it. It's the quickest way to send letters these days. Take someone with you if it's after sunset."

The parlour was busy with an older group of apprentices, so Prue went upstairs to write. Agapantha was sitting on the smallest bed in the room, and on the large bed nearest the window, where Agapantha had slept the previous night, sat Cora Duval.

"What are you doing?" Prue asked.

"This is my room too," Cora laughed.

"That's Agapantha's bed," said Prue hotly.

"It didn't have her name on it."

Agapantha stood up behind Prue. "I don't mind."

"There, see, she doesn't mind," said Cora.

"I mind," said Prue. "It's the principle of it."

"Would you like me to move?" Cora said to Agapantha, with her eyes wide and a sickly smile.

Agapantha shook her head.

Prue huffed and went to the desk. She tried to push it all aside and begin writing to Mum and Dad. Her pen hovered over the page for a painful amount of time before she decided to describe what it had been like to ride on the Gigantrak, what Medlock was like and even Deakins Entire. But she had to stop after that – she had so much to say, but the secrecy regulations prevented it. It felt as though she was even further from her parents, and this was a distance she would never be able to breach. She signed it *Sorry, Prue. P.S. Please address any envelopes to my official title, Apprentice Haywood. It's Guild rules.*

When she'd finished, she turned to Agapantha and said, "Would you please come to the messenger tower with me? Liddy said we should go in pairs after dark."

Agapantha's eyes flitted to the window. "It's getting late."

"Come on, the stars are coming out. Please?"

Agapantha nodded. Prue felt a bit bad because

she knew Agapantha's good nature made her easy to persuade, but she also knew it would be a chance to get to know her better.

"Don't be long," said Cora. "I need my sleep. Master Sollentude says Larkin is the brightest young apprentice the Guild has ever seen, and I intend to take his crown."

Prue resisted the urge to roll her eyes. "We won't be long."

They headed down the stairs to the pneumerator.

"Was it lever up to bring the pod this way or down?" Prue said.

"Up, I think, but it's already here because it's already up."

"Oh right, of course." Prue slid the door open and they climbed into the pod.

Agapantha looked around the curved metal interior of the pod. "It's a bit nerve-wracking doing this on our own, isn't it?"

"Silver lever to close the door. Come on, sit down, Ag." Agapantha sat beside her. "And we're..." Before Prue could finish, the pod shot forward.

Prue and Agapantha were soon at the transport hut. It was late evening and the factorium and forest were washed with a dove-grey light. The messenger tower, which stood alone to the right of the factorium, was almost as tall as the main building and looked something like a large brick lighthouse, with the only windows at the very top. They left the path and cut across the grass, which was damp with evening dew.

Prue noticed Agapantha glance nervously at the place where the personifate had been found dead the previous day. Prue shivered. "The library here is impressive, isn't it? I've never seen so many books," said Prue, to take their minds off the incident.

Agapantha nodded.. "The mathematics section is amazing. And I liked Phineas."

"Me too. He seems to really love it there. I wonder if he was a librarian in his first life?"

"I bet he was!"

"I must admit," Prue lowered her voice and made sure there weren't any personifates near, "I found the Hall of Lost Personifates a little creepy though."

"I suppose. But it's good to remember them, don't you think?"

"Yes, but what will they do as time goes on? Fill the whole of the factorium with pictures and personifate shells?"

"Maybe they'll build a new wing." Agapantha smiled.

Silence fell for a while. Prue was still thinking about what Cora had done. "Do you really not mind, you know, about Cora taking your bed?"

Agapantha shrugged.

"She should have asked you," said Prue.

"Honestly, it's fine."

Prue stopped walking and turned to face her. "It's not fine. Who does she think she is?"

"It means more to her than it does to me," Agapantha said, then continued walking.

At the messenger tower, a clackety door led to a metal spiral staircase that ran up the inside of the brick structure. They went around and around, until Agapantha said she felt quite dizzy. At the top, they emerged into a room with arched windows and a peaked high ceiling. The room was filled with comfy-looking sofas and tables covered in books and newspapers.

All manner of personifates lounged around: a great raven was reading on an armchair; a turquoise owl with pink eyes was in conversation with an emerald moth as long as Prue's arm, both perched on the window sill, and a giant black bat hung from the ceiling in front of them. It opened its eyes.

"Can we help you?"

Prue cleared her throat. "Hello. I have a message."

"Well, you've come to the right place," said an exotic, bronze-feathered bird with three sets of layered wings, as large as a golden eagle. "I'm Thackery, thunderbird personifate, the fastest in the tower."

"Fastest? Certainly the most something," said the green raven, looking up from his book.

"The most modest?" said the bat.

The owl and moth laughed and Thackery lifted his beak snootily.

"Nice to meet you, Thackery. I'm Frances and this is Agapantha. But I need someone who can take a message outside of Medlock."

Prue noticed a pigeon perched on the back of a blue velvet sofa. "Are you free?"

There was a moment of silence, then the pigeon looked around at the other birds. "Well, someone answer the girl."

Thackery extended his three sets of wings and gave them a little shake. "She appears to be looking at you, Lu."

"Me? I haven't had an assignment for many moons. It's usually the others who get chosen these days."

"I'm sorry," said Prue.

"No need to be sorry. I'm quite used to it," the pigeon said. "I know I'm slow, but that's because I was one of the original messengers. The craftsman used to go for the more traditional animals, based on what they knew, so a carrier pigeon was a logical choice for a messenger in the early days." She lowered her voice. "Urgent post rarely leaves Medlock, so lately, it seems the more exotic the better."

"What was your name?" Agapantha asked.

"Luella, but you needn't bother remembering it. My qwortzite has held out a long time, so it will probably fade soon and I'll just be another painting in the Hall of Lost Personifates." She shook her head softly and sighed.

Prue thought of the old machines seized up on the farm, recycled for parts. "Actually, I think you will be perfect for this task." She rolled the note and tied it carefully around Luella's neck, then gave her instructions on the farm's location.

As Luella flew from the tower Prue called after her, "Thank you for your service!"

Prue and Agapantha watched her fly away.

"Come on, Ag. We'd best get back before Cora decides she wants my bed too."

Chapter 14

AWEN

Home visits outside of Medlock were only allowed one weekend per moon cycle, so Prue, Edwin and Agapantha decided to go for a wander around the city. Craftsman Primrose had sent the thunderbird messenger with envelopes for her and Edwin, each containing a florin. Prue hadn't really thought about the idea that she might receive any payment as an apprentice. The three stepped out of the house into a sunny Sovereign Row.

"Shall we go to Medlock Fudge & Co?" Prue said eagerly. "I think it's near Deakins."

"Sounds lovely for you two, but seeing as I don't

eat, we'll need to find somewhere else for me to spend my florin," said Edwin, raising his brows.

"Of course, sorry, Edwin," said Prue.

"Art supplies?" Agapantha suggested.

"Hmm, I get everything I need from the Guild. I feel like doing something just for me, something different."

"Let's head for Smithy Door and see what we find on the way," said Prue.

They made their way to the bustling main square and then turned into Burlington West. Prue still marvelled at the smartness of the city people with their plush clothes and shiny buttons, precision in every stitch.

Edwin paused outside a shop called Denton Hats of Medlock – Suppliers of the Sovereign Chancellery. It had dark-green framed, multi-paned windows, behind which a machine whirled and crunched. A sign stated: *Made to measure to your specification and design in minutes*. They watched the cogs turn, piston's chuff, and belts turn, then a straw boater hat appeared out of a chute at the end.

Edwin smiled. "Wait here."

Minutes later, he appeared from the shop with a

bag. He took out a brown woolen flat cap, then put it on to model it for the girls. "What do you think?"

"Smart!" Prue remarked.

Agapantha smiled. "It suits you."

He tipped his cap to them and they all laughed, then he put it back in the bag. "Are you two sure you wouldn't rather buy a fancy hat?"

Prue shook her head. "Sweet treats win for me, Ed."

They headed on through the weekend crowds, along Pickwick and towards Medlock Fudge & Co.

"Isn't that Finblewick?" Agapantha said as he hurried past them in the street, ignoring them.

"Nice to see you again too," Prue called after him.

"It's like he'd never met us," said Agapantha.

Prue watched as he disappeared from sight. "Is it me, or did he look like he was up to something?"

Edwin glanced up at her. "I think it's just his face. I mean, he does look a bit peculiar."

"I can't imagine why they designed him to look like that?" said Agapantha.

Prue shrugged. "He must be an early model, perhaps when someone was learning."

They reached Medlock Fudge & Co and stood

open-mouthed, gaping at the glistening jars filled with candy twists, marzipan, jelly cogs, clove rocks, marshmallows, pear drops, coconut ice, liquorice, toffee, bonbons, chocolate limes and at least twenty flavours of fudge – ten times the choice of Peck's Supplies in North Owlcot.

They were about to go through the open doorway when they heard a voice from inside. "Cora, you will do as you're told."

Prue, Agapantha and Edwin looked between each other, surprised.

Cora stepped outside. "Oh, it's you," she said in a bored tone.

Behind her was a woman and man with the same dark eyebrows as hers and Larkin, immaculately dressed in highly-tailored outfits with a lavish mix of silk and suede.

"Cora, aren't you going to introduce us?" said Mrs Duval.

"These are apprentices at the Guild too," said Larkin.

"Cora, be polite," Mr Duval urged.

"This is Agapantha Young," said Cora.

Mrs Duval lifted her chin. "The Youngs of Medlock?"

Agapantha nodded. Mrs and Mr Duval shook her hand in turn.

"They've been away working with the MMD in Gawthorpe, haven't they?" said Mrs Duval.

"Yes."

"Be sure to tell your parents to visit us when they're back in town."

They turned to Prue.

"This is Frances Haywood," said Cora. "She's from a farm miles away, somewhere like Near Ollet?" said Cora.

"North Owlcot," Prue corrected.

"A farm worker?" Mrs Duval said, looking at Cora in disbelief.

"How … interesting," said Mr Duval. Neither of them moved to shake her hand.

"Edwin is an apprentice too," Prue said challengingly.

"Oh," said Mrs Duval, looking down and noticing Edwin for the first time. Mr Duval said nothing and glanced at Mrs Duval. "Well, it's a pleasure to meet you," said Mrs Duval, sounding merry on the surface, but Prue could hear the venom within her words. "Cora, perhaps you could invite Agapantha to visit while her parents are away."

Agapantha looked down to her feet.

"Remember to pass on our good wishes to your parents, Miss Young. Come along, Cora," said Mrs Duval, breezing away, closely followed by the others.

Mr Duval muttered something about falling standards as he walked away.

"Come along, Cora," Prue mimicked. As she watched them move along the street, she observed Mrs Duval snap her fingers at a small hedgehog personifate who had been standing imperceptibly at the side of the street beside Fortesque's Fanciful Footwear. Mrs Duval pointed to Cora's boots and the hedgehog hurried in with a cloth to clean and shine them.

"She didn't even talk to him, so I doubt there was so much as a please," Prue said, shaking her head. "Come on, let's go inside and get some fudge."

*

Later that day, Agapantha and Edwin were drafted in to help Lavender with dinner preparation, so Prue seized the opportunity to take the pneumerator to the factorium, as she wanted to make notes on the page numbers she'd marked down in the library previously. Also, another letter had arrived earlier in the day and she wanted an opportunity to read it alone. To her relief, when Lavender passed it to her, it was addressed to "Apprentice Haywood". She read it on the pneumerator. They were still cross with her, but it was less red hot than the previous letter and they'd included more general talk about the farm this time. Perhaps they were coming around to the idea of her being a Guild apprentice. But it was still written in her dad's hand, not her mum's.

There were still a few craftsmen, personifates and the odd apprentice to be seen as she headed for the library, but the factorium was much quieter at the weekend. She knocked on the door.

"Hellooooo!" said the cheery voice of Phineas. She pushed the door open and stepped inside.

The librarian was sitting among piles of books at the far end of the room with his great furry back legs crossed. He looked up. "Ah, Apprentice Haywood wasn't it?"

"I hope you don't mind me coming here at the weekend. I wanted to get ahead with some studies."

"Not at all, I greatly admire your dedication. Do excuse the state of disarray; I decided to reorganize the section on ancient history. Are you looking for anything in particular?"

Prue's skin prickled with expectation. It was the first time she'd been able to really research by herself. "I'd like to find out more about the harnessing process and the wildspark."

Phineas pushed himself clumsily to standing. "Harnessing is an advanced subject. Perhaps *An Introduction to Harnessing* by E.B. Sollentude, or *The Wildspark Frequency Guide* by Master Tinubu?"

"Yes, they sound good. But I was actually after some of the more *specific* areas too. For example, do you have anything on the theories of past lives of personifates, or … memory?"

Phineas scratched his head.

"It's just that I would like to try to understand all aspects of the process, if I possibly can."

"A noble pursuit, but I can't say anything comes to mind on memory… Ha! I can't remember books on memory! Get it?" Prue smiled and Phineas danced gawkily to a section and pulled several books from the shelf. "These are the two

I mentioned, and this one by Master Hannah Woolstenbury herself may interest you. But I'm afraid you can't take these from the library. You will have to read them here."

"Thank you," Prue said.

She sat at a table and opened the journal: *First Harnessings: Trials and Tribulations by Hannah Woolstenbury*. She skipped over the introduction and went straight to the diagrams of equipment. Most of them were for something called a spectral oscilloscope. It was fascinating reading, and she was thrilled to follow the calculations, but eventually they became so complex that she wished she had Agapantha to help her.

The door creaked open and Prue glanced up.

"Frances, I'm pleased to see you putting in extra time at the weekend," said Craftsman Primrose. "Very diligent with all the work that's to be done."

"I thought I'd get ahead." She hoped the half lie didn't show on her face. But maybe she was getting good at lying.

"I'm rather partial to a bit of weekend study myself."

"You must've read everything in these sections,

Craftsman Primrose!" Phineas called from behind the pile of books he was sorting. "Lucky I've just taken a new delivery!"

Craftsman Primrose walked across to Prue. "What are you reading?"

She showed him the book.

"It's certainly the most fascinating aspect of what we do here. The design and mechanics are crucial, of course, but the real magic is in the harnessing. Good to see you going straight for the tricky learning."

As he moved to turn, Prue hesitantly said, "Sir, I have a question."

"Yes?"

"I was just wondering if there might be a way to unlock memory in the ghosts."

Craftsman Primrose frowned, then pulled out a chair and sat opposite. "Memory loss is a by-product of the process. It's a curious thing, memory. Some say time leaves a trace in the frequency – all of our experiences stored in the very fabric of our imprint on the Universe." His eyes narrowed thoughtfully behind his thin-rimmed spectacles. "I've often thought if only there was a way to pull out a particular part of the signal after a ghost was brought back, we might—"

"You think there could be a way?"

"If there is, it will be a bright, enthusiastic young mind like yours who finds it." Craftsman Primrose stood up. "I'll leave you to your studies. I believe Phineas has just unearthed an excellent new book on Ancient Mercia for me. Fascinating culture; the way they looked at the after-life thousands of years ago was in many ways far advanced to our own thinking. Until the last eighteen years, of course, with the introduction of the Imperial Personifate Guild. To people of Ancient Mercia, death was only a temporary interruption, or pause to life. They believed in the existence of a person's spirit, that there was a unique spiritual characteristic of an individual. They called it the *awen*; we have come to know it now as the wildspark."

"So, this is why personifates retain their personalities?"

"Yes, I like to think so."

"Did the ancients have ghost machines?"

"No, their thinking and technology was greatly different, although they did believe that preserving the body was important because it was believed that the *awen* would return to it every night to receive new life. If you like, that was their version of our personifates!"

"Ah, here it is! I knew your book would be in the delivery somewhere!" called Phineas.

"Thank you, Phineas." Craftsman Primrose collected his book then called back to Prue. "Make sure you get back before dark, Frances."

As Prue read through her books, everything turned over in her mind. She felt she'd taken a big step towards finding out more about memory. She was certain that the answers were already there in the wildspark, she just had to find a way to reach them through building some sort of machine. Prue realized that in order to make real progress, she had needed to start experimenting with equipment, so she'd need a secret space to work in.

She said goodbye to Phineas and left the library. Through the glass ceiling high above, the coral glow of the setting sun tinged the clouds. The atrium below was now empty, and an eerie silence hung in the air. Her footsteps echoed as she took the walkway around the edge to the other side where the design lab corridor was. There were still voices coming from the main design lab, probably craftsmen working on the hundred. She hurried past to the very end, where there were a couple of storage rooms that she'd spotted the week before. One of them looked orderly and neat and the other was in more of a state of disarray, with a layer of dust covering the shelves. It was perfect: stacked with boxes which she could hide her journal in, and she could get her hands on any tools she needed. She opened some of the boxes and looked inside; one had synthetic fur, another had rolls of wire and various tools, and the next box had oddments of machinery marked "faulty".

Smiling, Prue said, "I hereby name you, *The Memory Lab*." It would be hard to get time away from the others to come and work here, but she'd try to find excuses to whenever she could. She glanced out of the window – it was dusk, and she had to get back for dinner or Lavender and Liddy would start to worry. At the door she took one last look and made a promise to Francis. "I'll be back to start work soon."

Chapter 15

TRAPS, HATS, WINGS AND WOES

The next day, Prue, Edwin and Agapantha headed straight for the forest to set the trap. Light shone in hazy beams between the branches as they trudged through mulchy leaves in and out of green-brown shadows. Prue touched the trees as she passed between them and recited their names in her head; Francis had taught her to identify the tree type just by the feel of the bark.

It was apparent that Edwin remained on edge, and he looked over his shoulder every few paces. "I'm glad we're at least doing something," he said, jumping over a moss-covered, fallen tree.

"It's a bit spooky in here," said Agapantha, giving Prue a quick sideways glance. She was wearing her worried "rabbit caught in the mechanicart lights" expression, just like the day they'd first met at Deakins.

Prue tried to smile reassuringly, even though she had to admit there was definitely something eerie about the forest. "It's fine. We're together. A wolf would be more scared of us, I'm sure."

Agapantha gave a little nod. "I've never done anything like this before."

"If there's anything out here, I'm sure we'll catch it," said Prue.

A short distance in, they found a suitable place where the trees were the right distance apart, then they spread out their equipment on the ground. Prue climbed up among the shifting leaves and creaking branches to hoist the ropes into place, instructing the others on where to tie and loop and thread the ropes and counter-balances. After a while, they finished and stood back to admire their work. Then Prue instructed them to carefully throw some leaf debris over the net, to disguise it.

On the way back to the transport hut, Prue caught the distant sight of Craftsman Primrose and Master White walking beside each other.

"They are definitely a thing," said Prue.

"You mean, together?" said Edwin.

"Totally. The way they look at each other, you can tell," said Agapantha.

"Gross," said Edwin, sticking out his tongue.

They all laughed, but as they walked through the forest back to the pneumerator, Prue glanced at Edwin. Did personifates love in their second lives? Could love survive from the first life into a second life? If she found a way to unlock the past lives, the personifates could at least remember.

Back at the house, the fire was lit in the parlour room, and the three of them stretched out lounging on the sofas, as for once they were the only apprentices in there. The relaxed Sunday mood was spoiled when Cora and Larkin returned from visiting their parents two hours later. Larkin went straight upstairs, but Cora popped her head around the door and burst out laughing at the sight of Edwin wearing his new cap.

"Nice try, but wearing a hat isn't going to make

you human," she said curtly.

Prue's mouth jarred in disbelief. "What did you say?"

Cora snort-laughed in response, then turned to Agapantha. "Don't forget, we must sort a date for you to come to my house." She gave a sickly-sweet smile then left the room.

Edwin took his hat off and threw it at a wall.

"She really shouldn't have said that," said Agapantha quietly.

"Sometimes she is just awful. Ignore her, Edwin." Prue went across the room, picked up his cap and put it beside him.

*

On Monday, the first lesson was rudimentary muscle wiring and signals in the laboratory. Master Sollentude was busy on the hundred, so to Prue's annoyance, Cora joined them.

"All thought and feeling signals come from the qwortzite frequency," Craftsman Primrose was explaining. "But it's not one-way wiring. The sensors send signals back to the qwortzite in a constant stream. As craftsman, and for you as apprentices, our most important skills are centred around the inner connections and workings of the machine."

Cora sidled up to Agapantha. Prue knew she was angling to work with her.

"It is our attention to detail that makes the Imperial Personifate Guild of Medlock stand head and shoulders above all the other cities and indeed the wider world, as a centre for invention."

When Prue glanced across, Cora mouthed. "Farm girl." Prue sighed and looked away.

"Ignore her," Edwin whispered.

"Once a ghost is harnessed inside the qwortzite, the first thing we need to do is establish the loop. So today we are going to be working on making simple loops. The movement data comes from the wildspark. But we can't practise with a real frequency, so in training we use signal simulators. Your task will be to create the looped wiring between the synthetic muscle and the simulator."

Craftsman Primrose bent down and took something from the cupboard below. It looked like the wing of a small bird, suspended by a delicate rod that had been mounted on a small base.

"Wings are used extensively in training and refining your skills. Elegantly simple, yet infinitely complex, they are the perfect choice for early studies. Have you all brought your copies of Master Tinubu's *Simulator Starting Points*? Good. And you all have your apprentice kit? Excellent. Then you will notice on your bench there is also an essential tool for all craftsmen for use with intricate mechanics." Craftsman Primrose slowly took off his thin wire-rimmed spectacles and folded them up. Then he carefully opened a wooden box about the size of a pencil tin and took out what appeared to be an elaborate pair of glasses with various interchangeable lenses on hinges. "These are magno-viewers." There was a soft hum as he put them on and looped them over his ears. When he looked around, the tiny cogs whirred and ticked, with telescopic cylinders extending and lenses slotting seamlessly in and out of place. "They follow the direction of your sight and auto-focus, allowing you to see intricate areas in the finest of detail."

Prue lifted her own pair up, trying to work out how they were powered, then saw a tiny cog mechanism.

"I want you to get used to the wiring, the structure, and the synthetic muscles, and perform the loop of a simple up and down movement. If you have read the first chapter, you can skip straight to page eight and begin. You may work individually or in pairs as it's your first time."

Cora's hand shot in the air. "Sir, may Apprentice Young work with me?"

"I'm honestly fine on my—" Agapantha began,

"Come along, Ag," Cora said.

Rolling her eyes at Cora's bossiness, Prue paired up with Edwin.

The connectors and tools were far more delicate than any Prue had used before, and the magno-viewers were a marvel. It took a while for her to get used to the difference in what she was seeing and her finger movements, but she shortly got the knack of it. After half an hour of careful wiring, their wing jolted, expanded, and rose.

"Bravo, Apprentice Haywood and Snow-Moon! That's the fastest I've seen it done by an apprentice since Larkin Duval, although I think he may still just hold the record," said Craftsman Primrose with a friendly wink. "You can move on to chapter three."

When Prue glanced over, she noticed that Agapantha was doing all the work, while Cora seemed to be expert at sitting back – then looking involved as soon as Craftsman Primrose looked over.

After a break, they were joined by Master Sabrina Tinubu for a lesson on personifate structure.

"Each personifate is based on a rigid primary structure, something akin to our skeletons but stronger. We compress and fuse flakes of grapheme to form a low-density, high-strength material."

"So, the skeletons are light but strong?" said Prue.

"Indeed. You will notice that while the bodies of the personifates replicate the natural world, they are generally faster and stronger than their animal equivalents."

Every part of it fascinated Prue. There was so much to take in, and she couldn't help but ask question after question about all the technology.

At the end of the lesson, Craftsman Primrose gave them all a worksheet to complete on the internal components of personifates, then informed them that the attendance of the new apprentices would be required at the factorium at eight in the evening in Master White's office. When they asked him about it, he wouldn't say any more.

As they left the lab, Cora was telling Agapantha how brilliantly they had worked together and how they should pair up all the time. Prue whispered to Edwin that they should skip dinner back at the house and check the trap, but they'd have to make sure Cora wasn't around.

"I think I'll grab something to eat here rather than go back," said Prue loudly. "Agapantha, can you stay and go over those equations you were showing me? Edwin's struggling with them too. We could go to the library."

Agapantha frowned, and Prue tried to tell her with her eyes to just go with it.

"You're skipping dinner to do maths?" Cora said in disbelief. "Mind you, I guess you need all the help you can get. I'll tell Lavender you're so behind you have to work on. See you later, losers." With that she breezed away.

"She's certainly a force," Agapantha said.

"That's one word for her," said Prue. "I guess she has quite a lot to live up to with Larkin being *super apprentice*. Not that that's an excuse."

"I shouldn't have let her get to me with the hat," said Edwin. "I know she just likes to push our buttons for her own entertainment."

Prue hooked Agapantha's arm. "Come on, let's check the trap. If we've caught a wolf, we could always put it in Cora's bed as a surprise."

Edwin laughed. "Looks like personifates aren't the only ones with a wild spark. I like it!"

They made their way to the forest.

"I wonder what we'll be doing later at Master White's?" said Edwin.

"I forgot to ask: where are the masters' offices?" said Prue.

"Top floor of the factorium," said Edwin. He leapt ahead, weaving his body this way and that.

"Don't go too far!" Agapantha called. "You know – what with hungry wolves and foxes and all that."

Prue watched him frisking elegantly, leaving a trail in the leaves, and tried to follow the pattern he was making with her own feet. She imagined what it would be like to be in the body of a stoat, to be so fast and athletic – she wondered if it would suit Francis. Having got to know Edwin, she was pretty sure if she came back for a second life, a stoat body would suit her well.

Suddenly, Edwin froze, rearing up on his back paws, his body rigid.

"Ed?" Prue whispered urgently. Her skin prickled.

He pointed upwards. "There's something in the trap!"

Prue rushed over. "If we're careful, we can keep it contained in the netting, and show the masters, then…"

Her elation quickly melted into disappointment as she took a closer look. It was a deer.

"I'm pretty sure deer are herbivores," said Agapantha, frowning at the writhing body above.

Prue sighed heavily. "We'd better release it."

They lowered the trap and after a few tense moments of untangling itself, the deer sprang away into the forest.

"Well, it's lucky we've got a spare hour to reset it!" said Edwin.

Chapter 16

HARNESSING

There was a shabby sophistication to Master White's room. It had a forest green, leather lounge chair, glass jars, red velvet curtains, and chaos lights in fringed lamps. Master White and Master Woolstenbury stood in their ruby jackets by a mahogany table where the machine body of a golden eagle lay beside a piece of equipment that Prue had seen pictures of before but had yet to see in real life: a spectral oscilloscope.

Prue's heart jumped. It was the full moon; they were at a harnessing!

"Please sit down," said Master Woolstenbury.

She had a voice which commanded in its assured, snipped tone. "You are here as observers, there will be no need to comment, or move, and no need to take notes. You are here to purely experience."

The four of them sat on the green lounge chair, hardly daring to breathe, while the two women proceeded to set up their equipment and talk to each other in hushed voices.

After a few moments Cora leaned in towards Prue. "Your boots look a bit muddy for library study," she said quietly, her mouth pinched.

"Oh, we—" Prue began whispering.

Cora put up her hand. "Spare me. If you'd rather gallivant around the grounds than study…" She paused while there was a brief break in the Master's conversation. "Then it just means that your exit from the Guild will come all the sooner."

Prue let out an agitated breath.

Master White sat on a chair beside the table and faced them. "This is the most important piece of machinery in the harnessing process, our spectral oscilloscope, or as we like to call it, the GODAR: our Ghost Observation Detection and Ranging device. This screen allows us to visualize the signals.

In time you will come to learn the inner workings of these systems."

Master White took the key from around her neck and went through a door at the back of the room. She returned with a small wooden box. Prue recognized it straight away.

Master White opened the lid and gently took the qwortzite out as though holding a fragile egg. It glowed with kaleidoscopic colours. She placed it inside the machine body.

A long time passed as the two women examined and adjusted equipment, with Master Woolstenbury wearing her magno-viewers. They attached something to the main machine that looked like a dish.

"This is a parabolic reflector. We use it to focus the signal into a feed point," said Master White.

Master Woolstenbury was adjusting the dials, looking at the signals streaming across the spectro oscilloscope. Prue strained to see them more clearly. She couldn't help but wonder: was one of those squiggly lines Francis, trying to come through?

"Signals, Prue. They're everywhere, we just can't hear or see them all."

Prue shook her head doubtfully. "How can they be there if we can't see or hear them?"

"Take rats, for instance."

"Did you say rats, Francis?"

"Yes. They communicate with each other at a range outside of human hearing."

"Really?" Prue said, dismounting her mechanimal horse beside the barn.

"I've heard it on the signal generator, when I was testing the homing transmitter. Silent signals are how the transmitter works. It sends a message through the air, and the receptor on the machine picks it up."

"That's brilliant!" Prue said, amazed.

"Come on. I'll show you how it works." Francis smiled.

"Agapantha, can you hold this for a moment for me, please?" asked Master White.

Prue looked to Agapantha, the spell of her thoughts suddenly broken.

After a sideways glance at Prue, Agapantha tucked her russet hair behind her ears and went to Master White. "Just hold that dial right there… That's it, give it a slight turn. Stop when it feels right."

The signals seemed to pulse a little faster. After

a moment, they became less tangled.

"Thank you, Agapantha. You have a knack for this. You can sit down now."

Minutes later, there was just one pure signal pattern on the screen. Master Woolstenbury glanced at Master White, her eyes gleaming.

Then she looked at the four. "Newly arrived souls are like infants, and in their panic about losing their memories, their sense of self, they can imprint on a person. This means they form an attachment that is deep, and very powerful. Here at the Guild we are very careful to prevent that from happening, because that affects the personifate's precious free will." She took a silver hand-held mirror from the table and held it before the face of the personifate eagle. "The first thing it sees, must be itself."

A wing twitched.

The next part of the process took Prue quite by surprise.

In the gentlest voice, Hannah Woolstenbury lay her hand on the chest of the eagle. "Welcome. Do not be alarmed. You are back in the world of the living, but you are something new now." Its eyes fluttered, then shut again. "You have no memory of what has come before. It is part of the process. Can you open your eyes?"

They waited for several moments before the eyes wavered and blinked. The bird's talons twitched.

"You were alive once. You were in the world of the dead. We cannot tell you for how long. Take your time, and when you feel ready, use your thoughts and feelings to try and speak."

After a while, the eagle opened its beak slightly.

Prue was leaning forward, barely on the chair, her heart thumping. What if it was Francis?

"You are in a different form, but the essence of you is the same," said Master Woolstenbury. "Can you see yourself?"

The eagle personifate gave a slow nod.

"Try to say something. Think, and it will flow."

Prue gave a little gasp of anticipation.

"He ... hello," came the quiet voice of the eagle, unmistakably older and female.

Grief twisted in Prue's chest. *Stupid*, she thought – she was so stupid. How could she have possibly thought it would be Francis? The disappointment bore down on her like a wave, crushing her chest.

Master Woolstenbury bent down to the new

personifate. "You bring with you understanding, but not history. You are in the body of a great bird, and in your new life you will work together with the living in a second, different life, striving for the good of all."

The eagle raised a wing and stretched out a foot, as though trying out her new body.

"We will give you time, but you are free to stay here in this form or return to where you were."

"Do I have a name? I don't remember."

"You may choose your own, or we can choose for you."

The eagle personifate paused then said, "Choose for me."

Master White looked to Master Woolstenbury. "Perhaps we should consult the apprentices?"

Master Woolstenbury nodded in agreement, but Prue's mind whirred with so many emotions she could barely hear what was being said any more. She wiped the sweat beading on her brow, her hands were clammy.

Edwin shrugged. "It's a big responsibility to name someone."

"Don't worry, the personifate can say if they don't like it," said Master White.

"Corabel?" said Cora.

The eagle winced.

"Maybe not," said Master White. "Agapantha, or Frances, any suggestions?"

But the room felt as though it was closing in on Prue. Her heart ached so much for Francis. She couldn't speak.

"How about Gisella?" said Agapantha.

Master White smiled. "I like it."

"So do I," said the eagle.

Green curtains were drawing over Prue's vision, her ears buzzed. Something soft brushed her hand. Edwin's paw was nudging her.

"Frances, are you all right?" he said.

"Francis," Prue whispered.

Then the curtains shut and there was silence.

*

When Prue woke, it was just her and Master Woolstenbury in the room.

"It's all right, Frances, you haven't been out for long."

The memory of the evening came back to her.

Master Woolstenbury must think she was useless, fainting at a harnessing. Panic hit her – if they contacted her parents to ask about her health, then she'd be found out.

"Here, have some sweet cocoa, it will help."

Prue took a sip. It warmed her and made her feel less hazy. "I'm fine, honestly," she said, swinging her feet around to sit up. The eagle personifate had gone, but she noticed Zareen was now in the room sitting quietly beside Master Woolstenbury's desk. "Silly, really; it must've been because I didn't eat much for dinner."

Master Woolstenbury narrowed her eyes.

Prue hoped if Master Woolstenbury was going to tell her she was too weak to be an apprentice, that it would be over quickly, and she could just pack her things quietly and disappear. Master Woolstenbury's eyes met Prue's, and much as Prue tried to hold her emerald stare, she found herself looking away. What if she'd already realized about Francis? Had she mumbled something accidentally while she'd been out?

Master Woolstenbury leaned forward. She spoke kindly. "You've recently lost someone, haven't you, Frances?"

For a moment, Prue felt the ground disappear beneath her. She thought it was all over.

Then she realized that Master Woolstenbury had called her Frances, which meant she probably didn't know everything.

Prue nodded.

"It's happened before with apprentices. An experience of loss can make the harnessing process difficult to deal with. If you need to talk to anyone, of course you have Craftsman Primrose, but I want you to know that my door is always open too."

"Thank you," Prue said quietly, her muscles relaxing with relief.

"One last thing. I'm aware of your interest at the library surrounding anything related to harnessing, especially with regards to theories of memory. No good can come of it, Apprentice Haywood. Memory loss is a natural part of the process. It's the way it is, and this is the important part; it is the way it *must* be. Can you imagine the chaos to society if the personifates could remember? Imagine the demand from people seeking their lost loved ones?" Master Woolstenbury sat back in her chair. "We are lucky with our current Governor and Sovereign Chancellery, but if events were different and the personifates went to the highest bidder, it could become extremely problematic. Imagine if there were personifates with memories who had vendettas on the living?"

Silence hung for a moment.

"The sooner you learn all this the better for you."

Prue nodded.

"How do you feel?"

"Much better, thank you."

Master Woolstenbury stood up. Their conversation was over. Prue walked to the door.

"Focus on your given tasks, Apprentice Haywood. Do I make myself clear?"

"Yes, Master Woolstenbury."

Prue was sure Master Woolstenbury meant well, but there was no way she would ever stop trying to get to Francis. She would just have to be more careful.

"If you could escort Apprentice Haywood back, please, Zareen, just in case she has any further dizzy spells."

Prue and Zareen left the factorium and headed across to the transport hut. It felt exhilarating to walk beside a creature which in the wild would have made her run for the hills. Prue's skin prickled with the thrill of it, and she couldn't help but keep glancing down.

"You know that she might not be completely right," said Zareen.

Prue looked at her curiously. "What do you mean?"

"Don't get me wrong, Hannah Woolstenbury is a genius, and there is no other first lifer I respect and esteem more, but…" She paused in her steps and glanced up at Prue. "Hannah Woolstenbury started all this, but it will be up to others to carry it on. Who knows, perhaps there are new things to come, things that need to be discovered by others."

Prue smiled.

Zareen escorted Prue back to the parlour, where Edwin and Agapantha were waiting, then said goodbye. A fire was smouldering in the hearth and there was a homely glow to the room.

"Are you all right?" Edwin said.

"Of course," she said, shrugging it off. "Must've been something I ate."

"Lavender said we could stay up until you came

back," said Agapantha.

"Honestly, I'm totally fine. We should all go to bed now."

*

The full moon hung motionless above the forest to the south, brushing every treetop with white in the night. Beyond, the streets of the forgotten village shone like silver streams. A chaos lamp glowed orange in the window of one of the buildings. Inside, something had awoken. The creature's body felt strong – formidable. It listened to its orders and felt anger and purpose surging through it.

It was here to kill.

Chapter 17

THE
INVENTORS PARADE

The rest of the week was busy with more muscle wiring and a new class that Prue found even more trying than design – administration lessons. They were being taught by Craftsman Ashby, who was about ninety years old and spoke in a single tone of voice that made Prue want to fall asleep within three minutes of being in the room. He told them that administration was of the utmost importance with the imminent hundred. Parts of it might have been interesting, had the delivery been a little more exciting, but words like "quota", "regulations", "accountable" and "non-expendable" trolled through Prue's brain. She was saved when she worked out it was possible to position her textbook upright on the table to look as though she was reading along, but was really making notes and plans for her memory machine. She decided her best shot would be to try and adapt a GODAR machine, which wouldn't be easy to get hold of – she'd been through all the boxes in her memory lab, so she knew there wasn't one there, but perhaps she could find an older model in one of the other storage rooms.

Cora was pulled away to assist Sollentude every day, so it was easy for Prue, Edwin and Agapantha to check the trap regularly before they made their way back from the factorium. Prue wondered if they should take it down, as they had only caught the one deer and the likelihood was the fox or wolf was long gone, but she liked the way it was a secret between the three of them; it somehow made it easier that she was keeping a bigger secret from them.

Soon it was the weekend again and the Inventors Parade. By the time they had left the Guild house, the streets of Medlock were already rapidly filling with people and personifates. They headed for the main square, which Agapantha had told them was the focal point; her parents had brought her every year since she was born. Prue noticed that often the people and personifates tended to stay in their respective company, but she also saw many first-lifers walking along together with personifates. An elderly lady in a feathered hat walked happily chatting and laughing with a sapphire-blue bird personifate on her shoulder. A little further ahead, two gentlemen held hands with a young girl and swung her in the air, while a large rainbow-coloured cat danced loops around them, singing a nursery rhyme with the girl.

"Hurry, Lavender said all the best spots get filled up quickly and I've thought of just the place for us," Edwin said, urging them across the road. He stopped at the rear end of the huge mechanimal bee.

"Edwin, I'm pretty sure that's a no-go," said Agapantha.

The great metal components whirred as the metallic wings lifted and lowered.

A grin spread on Prue's face. It was exactly the sort of thing she and Francis would've done together. She didn't need convincing. "Want a ride?"

She looked at Edwin and patted her own shoulder.

Edwin turned, and for a moment it looked as though he was scampering away, but then he turned and scurried forward, took an almighty leap up to Prue's shoulder – then leapt again on to the platform.

"You are one bonkers stoat." Prue laughed.

With a big jump, she grabbed the top of the platform. Prue scrambled her feet up the side and pulled herself up.

"Come on, Ag. Honestly, it's the best view in the square," she called down.

Agapantha shuffled uncomfortably, her cheeks ruby red. Prue noticed there were already other people looking at them and heading towards the statue.

"Take our hands and we'll pull you up," Prue urged.

After a deep breath and an awkward smile, Agapantha reached up and took Prue's hand. A couple of girls were trying to climb up on the other side.

"Quick, it's a race to get on the bee's back," said Edwin.

The great wings of the bee whirred, rising above them.

"We have to catch the down motion," he said.

One of the girls was already on the platform on the other side and was trying to pull her friend up.

"I'll go first," said Prue, jumping as the wing arced down. She almost slipped and fought to regain her balance. There were large rivets on the bee's body that she could hold, so without another thought, she used one to push herself upwards to grab another, and before she knew it, she was on the back of the great statue, the vibrations of the mechanics rumbling gently through her body as though she was now part of it. "Hurry up!" she said.

Edwin and Agapantha climbed up the other side and soon joined her. The three of them sat on the top and took in the view.

"Didn't I tell you it would be the best seat in the house?" said Edwin.

Prue looked around at the people and personifates starting to fill every inch of the busy square. She spied many blue jackets like their own and some mustard and ruby too. Barriers were keeping onlookers off the road and the windows on the upper floors were open, with colourful flags crisscrossing and people waving.

By now, others were on the statue's platform and a few climbed up to sit behind them where there was still room.

Prue had never been to a parade before. They had the summer fetes in North Owlcot, but nothing on this scale.

Somewhere, several streets away, music began playing; a thumping, booming, drumming with whistles trilling like excited birds.

"Yes! Here we go!" said Edwin.

Prue could feel her heart rate rising as the drums neared.

"The first cart is the showpiece, so be prepared to see some weird things," said Agapantha. "Most of it will never function in the real world of course; it's mainly for fun."

Soon a huge shadow fell on the street at the south end of the square. A band streamed in, playing their great rhythmic drums and blowing whistles. The crowd gasped then erupted with applause as a huge person, almost as tall as the surrounding buildings, stepped into the square. It was an automaton made entirely of cogs, which ticked and clonked as it stepped from one foot to the other, two huge arms slowly swinging forward and back.

Prue clapped and cheered, amazed at what looked like a great wind-up mechanism powering it.

The cog person was followed by a cart with chairs and tables which sprang into action and began dancing about each other.

"I suppose it makes it easier to play musical chairs," said Prue.

"Very practical," said Edwin, smiling.

Then followed a lady who was wearing great mechanical wings strapped to her body.

"I can't see that taking off anytime soon," said Agapantha. "Mathematically speaking, the proportions just don't work."

They watched and cheered as parade carts flowed around the square: peddle bikes powered by miniature engines, a giant self-playing piano with an advertisement on the float stating *Sponsored by Marvello's Automated Musicians*, a robotic trumpeter, a small house on wheels with the banner *Why stay still when you can move home every day?* Then a cart rolled in with enormous glass orbs high in the sky on great prongs.

"I don't get that one," said Prue.

In a moment, the glass domes filled with black, as though night existed within, then flashes of light exploded and the domes were ablaze with vibrant colours.

"These would make it possible to party anytime!" said Edwin.

Lastly, Governor Watson-Wentworth stood like a figurehead on a cart of personifates, waving and being cheered by the crowd. A banner was displayed: *All for personifates and personifates for all.*

"As the city's most esteemed invention, the personifates always take the final place," said Agapantha. "There's a personifate draw for which personifates are chosen to be on the cart. Everyone's name goes in and twenty are chosen."

"It is amazing, isn't it?" said Prue. "Those earlier machines were huge and impressive, but personifates are so much more advanced. It really shows how much further the Guild is, how brilliant Master Woolstenbury is…"

Suddenly, something flew through the air from the crowd – it hit the side of the cart and exploded red.

The parade wheezed to a stop and everyone

began looking around, wondering what was going on.

"Rights for personifates!" someone shouted.

"Look down there," said Prue, pointing to a leopard who raised herself on hind legs and threw a second paint bomb.

Then across the square a few individuals started chanting, "ASL! ASL!"

"Oh no, it's the Anti-Second Lifers," said Prue.

In no time, Sovereign Chancellery guards seemed to appear and bundled both the leopard personifate and the Anti-Second Lifers away.

"It's quite all right, nothing to worry about," Governor Watson-Wentworth called to the crowds.

"What was the leopard upset about?" said Prue, as the music started up again.

Edwin frowned. "Let's just say that some personifates aren't happy with being controlled by the first lifers."

"Oh, I've not thought about it like that before."

"That's the problem," said Edwin. "I'm not saying that the personifate was right in what she did, but…"

"But what?" said Prue.

"But you've got to admit there's an imbalance. How would you like to know you at best had fifteen years? Wouldn't you want to choose your path and to do everything you wanted to in that time rather than doing what the Sovereign Chancellery want?"

"Yes, of course, but even though it's not ideal, isn't it best to be given any chance at a second life?" said Prue.

"Without our memories, without any history, without any sense of who we are, we are putty in their hands, and they can tell us who we are." He huffed.

"But are any of us truly free?" said Agapantha.

Prue shrugged. "True – we all have to live with rules."

"I wouldn't expect you both to understand." Edwin jumped down from the statue.

"Edwin, wait!" Prue called.

"Let him go. We'll talk more when he's cooled down," said Agapantha.

Chapter 18

SPIRIT LIGHTS

The Inventors Parade had come to an end fairly swiftly after the incident, even though Governor Watson-Wentworth had waved the trouble away and ensured his personifate cart finished the full rotation around the square. The red paint bomb that had hit the side of the cart dripped like a wound down the side and was not so easily brushed away.

Prue, Edwin and Agapantha didn't talk any further about what had happened, but the incident continued to play on Prue's mind into the next week. She'd thought about what Edwin had said, and the leopard personifate had a good point. Even though all the personifates she'd met seemed perfectly happy, it didn't seem fair. When she eventually found a way to bring Francis back, she wouldn't want him to be assigned in a post as a messenger or kitchen worker. She wanted him back on the farm with her.

If she found a way to uncover the personifates' memories, surely that's what most of the personifates would want?

At breakfast on Wednesday, there was a lot of excited chatter around the table.

"What's going on?" Prue asked Yan, one of the other apprentices.

He indicated the mantelpiece where named envelopes were lined up. "See for yourself!"

There was one with "Frances Haywood" on in scrolled gold handwriting. She ripped it open.

Dear Frances,
You are invited to the Imperial Personifate
Guild of Medlock Annual Sahwen Celebration
on 31 October
Dress code: formal evening wear
Master Woolstenbury

Agapantha joined her. "What's going on?"

Cora breezed in, almost knocking Yan flying. She fanned herself with her invitation. "It will be so difficult to know what to wear. I only packed seven dresses." She threw a barbed glance at Prue.

Prue sat down at the table with Agapantha. "Well, I certainly didn't bring anything. What about you, Agapantha?"

"No, I wasn't thinking of evening wear when I packed for the Guild."

Lavender came in from the kitchen bearing a great tray of pancakes dripping with syrup. "Come on, girls, tuck in. Ah, you have your invitations, I see! Master Woolstenbury is confident they're ahead on the hundred. We were a bit worried it would be cancelled, to be honest."

"I don't think I can go. I haven't got suitable clothes," Prue said.

"Nonsense! Everyone attends the Sahwen celebration! Perhaps Cora can lend you something?"

Prue thought that she would rather face an angry bear than borrow something from Cora.

"I'd love to, Lavender, but I'm afraid I only brought a couple of dresses, and they certainly wouldn't fit her." Cora's face dropped in fake disappointment.

"Don't worry, we can go shopping at the weekend. We have plenty of time," said Agapantha, smiling at Prue.

Prue did have her apprentice money, but she wanted to send it home.

"It'll be my treat," said Agapantha.

Edwin glanced up. Things had been a little awkward since the parade.

"And you, Edwin. We can visit Bard's Precision Tailoring and get something made specially."

He smiled. "I'd like that."

Cora puckered her mouth. "How sweet," she said sourly.

*

The following few days were spent on repair duty – there was a backlog due to the craftsmen and masters working flat out on the hundred, so the apprentices were drafted in. They finished early on both days and Prue made excuses so that she could work in her memory lab. It also gave her time to sneak around and borrow all manner of equipment she thought might be useful, including an old GODAR which was left in a box in one of the labs. It was different to the GODAR she'd seen used in the harnessing, but she'd found books on older models in the library, so she'd been able to work out what needed fixing.

Prue sat behind a cluster of boxes in the memory lab and tapped a pencil on her journal. "The ghost machines process the movement data and thought data within the frequency ... but somehow the pre-harnessing history data is blocked," she muttered to herself.

Her journal was filling up fast with notes. She was convinced that the memory of the personifates still existed somewhere; either it needed pulling back from the spirit world, or it was in the wildspark harnessed by the qwortzite, possibly hidden in some way.

Sighing, she laid back on the floor and stared at the ceiling. Francis and home were on her mind. Her parents had written again on Monday, wanting to know why she hadn't been home for a weekend yet. She'd sent a note back with Luella explaining that they could only go on certain weekends and they were very busy at the moment with the hundred and promised to visit soon. Prue felt she was getting closer to finding a way to Francis, but there was one big problem; she would need a personifate test subject to get frequency readings from in order to take a closer look. Edwin was the obvious choice, and she thought he would probably leap at the chance of unlocking his past memories, but then again, she wasn't entirely sure on how he would take it after the Inventors Parade incident, or that she could ask him to risk his apprenticeship position, if they were ever found out. She had almost finished fixing the broken connections on the GODAR and she planned a few adjustments to make it more transportable, so next week she would be able to analyse the frequency and see if what she suspected from her research matched up.

At the end of the week, when they arrived back after lessons, Lavender had a hearty vegetable broth and still-warm sourdough bread ready for them. All the apprentices' winter cloaks were hanging on the pegs and there was a line of what looked like fishing nets, the sort Prue would use to skim the pond back at the farm.

"Everyone eat up quickly, then collect the light jars from the shelves and check your nets before we leave. You don't want any holes, or you'll have a very disappointing evening," she said, taking one of the light jars from the shelf.

"What in all of Medlock is she up to?" said Agapantha.

Martha, a year two apprentice, smiled. "Oh, it's the first new moon since you've been here, isn't it?"

"What does that mean?" said Prue.

"It's the collecting of the spirit lights."

"Spirit lights?"

She looked at the chaos lamps on the shelf – and realized they weren't chaos lamps at all!

"Yes, they're sort of like a wildspark, from beyond," said another apprentice. "But you can only briefly see them at the new moon. If you capture one, it stays until the next. We do it every moon-cycle. You'll soon see!"

"Hurry up now. Don't forget your jars!" Lavender called.

They ate hurriedly, then gathered the rest of the light jars and carefully packed them into backpacks.

Then they checked the gossamer fine nets lined up in the hallway to make sure there were no holes.

They all streamed down to the pneumerator. "Come along, ten at a time, we'll soon all be there, no need to push," said Liddy.

Once at the factorium they gathered on the front lawn. Everyone was instructed to take a jar and stood in a great line with Lavender in the middle.

The apprentices held their jars up to the sky. Prue looked at Agapantha.

"Well, this is a bit weird," said Prue.

Lavender cleared her throat and launched into a poem:

> *"At full moon's gate*
> *We wish you well,*
> *Spirit stars of light.*
> *We thank you for your everglow*
> *And return you to the night."*

Then she unscrewed her jar and the light shot out. With a fizzle it was away.

Everybody else started unscrewing their jars. It was suddenly as though fireworks had been set off and the lights shot into the air, leaving a shimmering trail in their wake, dancing off into the night air. Then the apprentices all sat on the lawn and waited until the very last sliver of sun had disappeared somewhere behind Medlock.

"All right, spread out everyone. Nets at the ready," Liddy said.

"What are we waiting for?" said Prue.

"Why, for the lights to return, of course!" Lavender laughed.

"So, we released them, and now we're going to catch them again?" said Prue.

"Not the same spirit lights! Oh, dear no, that would not do. They stay with us until the next full moon is approaching then we release them back and catch a whole new set of spirit lights. Just wait, they'll be here soon."

Prue watched the night sky, eagerly looking for more lights. In Staplefield, when it was the end of the harvest, fireworks were set off. She and Francis would climb out of his bedroom window where the ledge made it possible to edge along to the roof, and scramble to the top.

"Francis, Mum is going to kill us if she finds out."

"Best not tell her, then." He laughed, swung his other leg out of the window, then disappeared.

"Francis!" Prue whispered urgently. She heard the door to her parents' room close.

Francis's hand appeared back in the window and beckoned her. Prue took a breath and climbed out. They edged along, Prue's heart juddering like cart wheels over dry tracks as they passed the window of their parents' room. They clambered up the roof tiles to sit atop the ridge of the roof, just as the first fireworks of Staplefield began. They were just distant pinpricks of sparkle in the night sky, but Prue knew to her and Francis they represented possibility.

A grey speck caught Prue's eye; it was Luella flying towards her. She landed clumsily at Prue's feet. "I'm sorry I'm so late with this letter. I had a lovely chat with your father about the barley harvest, and he showed me all the fascinating machines you and your brother had created."

Agapantha looked over at Prue. Prue hoped Agapantha hadn't heard and put the letter in her pocket for later.

Prue spoke quietly. "Wait, you chatted with my father?"

"Oops, well, he was making a rather interesting pie and I was curious about the ingredients – I thought I could pass it on to the personifate chefs at the factorium who cook for the masters, and I completely forgot myself and asked, then had to explain about being a personifate. He was very nice about it."

A whirlpool of panic churned inside of Prue. "And he spoke about me and my brother … by name?"

There was a moment of awkward silence, then Luella said quietly. "Frances or Prudence, I can tell a good person when I meet one. I'm sure you have your reasons and it's no business of mine. I shan't be passing the knowledge on to anyone. You're Apprentice Haywood to me." She winked.

Prue smiled. "Thank you."

"Your dad said that they had accepted that you need to follow your own path, although he said your mum has taken some convincing. And he told me about—" She paused. "I'm sorry about your brother."

All Prue could do was nod, because if she dared to open up, she feared it would flood out of her like a burst dam. She was pleased that her dad had seen how amazing personifates were – she was certain he would love them. "Did you meet my mum too?" she asked tentatively.

"Your dad said she was busy in the fields."

Prue sighed, but she wasn't sure if it was relief or a slight disappointment – she was worried about her mum's reaction, but also wanted her to see how amazing the personifates really were.

"I stopped off in Batterthwaite on the way back. It was rather strange; I felt a sensation which I can only describe as being pulled away, which was odd. It was like one minute I was there, then for a moment I wasn't."

"Perhaps you should rest, Luella," said Prue. Then a tiny spark of light caught Prue's eye in the grass. Then another, and another.

"Here they come. Give them a moment; we don't want to scare them off," Lavender called out.

"Nonsense. Let's go!" said Liddy, leaping after them.

"Quick, Luella!" said Prue, tearing off after Liddy. Luella took flight beside her.

Lights were now flickering all over the lawn, like a star-spangled sky turned upside down. Prue darted around, with Luella laughing in her ear.

"This is the most fun I've had in many moons! Hurry! To the right, there's one!"

They dashed about catching the lights, filling the jars and laughing until Prue's legs felt like jelly and she slumped on the floor. Then Prue had an idea. "Luella?"

"Yes, dear?"

"I wonder if you would mind helping me with a little project."

"Of course, although I'm not sure what use I can possibly be?"

"It's nothing difficult. I'll call for you before lessons tomorrow."

Luella stretched out her wings. "I shouldn't think I'll have anything else to do, I'm hardly in demand."

"Then I'll see you then," Prue said quickly as Edwin and Agapantha bounded over.

"Lavender, Liddy and the apprentices are heading back," said Edwin.

"I'd best be getting back to the tower. I'll see you all later," Luella said, taking flight.

Agapantha stood beside Prue. "Lavender said there'll be hot cocoa waiting for us at the house."

"If there's one thing I wish I could try, I think it'd be that," said Edwin.

"It's a hug in a mug," said Prue. "I hope there are cookies too." Her stomach growled at the thought and she made exaggerated groans of hunger.

"Come on," Agapantha said, glancing towards the transport hut. "Everyone's gone back now."

But Prue's eye was caught by a flash of light at the forest tree line. "Look! There's one more!" She grabbed her net. "It's mine."

"Not if I catch it first!" said Edwin leaping after her.

"We really should go," said Agapantha.

Without moonlight, the forest was a complete and dense black, apart from the spirit light which brightly illuminated the immediate area at the edge. It flitted through the ferns like a gleaming dragonfly, with Prue, Agapantha and Edwin leaping after it.

*

Behind a tree, a short distance away, the creature watched the children. They were the enemy. If it was to stay alive there was one order to obey – *you will need to kill.* He wanted to give his new body a try. He was meant to await command, but what difference would two small girls make? Perhaps the master would be pleased? This new body was powerful; it would be practice. The others had gone – two girls and a little white creature could be quickly disposed of. It flexed its clawed hands and edged closer. A branch cracked beneath its feet.

"What was that?" said the pale girl, suddenly looking his way.

"Got it!" called the other girl. "Feisty one, this!"

"We should go," said the pale girl, weakly.

The creature took another step closer, behind the next tree. The leaves shook.

This time the other girl, the one with the wild hair, looked over her shoulder, into the forest. "Did you both hear that?"

She was barely ten metres away. The creature crouched, ready to spring. The ferns crunched.

"We should go," said the small white animal.

"I think you're right," said the girl.

*

The creature surged forward, thundering through the undergrowth towards them.

"Run!" Prue cried, but Edwin and Agapantha were already dashing across the lawn towards the transport hut.

Prue sped after them, dropping her net so that the spirit light fizzed away, her heart suddenly felt like a rotary engine thudding in her chest. The rush of leaves and pounding of feet came from the forest behind, or was it her own hectic steps thumping, and what in Medlock was that great snorting sound? She willed her legs to charge faster through the dew-soaked lawns and sprinted onward, her eyes firmly on the glow coming from the door of the transport hut. She was fast – she'd always been able to beat Francis – luckily, Ag and Edwin were too. Prue risked a swift look over her shoulder and caught a glimpse of something. A horned creature. Was it just a stag?

Then, with a terrible rasping hiss, it called, "*Need to kill.*"

Blood whooshed in her ears and she doubled her efforts, not even daring to look again for fear it would slow her down by one moment. The group hurtled inside the transport hut and Prue slammed the door behind them. Agapantha rushed to pull the lever to bring the pneumerator their way. There was an immediate whirring sound.

"What was out there?" Agapantha said, her chest heaving.

"You ran, so I ran! What happened? I didn't see a thing!" said Edwin.

Prue's legs felt like the bones had disappeared. "Hurry up!" she said, willing the pod to appear, glancing back at the door.

Agapantha stared at her, emerald eyes glistening and as wide as one of Lavender's dinner plates. "What did you see, Frances?"

"It was like a stag, but not. Worse. It was hard to see in the dark, but there were antlers. I think it stopped not far from the forest edge. I couldn't see properly."

The pneumerator appeared – they hurriedly opened the hatch and clambered inside. Prue sat down and put her hands on her knees, taking several breaths, trying to reassemble what she had glimpsed. They all sat in silence for a moment.

"So it was just a stag?" Edwin said, letting out a

232

small laugh of relief.

Agapantha huffed out a lungful of air. "Yes, must've been."

Prue shook her head. "No. It said something to me."

Agapantha looked to Edwin. "Maybe it was a personifate, then – a guard. Are there any stag personifates?"

He thought for a moment. "I don't think so. Not that I know of."

"But it wasn't like a normal personifate. It said…" Prue shook her head.

Edwin put a paw on her arm. "What?"

The pneumerator slowed to a stop at the house.

"What did it say, Frances?" Edwin asked, as they all climbed out.

After drawing a long breath, Prue said, "'Need to kill.'"

Agapantha shivered her shoulders. "We should tell someone."

Prue shrugged. "It's going to sound pretty ridiculous. I mean maybe it was a deer, or a personifate guard thinking it was funny or something."

There was a whirring sound as the pod disappeared. They climbed the stairs back into the hallway of the house. Chatter was coming from the dining room and the sweet waft of cocoa and cookies filled the air.

"Perhaps we should keep this between us," said Prue. "I mean, what evidence do we have?"

"I agree. Cora would probably only jibe us about it and say we'd made it up," said Edwin.

Then footsteps sounded behind the mouse painting. Cora and Larkin appeared, laughing.

"What are you three doing lurking in the hallway?" said Cora. Larkin carried on to the dining room.

"Where have you been?" Prue said, narrowing her eyes.

Cora raised her eyebrows and said, tight-lipped, "We had to run an errand for Master Sollentude." She pushed past them and carried on to the dining room.

Prue stared after her.

"Do you think they saw it too?" Agapantha whispered.

Prue and Edwin exchanged a look.

"Think about it, Ag. They arrive not long after

234

us. Don't you think that's a bit strange?" said Edwin.

Prue nodded. "Exactly. I think it was their idea of a joke. I mean it's not exactly hard to find the materials to make you appear like a scary animal around here, is it? Well, we're not going to let them see it got to us one bit. Come on – cocoa's waiting." Prue strode forward to the dining room.

Chapter 19

TRAPPED

The next morning, Prue sneaked out of the room before Cora and Agapantha woke up. The events of the previous night seemed silly in the light of morning. She was pretty certain it had been a Cora and Larkin joke, and she'd decided not to get drawn into Cora's games and focus on her memory mission. She hurried down the stairs, hoping Edwin was still resting in his room. Her stomach twisted uncomfortably – it was horrible having to lie to both of them, but she needed to keep on track with her plans to get to Francis, before she was found out.

She was about to open the door to the

pneumerator staircase, when a cough came from the dining room.

"Where is one off to so early, Frances?" said Queen Adelaide

Prue turned to see Queen Adelaide sitting on her golden chair.

"Oh … one is, I mean, I'm off to the library, to get some study in before lessons."

"I commend your conscientious nature, but if there is one thing a queen has, it's an excellent sense of when something is going on in her court that she should know about."

"Honestly, there's nothing to know about," Prue said, then quickly added, "Oh, is that a new dress, Your Highness? It looks particularly magnificent."

Queen Adelaide raised her chin and smiled. "The finest velvet from Augustine."

"It's very nice," Prue said, hurrying out of the door.

But as she made her way down the steps to the pneumerator, Prue's mind began to turn. Perhaps she would be able to persuade Queen Adelaide to work with her on her memory project? Everyone had her down as a deranged personifate, but what if there was something different in her that was unlocking real memories?

When Prue finally reached the messenger tower, Luella was perched in the window. With a few beats of her wings, Luella flew down and landed on her shoulder.

They hurried through the factorium to the memory lab.

"This is very intriguing, Prue, but are you sure you should be in here?"

"No one has said I can't," Prue said carefully. She took out her journal from her hiding box and the GODAR she'd managed to fix. "I'd like to take a reading of your wildspark signal, if possible. But I must warn you there are risks involved. I've never actually used this machine before."

"How will you do it?"

"If I attach these wires through your synthetic skin, I believe I'll be able to get a reading on this machine here. Don't worry, you won't feel a thing."

"I never do. It's a funny thing, missing pain. Missing something unpleasant. Missing something you can't even remember. Tell me, Prue, why exactly are you doing this?"

Prue paused then lowered her voice. "Luella,

promise me you won't tell another soul."

Luella thought for a moment. "You're a clever girl, no doubt about it, and you have a kind heart. I promise you."

"You're the only one who knows what happened to my brother. I want to find him, and I'm not sure how, but if I can unlock memories at least it'll be a first step."

Luella was silent for a while. Then she nodded. "So, you want to analyse my frequency as part of your search?"

"Yes."

"Well, my dear, I feel this is a rather personal request, but it's a noble pursuit indeed and I would be happy to play a small part in the process."

In a moment, Prue had swept her up and hugged her close. "Thank you!"

Then Prue lay her equipment on the floor. "I want to attach a receiver wire to your chest, close to the qwortzite."

Luella nodded. Prue gently inserted the wire, just a millimetre or two so as not to risk any damage, then she switched on the GODAR. It crackled, then she slowly twisted the dial. A frequency appeared on the screen.

"Well, I'll be darned!" said Luella.

"Hold still, I'm going to make some notes." Prue hurriedly sketched the shape in her journal. "Right, I'm going to zoom in a bit."

Prue's breath caught in her throat. There were complex patterns within the wave: waves within waves, within more waves. Some curved, another like saw teeth and another like a series of steps. She hurriedly copied it all into her journal.

"Will you move a wing for me, please?"

Luella did so, and the square wave contracted and expanded.

"Now could you imagine how it feels to fly?"

The saw tooth wave moved.

"Fascinating," Prue breathed. "That must be linked to emotion."

"I've no idea what you're making sense of in all those squiggles, but I'm glad it's of some use!" Luella laughed – and as she did so, the saw tooth signal rippled again on the screen.

*

Afterwards, Prue hid her journal back in the box and then popped her head out the door and checked the coast was clear before sneaking back out. She hurried to the mechanics laboratory for her lessons, and found apprentices of all levels were already there, bustling inside.

"Where have you been?" asked Edwin.

"Library."

"That's funny," said Cora, "because the library is in that direction."

Prue's cheeks burned.

"And I thought you three were such good friends."

Edwin and Agapantha went quiet and they all hurried inside.

"Why don't you sit with me today, Agapantha? We both know we're the only two who are going to make it here," said Cora.

Prue ignored her and found a free seat. Master Tinubu was at the front of the class waiting.

"Apprentices, we are, as you know, all hands-on to prepare for the blood moon. The masters have decided that a suitable task for the apprentices will be to work on the mechanical voice boxes. The specification is uniform for each personifate, so this is the best task to get started with."

Prue had read a little about voice boxes in her library studies.

"Apprentices who have been with the Guild for a year can proceed on the projects, and I will check your work. Apprentices who have been here under a year, please come to the front table."

Seven apprentices came to the front. Master Tinubu placed a cube, about the size of a dice, on the table. Prue had certainly been expecting something a little bigger.

"While our own voice boxes, our larynx, controls the flow of air, the mechanical voice boxes we make at the factorium control the flow of signals and translate that into sound. The ghost's own frequency results in the voice so there is only one possible, unique sound. If we don't get the mechanics quite right, it results in static or silence. The voice box is complex micro-engineering, but the mechanics are easy to follow if you stick with the step-by-step instructions."

Master Tinubu looked to the door. "I had hoped Master Sollentude would join me to get you all started." She glanced at her pocket watch and sighed. "Well, we'll have to just get on with it. She went to the cupboard then gave them all a copy of *Inner Mechanical Workings of the Personifate by Hannah Woolstenbury, Volume III*, which was as thick as one of Lavender's spelt loaves.

"Chapter Eleven onwards. You'd better get reading, then tomorrow you can make a start on the mechanics."

*

By the end of the afternoon, as they walked back to the transport hut, there was so much information going around in Prue's brain that she longed for sleep just to give it a rest. The voice boxes were fascinating, but it had been difficult to concentrate when her mind kept drifting back to her memory research. She looked back at the factorium, then she realized with a bolt that they hadn't checked the trap in two days!

"We'd better check the trap. If some poor animal was stuck there, I'd feel terrible."

"I'd almost forgotten about it, what with that

business at the spirit lights," said Edwin.

"It's time to take it down anyway. Whatever killed the personifate is probably long gone," Prue said, although there was still that seed of doubt in her mind. What if it hadn't been a joke? What if there was more to the creature she'd seen? "We need to keep an eye out, in case Cora and Larkin try anything again," she added.

The evenings were drawing in earlier by the day, and the light already had a murky gloom to it as they entered the forest. They walked silently, eyes flitting in all directions, on their guard.

They were approaching the trap when they suddenly all froze, hearts thumping in their chests with both fear and elation: there was something in it!

"Is it another deer?" asked Edwin.

But Prue had already seen that the long leg sticking out of the net was not that of a deer. Her body slumped with a terrible realization. "Oh no," she stammered.

The three of them stepped into the clearing and looked up.

They hadn't caught an animal.

The net gently rotated. A human face pressed

against it and slowly swung towards them. "What in all of Medlock is going on?" he rasped.

It was the unmistakable ashen face of Master Sollentude, ten feet from the ground.

"Oh dear," Prue said breathlessly.

"Well, I guess we know why he didn't show at the lab today," Edwin whispered.

"Get. Me. Down … immediately!" he said, his voice furiously quiet.

They rushed to release the trap, with Prue stuttering instructions and pleading to do it as gently as possible. Even so, Master Sollentude landed with a bump.

He stared at them. "The Duval apprentices warned me about you three. Cora said you were up to something in the forest. I'll be speaking to White and Primrose and you can expect severe repercussions."

They gathered the trap netting, then were marched back through the thick ferns to the forest edge.

"Leave the equipment there for now and get back to the house, out of my sight," said Master Sollentude. "You've not heard the last of this."

The three made their way solemnly back to the transport hut.

"We should probably start packing," Prue said gloomily.

"Do you think?" said Agapantha.

"Look, we don't know," said Edwin.

But their sagging shoulders and shuffled steps told each other that it wasn't looking good.

Not another word passed between them as they rode the pneumerator, then they glumly made their way across the hall.

The bottom of the staircase was barred.

"Had a nice evening?" Cora had a smug, pinched expression which made Prue's hands clench. She felt Edwin's paw tap her as though to say *don't*.

Prue barged past and stormed up to the bedroom and slammed the door. She was likely to be sent home and she'd barely got started on finding a way to Francis. Moments later, Agapantha gently opened the door.

"Frances, Lavender said there's tea downstairs."

"I don't want any. Tell her I'm not hungry."

Agapantha closed the door.

Prue felt so many emotions, but the worst one was

246

knowing that it was her fault; she'd come up with the net idea and persuaded the others to do it. She'd let down the best friends she'd had since her brother. If only she hadn't been so keen to prove herself.

She hurriedly changed into her pyjamas, got into bed and pulled the covers tight around her.

Chapter 20

WARNING

The next morning, Prue, Agapantha and Edwin were told to report to Master White's office at eight o'clock sharp.

When they knocked on the door, Craftsman Primrose answered. Prue hardly dared to look him in the eyes, but when she did, he smiled awkwardly, and it made it all the worse that he'd taken a chance on her and she'd let him down.

Masters White and Sollentude were both sitting behind the large desk. Master White beckoned them to come forward.

"These three have been up to all manner of

shenanigans, blatantly disregarding—" Master Sollentude began.

"With respect," Master White interrupted, "you have already detailed the events, and I'm sure the three concerned are not experiencing any random memory loss."

Prue noted a small grin at her words from Craftsman Primrose, who, as the least senior Guild member in the room, was sitting just to the side.

"Do you have anything to say?" Master White asked the apprentices.

Prue raised a hand. "It was all my idea; if anyone is getting thrown off the apprenticeship it should be me."

"But we went along with it," said Agapantha.

Edwin nodded in agreement.

"I see," said Master White.

"So, she's the ringleader. I told you it was one of Primrose's apprentices to blame; he's obviously chosen unfit individuals for the trade and let them run amok," said Master Sollentude.

"The smaller personifates were shaken up after what happened to Rayana," said Edwin. "We just wanted to make sure they felt safe, so we thought we'd try and catch whatever it was."

Master White tilted her head. "Taking heroics upon oneself is not a sensible course of action. The Guild searched the area and found nothing. It's likely long gone and just a unique, tragic occurrence."

"Reckless actions have no place in the Imperial Personifate Guild," Master Sollentude chimed in.

"They were just trying to be helpful, surely?" said Craftsman Primrose.

Sollentude scowled at him.

"Anyway, Sollentude, what were you doing lurking about in the forest?" Craftsman Primrose asked, taking his glasses off and wiping the lenses with his pocket handkerchief.

"My apprentices alerted me to the fact they'd seen your lot prowling suspiciously about the woods a week or so ago, so I decided to take a look."

Craftsman Primrose stood up. "Perhaps you could alert me to the fact, should the occasion ever arise again – which I doubt it will. As you say, two of these are *my* apprentices. And I'm sure Master White would feel the same."

Master Sollentude narrowed his eyes.

"Imagine if they had happened to catch the bear, or wolf, or whatever it was that preyed upon our dear Rayana. Perhaps they'd be heroes."

Master White turned to Master Sollentude. "Master Sollentude, I am in agreement with Craftsman Primrose."

"Of course you are," said Master Sollentude accusingly.

"Master Sollentude, I can assure you I am quite capable of an independent opinion. I think the apprentices have learnt their lesson. I will explain to Master Woolstenbury and, as Guild rules stipulate, the choice of consequences for any minor inappropriate behaviour from apprentices lies with the direct mentor. Perhaps you should question why your own apprentices took over a week to report to you that they thought the three were up to something in the woods? If they suspect fellow apprentices to be in any danger, it is their duty to report that immediately."

Master Sollentude's cheeks burned.

Prue could feel Edwin stifling a grin beside her, and her own shoulders relaxed for the first time all morning.

Master Sollentude stood up stiffly, nodded and left the room, flashing a last look of disapproval in Prue's direction.

"We didn't mean to catch him. We're sorry," said Prue, once the door had closed.

Master White clasped her hands together. "There's plenty for us to focus on with the blood moon approaching; we really don't need these distractions. There are still one hundred personifates to finish, and I trust you will be too busy with the voice box task to get up to anything else problematic. I will assign a suitable task as a matter of consequence for your actions when I have a moment to think. In the meantime, you may go."

They all left Master White's office, Master Sollentude glaring at the apprentices as he waited for the lift.

Craftsman Primrose walked with them across the atrium.

Edwin repeated how sorry they were.

"Look, there's no harm done, really," Craftsman Primrose said, pausing. "Except when it comes to apprentices being kept on long term, it's not just me who gets a say. The masters can collectively overrule any decision I make. While Agapantha is at a slight advantage being apprenticed to a master, I'm afraid I don't yet offer you two that benefit. I don't want you to go near the forest again. Is that understood?"

They nodded.

"If it makes you feel better, I'll ask Master Woolstenbury to ensure the woods are searched again by the guard personifates, but I really think what happened to the poor jackalope was a one-off. Now, off to mechanical lab three with you all. I have some business at the Sovereign Chancellery – the usual trouble in the city with the ASL. Honestly, these people." He hurried away.

The three headed up the stairs towards the mechanical labs. Zareen was walking along the corridor, her golden fur bright in the morning light streaming through the sky-light above.

"Ah, the three net busters," Zareen said.

"Word gets around here," said Prue awkwardly.

"I'm not judging you. Many of the second lifers here think the intention was actually very nice of you," Zareen said. "But be careful. There's been reports of a strange animal roaming the streets of Medlock after dark. Two sightings in one week."

"Really?" Prue said.

"The ASL are saying it's the guard personifates getting above themselves and scaring first lifers for fun."

Prue wondered if that was the business Craftsman Primrose had been talking about.

"Personifates wouldn't do that, would they?" asked Edwin.

Zareen shook her head. "It's probably just rumours the ASL have started purely to create fear of personifates. Even so, Master Woolstenbury is going to send a note over to the house to ensure everyone is extra vigilant. I just thought I'd tell you three, as you seem prone to trouble." Zareen raised her eyebrows and carried along the corridor.

"I wonder what that was all about?" said Agapantha.

Edwin shook his head. "Probably just the ASL, like Zareen said."

*

In the mechanical lab, Prue was glad to focus on something technical for the day. She still felt responsible for what had happened with the trap, and if she got caught for lying about who she was, or for the memory lab, she didn't want the others to get into more trouble on account of her. She decided she'd have to keep her distance, for her sake and theirs, starting from that moment. She set up on a bench of her own and worked quietly by herself, then sneaked out before the others for lunch break.

When it got to the end of the afternoon, Edwin came and sat next to her. "Frances, you've barely said a word all day. If something's bothering you, you can talk to me and Ag. I know we got into trouble with the trap, but it's not that bad. I'm sure they'll forget about it soon enough."

Prue shrugged. "I'm fine. I'm going to take the trap equipment back – I just remembered we left it by the forest edge."

"We can all go," said Agapantha.

"No, honestly, it won't take me a moment. I'll see you both back at the house soon." And she hurried off before they could disagree.

Once outside, Prue hurried to the forest edge to collect the netting. A rustling came from somewhere in the trees. Pausing, she squinted, staring into the dark mossy green. There was nothing there.

She carried the netting back to the shed, but as she shut the door and turned, something caught her eye past the orchard, a shadow darker than the rest. Someone or something *was* there. She strained her eyes to see – perhaps she was imagining it?

"Hello?" she called.

But whatever it was had disappeared back into the forest.

Chapter 21

BACK TO THE FARM

Learning the mechanics of the voice boxes took every moment of the following days. As Prue worked on the tiny machines, she wondered if she would recognize Francis's voice when he came back? Even though they didn't know for certain if the personifates' voices were the same as their previous lives, it was thought highly likely.

Sometimes she couldn't even picture his face, and it terrified her.

Now she'd decided to distance herself from the others, Prue found herself feeling increasingly alone in her thoughts of Francis. She sneaked off to her memory lab at lunch and before tea, but the calculations were getting tricky, and she longed for Agapantha's keen mathematical brain, and Edwin's talent for creative solutions. Somewhere in her workings there was a missing piece that she just couldn't seem to find.

In the late afternoon after a day at the factorium, Prue took a detour to the messenger tower to see Luella.

The pigeon was sitting on the open window looking a bit sorry for herself. "Oh, hello," she said wearily.

"Is everything all right?" Prue asked.

Luella slowly outstretched a wing. "I think my mechanism is broken."

"Shall I take you to repairs?"

"Oh no, dear, they're very busy. I don't want to be a bother."

"I can have a look if you like? I have my toolkit."

"That's very kind of you, but honestly, you have enough to do."

"I insist."

Prue set to work. She was a little nervous, but was familiar with the workings of the wing from her time working on them in the labs.

"Not long until the Sahwen celebration," Luella said, while Prue carefully adjusted the mantle.

"I quite forgot. It sounds wonderful."

"It is magical. And a big coming together of all the personifate workers at the factorium with the masters, craftsmen and apprentices. So much fun. I don't expect you've had much fun since you lost your brother. It sounds like you two were very close."

"We were."

"Maybe he'll come back as a personifate one day."

Prue swallowed. "I hope so." She picked out her micro screwdriver and got to work.

"Now, what was I going to update you on?" said Luella. "Oh yes, the apple harvest is bountiful, and they've sold lots at North Owlcot market. Your father has made about two-hundred jars of apple chutney from what I could see! Your mother says" – she stopped for a moment – "not to worry about the oiling of the mechanimals for winter, she's taken care of it."

"You've spoken with Mum? Is she all right with you?"

"She's not as chatty as your dad, that's for sure,"

Luella chuckled. "But cordial enough. She said the mechanical plough needs fixing, and she can't work out what it is."

"Probably the rotary belt again. Thanks, Luella. I feel better knowing you're keeping an eye on things for me."

Luella blinked and smiled in the best way a pigeon can smile. "Now there was something else. The hoppity—"

"Hoppity-wrench."

"Yes, it's escaped again, but this time they can't find it."

"Oh dear, it always did seem to have a mind of its own."

"They are rather desperate for you to visit, dear."

Prue stood up and retied her hair. She missed the farm more than ever. "I'm going to visit home this weekend."

"Good, I think they'll like that."

"Me too."

After a while, Prue finished. "There. All fixed and good as new," she said proudly. "How about a test flight?"

Luella extended her wings, then Prue watched,

her grin wide, as Luella flew out of the window and zoomed at twice her usual speed around the factorium grounds.

"That was brilliant, thank you!" Luella said, flying back inside.

They sat together in silence for a while, watching the sun disappear behind Medlock in the west. The east side of the buildings became shadowed, while the tops blazed with rosy light.

"You should be getting back, dear. It's a new moon and will be a dark evening and … bad things come out in the dark. There's talk of strange things in the streets of Medlock."

"That's just silly ASL rumours."

"Let's … hope so."

It was as though Luella's increasing blank moments were momentarily taking her out of the world. At least soon, Prue would have a machine ready to test, and she would hopefully help Luella remember everything.

*

It was strange putting her dungarees on again.

They felt familiar to Prue yet somehow awkward, as though they weren't a part of her any more. Prue said a quick goodbye to Agapantha and Cora, then let herself out of the front door and made her way to the main square and station. Outside, a retriever personifate had a tray on the ground in front of him.

"Rights for Personifates, display your allegiance," he called.

Prue paused. His tray was full of badges with the symbol she'd seen before of the human hand with a paw in its centre.

"I'll take one, please," she said, putting a coin in his pot. "What happened to your fur?" she asked, noticing bare patches on his body where you could see through to the synthetic skin.

"I got brought back as a companion, for a lady in the north of the city. Turned out she was secretly ASL. Liked to lock me in a tiny cupboard for days on end – she said I needed to learn my place."

"That's terrible."

"It near drove me mad being confined like that. I tried desperately to escape, of course, and nearly made it," he said, glancing down at his skin. "Luckily the Chancellery got me out when they realized. They reassigned me, but now I use my spare time for the cause."

"You could get it repaired at the factorium, you know."

"I know. But the marks remind me it's worth trying."

"Trying?"

"For better."

She pinned the badge to her dungaree pocket and made a note to tell Craftsman Primrose on her return. He was sympathetic to personifate rights, and she wanted to make sure the awful person who had done this had been dealt with, so she took the address from the retriever personifate before carrying on her way.

The Gigantrak was waiting for the first journey of the day. Prue bought a ticket from the kiosk, then presented it to the conductor and found a carriage. At Batterthwaite she found an available mechanicart, which was painfully slow after the Gigantrak and the pneumerator. The mechanicart dropped her in North Owlcot at midday, and she began the long walk up Lane's End towards the farm. She paused on the path. Harvest bales now dotted the golden fields, and the leaves of the oaks were browning. She bent and picked up a fallen acorn and put it in her pocket; it was what she did every autumn when she saw the first, for luck. She had a feeling she might need it.

Especially for when she would see Mum.

Someone was in the top field riding on the mechanimal horse, but she couldn't quite see if it was Mum or Dad. As she reached the path to the farm she paused, thinking of the moment she'd left and how in one way it felt like years ago and in another way just as if a few moments had passed.

The door was unlocked, as always. Prue breathed in: island plum pie – she'd not smelt that in perhaps two years, when Dad had traded a whole casket of apples for twenty island plums. Mum had been mad at him for the whole week, but he had said it was worth it. Prue looked around at the kitchen – all the familiar objects were in their place: iron pans on shelves, baskets on hooks, utensils in painted jars, and on the table, a sky-blue ceramic saltcellar and mustard pot beside a neat pile of napkins delicately embroidered with a small oak tree in the corner. Suddenly she heard a clatter, and Mr Haywood's great smiling face appeared around the corner.

"Dad!" Prue dropped her bag and ran to embrace him. They broke their hug and looked at each other. She'd missed his warm grin, but it also brought Francis straight back to her.

"Well, look at you! You've grown!"

"Dad, I haven't been gone *that* long."

"Then you're walking taller, eh?"

Prue glanced at the stove. "Is that island plum pie I smell?"

He winked. "I met a trader passing through North Owlcot this week – I paid a fair sovereign or two, but don't tell your mother. I may have distorted the cost just a little, between you and me." He tapped his nose. "Our secret."

Prue noticed the note she'd left was still on the dresser, now pinned beneath a ceramic owl salt pot.

"Better call your mother. She's up in the top field. I'll go and put the cart away and see you in a minute."

Prue went out of the back door and called. Mrs Haywood looked over then changed the mechanimal horse's direction and began trotting down the hill. It looked so clunky and old-fashioned compared to the technology in Medlock. Prue's mind raced with the improvements she could make, with all that she had learned at the Guild. Perhaps she could use synthetic muscles for greater power, and grapheme to make the joints stronger?

Mrs Haywood switched off the horse, and jumped from it, her blonde hair neatly tied up as ever and her light blue blouse without a crease. Prue smiled awkwardly and Mrs Haywood embraced her.

"I missed you," Mrs Haywood said, taking a clip from her hair and pinning back one of Prue's curls. "What were you thinking, disappearing like that?"

"Mum, please."

Mrs Haywood held up her hands. "All right. I understand you've just got back, but things need to be said. In person."

They walked inside, and Prue sat at the table while Mrs Haywood put the kettle on the stove. Dad was still outside putting the cart away.

"I think I know why you went, Prudence." Mum only ever called her by her full name when she was cross. "You forget that I know how your mind works. I watched your first determined steps walking. You went from crawling to walking within days, just so you could chase your brother into the fields."

Prue fidgeted with the sleeve of her jacket, not knowing what to say – trying not to think of Francis, trying not to fall to pieces.

Mum clattered with cups at the sink. "You want to bring Francis back at that Guild, don't you?"

Prue opened her mouth to make some excuse, but Mum had always been able to read her thoughts.

Her mother turned from the sink to face her. "What good do you think will come of it? Things should be left well alone. I don't want to see him as some animal, some clickety-clackety monstrosity!"

"You don't understand what it's like, what they're like!"

"I understand perfectly, Prue. Life is life and death is death. It's tampering with things that shouldn't be messed with. It can only end one way, and that's badly."

"But if we thought like that about all technology, then we'd still be living in mud huts and caves! We use machinery on the farm to help us, don't we?"

Mrs Haywood sat opposite her. "Don't be contrary, Prudence. You know very well that's different. Machines are machines; mixing it with the other side is wrong."

"But they aren't monstrosities. They're brilliant, advanced, completely life-like machines that contain *people*. You've met Luella – she's lovely!"

"Well, of course I'm civil to her, she's nice enough and it's not her fault she's been brought back."

"But—"

"Prue, I don't want to hear another word of it. Now, you can continue there, I shan't stop you, but you let go of any thoughts of messing with Francis."

Prue screeched back in her chair and stood up. "You don't understand!" she shouted. "We need this, we need Francis back."

She paced back and forward a couple of times before stopping at the dresser where a picture of the four of them together rested behind a small jug. Below, among a pile of paper, Prue caught sight of a flyer. The symbol of the ASL was on it and it simply stated *ASL. For natural order.*

"You're not falling for this nonsense, are you?" Prue snapped, snatching up the paper and throwing it on the table.

Mrs Haywood looked at it. "My opinions are mine and I don't need anyone else telling me."

"Everything all right?" said Mr Haywood walking into the room.

They both fell quiet.

"Perhaps it's time for tea," he said.

*

In the evening, Prue took a stroll to the shed to check on the mechanimal sheepdogs and horses. She had a quick look at the broken plough, but decided she'd mend it after a ride around the fields on one of the mechanimal horses. She stopped off at Haywood's Oak and climbed into the branches, looking back at the farmhouse.

Beneath the indigo-blue of night, the setting sun burned with apricot and vermillion fire, casting thick orange roads of light between the trees across the fields and blazing the tips of the branches around her. She couldn't count the times she'd sat in this exact place with Francis beside her, him teasing that she hadn't climbed up as quickly as him, watching the sunset together, arguing over the last oat cake, dreaming of faraway cities and what the future would be. It was good to be home, even if Mum was suspicious of her intentions and they'd argued, and supper had been tense. She could feel Francis all around her, and memories of the farm and this made her more determined than ever to complete her mission.

*

The morning came all too quickly, and Prue had to set off early in order to make it back.

"Such a short visit. I wish you could stay longer. Here, take some island plum pie back for your friends," said Mr Haywood, filling her bag with treats from the kitchen.

Friends who probably thought she was *anything but* at the moment, Prue thought.

Mr Haywood sighed. "I'm sorry, Mum went to the west field early. It might take her a while to come around."

Prue swallowed back her emotion and smiled. "It's all right, Dad. I just have to show her. And I will."

"Mum always said, once you make up your mind, it's like trying to tame a storm. You're more like her than she knows."

Prue hugged her dad and picked up her bag. "I'll write soon."

"Have a safe journey."

"Oh, I forgot to fix the mechanical plough while I was here!" Prue said hurriedly. "I had a quick look, and I'm sure you can do it – the gear box has seized. You just need to separate them and isolate first gear."

Mr Haywood held up his hand. "Slow down – do what?"

Prue grabbed a piece of paper from the dresser. She sat at the table and drew a quick diagram. "Take out the reverse cog, then remove the second, that's this one. Put the gear box back together. It will still move forward because you've isolated first gear and..." Prue paused mid-flow, her own words suddenly like the missing pieces she'd been looking for. *Move forward ... Isolate first gear...* Prue's mind began to race.

"Prue? Are you all right?"

She suddenly leapt from her chair with a cry. That was it! The key to adapting the GODAR. She'd been trying to interpret a signal with three parts. What she needed to do was separate them out; to cut off the other frequencies completely so that there was no interference then isolate the one she needed!

"Dad, you're a genius!"

"What did I do?"

"I've got to go back – I'll visit again soon, I promise. Perhaps with great news!" And with that, she grabbed her bag and ran out the door, not stopping until North Owlcot.

Chapter 22

GODAR

When Prue arrived back at the Guild house it was suppertime, and everyone was sitting in the dining room chatting.

"Prue, we missed you this weekend!" said Lavender, enveloping her in a warm hug. She hurried her into the dining room.

Cora was sitting beside Agapantha. Seeing Prue, she hooked Agapantha's arm. "I hope you had a lovely weekend back at the pig sty. I decided to stay here and keep Agapantha company. I think I might take her under my wing."

"I'm glad you're back," Agapantha said with

pleading eyes for Prue to sit the other side of her.

Prue smiled – she hated distancing herself from Agapantha, but she had taken a decision to keep her friends away from any trouble, and that was what she had to do. "I'm tired after the travel; do you mind if I go straight up?"

"Of course not," said Lavender.

Prue peered into the parlour as she passed. Edwin was in conversation with Samir, his roommate. Samir was gesturing with his arms and Edwin laughed in response. Prue felt as though an invisible thread connected her with Edwin, and that it had suddenly been tugged, making her long to share all the thoughts bursting in her brain with him. She hurried along.

The next morning, they continued working on the voice boxes until lunch, when Prue sneaked away to the memory lab. She started a new set of calculations in her journal and began re-wiring the GODAR, building in a high-pass filter and taking out unnecessary parts. It was now much smaller so she could transport it easily.

By the following Saturday, Prue was ready to test the modified GODAR, which was perfect timing as the house was quiet. Cora had tried to drag poor Agapantha off to meet her parents, but Agapantha had managed to come up with an excuse of having promised to read the history of Medlock to Queen Adelaide (all five volumes), an excuse that Queen Adelaide obliged in going along with and had proceeded to make Agapantha do exactly that.

"So many memories to relive," she had said, sighing happily.

"Honestly, I'm beginning to think I took the harder option," Agapantha whispered at breakfast.

Edwin seemed to be behaving a bit strangely towards Prue, which she couldn't blame him for, what with her disappearing all the time.

After Lavender had insisted she at least eat a pumpkin pancake for breakfast, Prue hurried over to the main building.

She walked in just as Craftsman Primrose was leaving the building. "Studying again, Apprentice Haywood? There's no stopping you! The good news is we're about to meet Master Woolstenbury's expectations on the hundred. Mind you, this news is top secret; if Governor Watson-Wentworth gets wind of it, he'll likely add another ten personifates on to the list!"

He peered at her for a second. "Is that a Rights for Personifates badge?"

"Oh yes, is it all right to wear it?"

"Well, some here might prefer a more neutral stance, but I can't say that I mind at all," he winked kindly.

She told him about the poor retriever and handed him the address of the personifate's companion.

"Dear me, how terrible. I'll make a few enquiries and check whoever was responsible was charged. Right, best be getting on."

He hurried away. Prue waited for a moment, then went up the stairs to the memory lab. With a quick glance over her shoulder she hurried along, rushed through the door, then shut it gently behind her.

She froze.

Edwin was sitting in the middle of the room staring at her.

"What are you doing here?" she asked.

"I've been following you for days."

Her words jammed in her throat.

"You've been avoiding me for a while now. What exactly are you up to, Frances?"

"I'm not avoiding you. I've just been—"

"Busy?"

"Yes, well, it's a nice quiet room for studying."

"And for experimenting with equipment." He pulled the sheet from the box where Prue had hidden her modified GODAR.

"Please, you haven't told anyone, have you?"

He looked at her curiously. "I thought we were friends?"

"We were friends, I mean we are. It's just…" She thought of Francis and the wound felt new again, and the emotion of it all rose in her chest in an overwhelming surge. She felt tears filming her eyes. She didn't want to cry, but she'd been caught, and she suddenly felt laid bare and exhausted from having to keep secrets.

"What's going on?"

She sat down beside Edwin and drew in a long breath. "I had a brother. He got sick, just a silly bug, the sort that most people get over, except he didn't. He was the one from *one in a thousand* who died from it."

Edwin looked up at her. "I'm so sorry to hear that."

Prue didn't want anyone to be sorry, she just

wanted things back to how they were.

"I know what it's like," he said after a while.

"Edwin, how can you possibly know what it's like? You don't have family."

He moved to face her, paws on hips. "It might not be exactly the same, but I do know what it's like, because I'm dead. I've lost *everything* – any brothers and sisters I may have had – but I've also lost myself. Who was I? I have no idea, and that's not easy to live with. Ever thought of that?"

She shook her head, angry with herself for being so thoughtless. "Edwin, I'm so sorry."

He put a paw on her knee. "What was his name?"

"Ah … that's another thing." She bit her lip, then said, "He was called Francis."

Edwin frowned at her. "But that's your name? You both had the same name?"

"No. Frances Haywood isn't my real name … I'm actually Prue Haywood." She explained what had happened when Craftsman Primrose had first arrived at the farm, and how he'd heard about a talented young mechanic called Francis.

Edwin listened intently. "Wow. Do you ever count how many risks you take in a day?"

"You can see why I thought it might be best to distance myself from you and Ag."

"So, Prue – which I must say suits you better as a name – are you going to tell me what the machine is all about? I promise I won't tell a soul. Not even Ag, if you don't want me to."

Prue showed him her journal and explained how she'd worked out her theory of history data being isolated in a different part of the overall wildspark signal.

Edwin listened intently and nodded. "Have you tried it yet?"

"No. I was going to ask Luella; she knows about Francis, and she wants to help."

"Try it on me."

"What?"

"Right here and now."

"Are you serious?"

"Deadly."

"That's not funny. What if it goes wrong and I do something to your frequency? Luella doesn't think her qwortzite will hold out for much longer, so she says she's got nothing to lose, but you're young in your second life."

"Then we'll not need to say another word about it, because I'll be dead. Again." Edwin saw Prue's stricken face, then sighed. "Look, I'm just joking. I won't die." He gestured towards the pages of her journal. "Your calculations look sound. I trust you. And if there is the remotest chance of me finding out who I really am, I could be the first personifate to ever know."

"You should know that after I fainted in the harnessing, Master Woolstenbury warned me against messing with memory. If she found out what I've been up to, we'd both be thrown out of here."

"The fact you carried on tells me that it's a risk you're willing to take."

Prue nodded.

"Then I am too." He smiled. "How do we hook up this machine of yours?"

Prue got to work checking everything then gently put the wires a millimetre into Edwin's stomach.

"Ouch!"

"Oh, I'm sorry!"

"I'm kidding. We don't feel pain, remember?"

"Not a good time for joking, Ed."

She stopped speaking and concentrated on

creating a loop wire. When she was happy, she said, "When the signal is isolated, I'm hoping the machine will read it, but also that you'll be able to directly feel the memory when the isolated signal is sent back."

"An interesting thought. There's only one way to find out. Press the button, Prue."

For a moment she thought she saw the flicker of nerves in his eyes, but she forced herself to look at the GODAR and focus. Within moments, the frequency was being displayed on the monitor unit. The shape had a different pattern to Luella's; it had a strong, yet elegant, movement. With a turn of the dial she isolated what she hoped was the history data. The reading fizzed and blurred for a moment, then there was one very thin, clear rise and fall.

She looked keenly at Edwin. "Has anything changed? Edwin, do you feel anything?"

Edwin shook his head.

Prue's heart sank to the floor. "Of course. It was ridiculous to think it would work on the very first try."

"I wasn't shaking my head because I don't feel anything. I was shaking it because Edwin isn't my name."

"What do you mean?" she said in barely a whisper.

"It's strange. I don't remember any other details, but suddenly I do remember my name."

Prue was aghast.

"My name's Jack. Jack Swift."

 **Chapter 23**

CONFESSIONS

Prue and Edwin made their way out of the factorium. They were both buzzing about the revelation and needed to get some fresh air and take it all in. Edwin hopped across the lawn with extra spring in his paws.

Prue thought that Jack Swift was the most brilliant name and it somehow suited him perfectly.

"I know my name is just one detail to remember, but it feels huge. Like all of a sudden I've reclaimed a piece of me."

"I'm happy for you, Edwin – I mean, Jack. Gosh, what do I call you now?"

"Best stick to Edwin for now or people will start to wonder, and we don't want the masters to find out about it. And I'll obviously stick to Frances."

"Yes, you're right."

"Imagine if your brother had a second life; you would know it's him if he could remember his name. And perhaps we could work on a way to restore more memories. I mean, it's obviously going to take time. I know so many personifates who would want this more than anything. We must be cautious, but this is amazing! For the first time in my second life I feel properly connected to what's come before. Like a part of me has been unlocked."

"That's great." Prue beamed.

"I could put the word out to some of the personifates. Covertly, of course," said Edwin.

"That's a good idea. Perhaps if we can persuade Queen Adelaide to try it, then it could be the key to finding out more. Imagine if it turns out she really was a queen all this time, while everyone around her has been laughing behind her back and humouring her? And if she's had her memory the whole time – think what it might mean!"

Edwin paused. "It's a good idea, but remember

Queen Adelaide talks to everyone about everything. I'm not sure she has it in her to keep it quiet. Are you going to tell Agapantha?"

"I'd like to. I don't want to put her at risk, though. And I feel a bit daft for never mentioning my brother and for being so off with her lately."

"She'll understand."

Then something caught her attention at the forest edge; a tall and slim figure walked from the orchard and disappeared into the trees.

"Is that Sollentude?" Prue said.

Edwin looked to where she was pointing, but the figure had gone. "It could be. He's probably seeing if he can catch us laying traps again."

But something about it struck Prue as odd. "He seems to do an awful lot of lurking around the forest," Prue said suspiciously. Then her eye was caught by Luella in the window of the messenger tower and it was clear who would be next. Prue whistled and Luella flew down to them.

"What are you two up to? If you've got messages for me, I'm not sure … I'm feeling up for it."

Prue explained her latest developments.

"Oh! My previous name? I'm rather used to *Luella*,

dearie ... but wouldn't it be a thrill to find out!"

"You must promise not to tell anyone."

"Of course, cross my feathered chest."

"Then there's no time like the present!"

The three of them headed back to the memory lab, making a slightly awkward diversion to the library after bumping into Craftsman Shad in the atrium.

When the coast was clear they hurried around the walkway to the memory lab.

This time, Prue was quicker with the equipment.

"I hope it's something exotic." Luella giggled.

"Keep still. When you laugh, the emotion signal goes wild. Almost there." Prue isolated the memory wave. She wondered if this time more might be revealed.

After a few moments, Luella blinked. "Well, I'll be darned. My name is Edith Scamp." Then she giggled. "I wasn't sure what I was expecting, Prue, but it wasn't Edith Scamp!"

"Is there anything else?" Prue asked keenly.

"No dear, not a thing. But that feels like quite enough for now!"

"It's a brilliant name. You sound adventurous," said Edwin.

"Or perhaps I was a dangerous criminal mastermind!" Luella laughed.

"Maybe we could start looking for other Scamps in Medlock? Or Swifts? You might have living relatives!" said Prue.

"Family?" Luella said, shocked. "I should like that. Although, I'm not sure what they'd make of having a pigeon as a relative!"

*

Back at the house, Prue and Edwin found Agapantha in the bedroom and made sure she was alone. Prue sat down opposite her with Edwin.

"What's going on?" said Agapantha.

"I want to say sorry. I've not been very much of a friend at all lately. Since the harnessing, then the trap, I thought it would be better if I just went it alone and focused on what I came here to do." She took a breath.

"Over a year ago my older brother died. We were close and did everything together. He was a better mechanic than me."

Agapantha's shoulders dropped. "I'm sorry. It

287

must've been so hard for you to lose him so young," said Agapantha. "I've never had any brother or sisters, but I can imagine it's heartbreaking."

Prue could feel the crack in her heart. "There's one other small detail," she said. "When Craftsman Primrose visited the farm to offer an apprenticeship, I pretended to be him. Or, at least, Frances. Francis was his name. Mine's Prue. I came here to find a way back to him."

"Crikey, Frances!" she looked over her shoulder to make sure no one else had come into the room. "I mean, Prue," she whispered. "Although, I'm not sure on one thing,"

There was an awkward pause.

"I can't see that he was a better mechanic than you, because I refuse to believe that's possible."

Prue smiled and took a breath. "I've got something else to tell you." She explained about the adapted GODAR and how it revealed the first life names.

"Meet Jack Swift," said Edwin proudly, taking a bow.

Agapantha was wide-eyed. "It seems I'm the only one without a new name!"

"That's because you've already got the best

name in the house. We need to keep this all top secret," Prue said seriously. "It's going to take lots more research to find a way to Francis. I know the odds are against me, but I need to try. And perhaps there's a way to read the wildsparks from beyond; we all saw the signals when Master Woolstenbury harnessed the ghost. We may be able to read them and select who comes back."

"Prue, this is amazing. Can I help? We might be able to improve it, if we all put our minds to it," said Agapantha.

"I can show you my memory lab at the Guild tomorrow, if you'd like? Everything is hidden over there, and it's where we can work in secret."

"Memory lab?" Agapantha said in awe.

"It sounds grander than it is. It's really just the end storage room on the design lab corridor."

They heard shuffling outside and fell silent.

The door swung open. It was Cora.

"What are you three up to?"

"Just chatting about Sahwen. It's next weekend, you know," said Agapantha, flashing the others a quick grin. "We were just saying that we still haven't sorted out what to wear."

Cora breezed over to the wardrobe. "I know the feeling. I have to choose between six outfits." She took one out and held it against her. "I overheard Queen Adelaide say there has been another sighting of a weird creature in the streets of Medlock. Something with horns, apparently."

"Horns?" said Edwin, throwing Prue and Agapantha a frown.

Prue knew he was thinking of what she'd seen the night of the spirit lights.

"Strange," Prue said, giving a sly sideways glance in Cora's direction. She was certainly trying to press their buttons. "Anyway, what *are* we going to wear to Sahwen?"

Agapantha stood up. "I can't believe we forgot. Come on, there's still time to go to the shops before sundown."

Edwin jumped from the bed. "We'd best get going then."

Chapter 24

STAG-MAN

"So, this is where you've been sneaking off to," Agapantha said, looking around the memory lab.

Prue went to her hiding place and opened the box. Her heart missed a beat. "It's disappeared!" The GODAR was there, but her journal had gone.

"What?" said Edwin, hurrying over.

"My journal – it's got all my notes on restoring memories! Check the other boxes!" said Prue.

"But no one knew about any of this, apart from us three and Luella."

Prue put her hand to her mouth.

"What?" Edwin urged her.

"Cora; when she came back yesterday. What if she heard more than we thought before she came into the room?"

"You should search her things back at the house later," said Edwin.

Prue stood up. "Or now."

They hurried back along the corridor.

"Halt!" someone called.

They looked up to see Sollentude on the staircase below. He narrowed his eyes. "Well, this is timely; Master White has decided on a suitable consequence for your antics in the forest. Some of the apprentices have been clearing out the archive rooms to facilitate the harnessing of the hundred and there is all manner of old machinery for oiling, cleaning and testing. It's now your responsibility." He smiled meanly. "It's been sent over to the shed."

They exchanged looks of despair.

"Well? What are you waiting for?"

*

The machinery was a tangled pile of metal.

Prue felt a tightness in her chest at not being

able to go and find her journal straight away, but there was nothing she could do. "Come on. The sooner we get stuck in, the sooner we finish," she said.

"These things look ancient," said Agapantha. "My parents would have these in a museum."

But to Prue there was a certain beauty in the broken. "There's nothing wrong with them. With a bit of adapting and imagination they can become whatever you'd like them to be," she said, recognizing some as similar to those they used at home. "This hasn't been touched for a year, maybe two." Prue pulled a hunk of metal from the pile. "It's just like the hoppity wrench we have at the farm!"

It had completely seized and was battered and bent, but she instructed the others on which tools to fetch and they began untangling the pile and laying out the parts on the ground beside the vegetable patch. Prue found some oil in the shed and Agapantha and Edwin started helping her clean and grease the joints of the hoppity wrench, while she reconnected and straightened components. When they had finished, Prue rooted around in the shed and found an ion battery plate.

"It's had a rough life, but you never know," she

said, slotting it into place.

Nothing happened.

"Well, that was a waste of time." Edwin huffed.

Then there was a whirr of cogs within and a squeak as the hoppity wrench slowly bobbed down, then straightened.

"Wait, it's the restrainer!" Prue unhitched it.

Its legs suddenly sprang into action and it dipped up and down a few times, making them laugh, then with unexpected speed, it hopped off towards the orchard.

They ran after it, giggling and shoving each other.

"Whoever catches it gets all of the apple doughnuts Lavender left for us!" Prue called.

"That's hardly fair to someone who doesn't eat!" Edwin said.

"All right, we'll buy you a new hat!" Agapantha laughed.

Before they knew it, ferns were whipping at their ankles and they were jumping through the low-lying forest fog and mulchy leaves.

"Where's it gone?" Prue called.

"There!" Edwin said, pointing east where the hoppity wrench sprang above the fog line, hopping deeper into the trees.

"Out of the way, those doughnuts are mine!" Prue called as they dashed on.

But the fog was getting thicker, making it nearly impossible to see. They came to a standstill and looked around.

"I can barely see you," Edwin called.

Prue scanned the clearing. She couldn't hear the hoppity wrench any more. She caught sight of Edwin, low to the ground a short distance from her feet, then the shapes of Agapantha and ... she froze. There was another shape in the white.

Around ten paces away, the branches moved, twisting as though suddenly alive. The hair on her arms rose. She watched the trees intensely, trying to see through the fog. There wasn't a breath of wind, yet she was certain they were moving

"I think we should go back," Prue whispered.

There was a rustling sound.

The branches moved again, separating from the trees. A creature emerged from the thick fog and stood facing them just ten paces away. It looked almost human in body, but taller and sinewy, with hard lines and skin tough and cold as bone. Great stag-like antlers extended from its head, its face a featureless skull with hollow eyes a glow of blood red within. Its extended arms hung at its side. Great clawed hands twitched.

There was a terrifying moment when none of them could move, then Agapantha cried out and it bounded towards them and they were running back, frantic breath steaming into the chill air. Branches snagged and snatched at them as the crunch of pounding feet and the whip of branches chased them through the undergrowth. Agapantha fell and Prue turned swiftly to help her, catching another glimpse of the fearsome stag-man in the fog hurtling towards them. But there was no time to take anything else in. Agapantha was up, and again they ran, but where was Edwin? Branches were coming at her suddenly through the mist and she took a swift turn away from Agapantha to dodge a fallen tree. Onwards she ran, but she was tiring rapidly and stumbled on a rock. Her knees buckled. She fell, hitting her head. Pain seared. She put her hand to it; thankfully, there was no blood. Hurriedly, she looked to her side for one of the others, but there was no one there.

No one except the stag-man, which was now standing barely ten paces away and looking right at her.

Her belly tightened as she took in the terrifying creature.

It let out a rasping, angry sound and stepped towards her.

She edged backwards, her muscles weak with fear, her heart hammering against her ribs.

It took another step. Its antlers were like sharpened chisels. It drew back, about to jump.

Then something flew from the trees. A stone bounced meaninglessly off the creature's black chest, but it was enough to distract it and kick Prue into action. She scrambled to her feet. It lunged and swiped at her, but she arced backwards, and its antlers missed her by a whisper, just snagging on her jacket. Then something grabbed her hand and pulled. She didn't resist, and began running alongside—

It was a long, thin hand holding hers, not Agapantha's or Edwin's. "Finblewick?" she managed to splutter between great gasps of air, then they twisted sharply, and she saw Agapantha to her left.

"Keep running that way!" Finblewick called. He jerked his hand away and leapt off in a different direction.

She dashed onwards, calling to Agapantha, then Edwin appeared just ahead, crashing through the thickets. With a rush they emerged from the forest and didn't stop until they reached the factorium. Panting, hands on knees, sweat pouring, they looked back at the forest.

It was silent.

They watched, unable to take their gaze away, until Prue said, "Finblewick, he was there."

"What?" said Agapantha.

"He saved me; I've got to go back."

"Are you bonkers?" said Edwin.

"Let's get help," said Agapantha, but Prue was already heading back. Then Finblewick stepped out from the trees.

"What were you all thinking, larking about in the forest!" he spat. He looked at each of them. "You can all stop looking like scared rabbits; you're quite safe."

"Quite safe?" Prue repeated. "What *was* that?"

"Weren't you told to keep out of the deep forest?"

"Yes, but our hoppity wrench escaped and...

Wait a minute … what were you doing in the forest? It's a long way from Deakins."

"Never you mind. Your concern should be that no one finds out you were in there."

"Finblewick, what was it?" Agapantha said.

He huffed and swayed hands on hips for a moment, lips contorting as though fighting to keep something inside. "It was … a guard. A guard to protect the Guild against snoops like you, and small personifates from wild beasts."

Prue narrowed her eyes.

"You'd better get back to whatever you should be doing and hope that I don't tell on you for nosing about where you shouldn't be!" Finblewick said haughtily.

"Let's go," Prue said.

Sick with relief, they took the pneumerator back to the house and went up to Prue and Agapantha's room. Prue insisted on grabbing a few apple doughnuts from the kitchen. "I feel like I need something sweet after that!"

"Do you think Liddy and Lavender know there's such an awful guard out in the forest?" Agapantha asked.

"If they knew, they would surely just say, 'Don't go into the forest because the antlered monster guard might attack you,'" said Prue. "But I suppose it's plausible that the masters would protect the forest from spies. Maybe Cora and Larkin had heard of the stag guard and that's why they scared us like that?" She looked to Edwin. "Have you ever seen anything like this before?"

He shook his head. "Only in books. It's like something in the Ancient Mercia books – some god of the underworld, I think."

"Maybe Craftsman Shad has been experimenting?" suggested Agapantha.

Edwin frowned. "You've seen his designs. They're mythical and over the top, but they aren't evil-looking! That thing was horrific!"

"Hang on," Prue took a bite from her doughnut and thought. "When we were being reprimanded in Master White's office, surely White and Primrose would've mentioned the guard? And what was Sollentude up to when we caught him in the trap?"

"Actually, that's a good point. What do we do?" Edwin asked.

"We should speak to Craftsman Primrose about the guard. If it's gone a bit rogue, they should know, as maybe it's the thing responsible for the sightings in Medlock. But we don't want to all get into trouble again for going into the forest," said Prue.

"Perhaps an anonymous note?" suggested Agapantha.

"I'll write it. I'm good at disguising my handwriting," said Edwin.

"Good. We'll send it to Craftsman Primrose – he's least likely to get us into trouble if he does realize it's us, or if Finblewick says anything. And he's not keen on Sollentude, so I doubt he'll bring it up with him." Prue thought for a moment. "I still can't imagine what Finblewick was doing there, though."

"Maybe he helps with the guards?" Agapantha suggested.

Prue shrugged. "Perhaps. But there's one other thing I need to focus on first; I want my journal back from Cora. Quick, help me look before she comes back."

But after rooting through Cora's things for half

an hour, they had to concede: the journal was nowhere to be found.

 **Chapter 25**

CORA

On Monday, they stopped by the tower on the way to lessons and asked Luella to take the note anonymously to Craftsman Primrose. Cora was unusually quiet, which made Prue even more certain that she was up to something. She searched her things again in the evening, but there was still no sign of her journal.

Over the next few days, Prue, Agapantha and Edwin were keen to know what Craftsman Primrose had done about their note and what would happen, but they could glean nothing from his behaviour. He did seem preoccupied, but all of the craftsmen and masters were at the moment. The apprentices were working on some of the finer details of aesthetics with Rami Shad. The hundred personifates had filled up the huge open space of the design studio in orderly lines, and any final touches were being made.

Edwin had begun to approach discreet personifates who he thought may be open to finding out their first-life names. So Abel the garden mole became the next to discover that his original name was Maurice Montgomery. Prue thought it gave him an air of distinction, and she noticed he seemed to be rising up on his hind paws more and carrying himself with pride.

That evening, Prue lounged front-down on the parlour rug by the fire, writing a long letter home. Her thoughts were back on the farm, as the upcoming weekend was Sahwen. The only year they'd not celebrated Sahwen as a family was the previous one – the year when celebrating stopped. On their farm, the changing of the seasons was usually a big event. Francis and Prue would carve faces into the great pumpkins they grew in the north field, then they would place them around the house, lit by candlelight. Their parents made delicious pumpkin soup and pie, spiced with cinnamon; it tasted like autumn. In the evening the great orange faces burned brightly and the whole family danced around a scarebot, singing harvest songs together.

Agapantha sat crossed-legged beside Prue reading a note, and Edwin was on the other side with his face buried in a book on Ancient Mercia.

"My parents are in Medlock tomorrow," Agapantha said.

"That's good," said Prue, not looking up from the letter she was writing.

There was a pause. "I'm going to meet them for dinner."

"Nice," Edwin said absently.

Agapantha cleared her throat a little.

Prue and Edwin both looked up at her.

"Spit it out, Ag," said Edwin.

"Well, I wondered if, only if you'd like to, no pressure, but would you, maybe, like to come along and meet them?"

Prue smiled. "Of course – why wouldn't we, you

ninny!"

"Great!" she said sounding surprised, "I'll send a note straight back."

*

The Grand Principalia was the most exclusive hotel in Medlock.

"I feel massively underdressed," said Prue.

"Imagine how I feel," Edwin said, surveying the room of immaculately dressed people in plush dresses and suits.

They were greeted by an elegant white peacock. "Mrs and Mr Young are waiting for you, do follow me," she said smoothly.

They followed the peacock past exotic palms and tables with smooth ivory tablecloths and silver cutlery. Crystal flutes sparkled beneath chaos lamps suspended from the high ceiling in glittering orbs.

Mrs and Mr Young stood as they approached the table. Prue could see that Agapantha inherited her fiery hair and red cheeks from her dad. Her mum had the same pointed chin and amber eyes, and she had a neatness to her blouse and trousers which, with an ache to her heart, reminded Prue of her own mum.

"Ah, here they are!" said Mrs Young. "We've missed you so much, Ag!"

They both embraced Agapantha warmly.

"These are my friends from the Guild, er … Frances Haywood and Edwin Snow-Moon."

Mr Young laughed. "Oh, Ag, for a minute I thought you'd forgotten your friends' names!"

Mrs and Mr Young fussed over them, making sure everyone was happily seated and had drinks and food, even ensuring Edwin had a plate and cup even though he wouldn't be eating. "We want you to feel part of the evening, dear." Mrs Young smiled.

"How are things in Gawthorpe?" asked Agapantha.

"Well, technology is taking some extraordinary twists and turns. Between us, I think it's highly likely a personifate Guild will be opening at some point in the near future," said Mrs Young.

"Really? But I thought the technology was exclusive and patented to Master Woolstenbury and Medlock," said Prue.

Mrs Young nodded. "It is, but they are developing

their own theories, presumably in different ways."

Prue thought of the stag-man in the woods. Perhaps it *was* just an extreme deterrent against spies, or perhaps it was something from a rival city?

"Where do you work in Gawthorpe, Mr and Mrs Young?" Edwin asked.

"We're at the MMD," said Mr Young.

"That's the Mechanimal Model Development," added Agapantha.

"Oh, I've heard of that. Our mentor worked there before he joined the Guild," said Prue.

Mr Young sat forward. "How wonderful, what's his name? Mia has worked there for fifteen years, she'll probably know him."

"Come now, Archibald! You make me sound like I'm dreadfully nosy, which I am of course." Mrs Young laughed.

"He's called Craftsman Primrose, Charles Primrose."

Mrs Young looked thoughtful for a moment. "The name doesn't seem at all familiar, I'm afraid... No, I'm quite sure, I don't know him. Perhaps he worked for the MMV, the Mechanimal Model Vicinity?"

"Yes, sorry, it must be, perhaps he said that."

They ate and chatted mechanics and invention. They were warm and friendly, and the sort of people Prue thought her parents would like.

Prue excused herself to visit the bathroom, but on the way, she heard a voice she knew too well; Cora. She and Larkin were sitting at a table in the next room with their parents. Prue ducked behind a leafy plant.

"We'll have to have words with the Governor. If they start having *anyone* as apprentices, they'll lose all credibility," Mrs Duval was saying.

"Your mother is quite right. Being an apprentice at the Imperial Personifate Guild of Medlock affords you the highest esteem from the Sovereign Chancellery, but if they start to lower their entry standards it'll soon falter," said Mr Duval.

"Well, for now, it will secure your future and the good name of the family. If you think for one minute you can make any sort of future from your own ridiculous notions!" said Mrs Duval.

"But Larkin is the one who's good at all this invention nonsense!"

"And so are you."

"She's not that good," said Larkin.

"I hate it there."

"You don't have a choice and that's the end of it. I paid good money to Governor Watson-Wentworth to secure your apprenticeship."

"Listen to your mother, Cora. You are a Duval and you will do as you are told, young lady."

There was a screech of a chair and Cora stormed past inches from where Prue was hiding.

Prue almost felt sorry for her. Her parents hadn't wanted Prue to come to the Guild, but they respected her choice when she ran away. It sounded like Cora wanted to do something else and didn't actually want to be there at all. She hurried back to her table with the Youngs.

"Everything all right, Frances?" said Mrs Young.

"Yes, thank you," she said.

*

On the way back, Prue, Edwin and Agapantha bumped into Craftsman Primrose on the steps of the house.

He opened the door ahead of them. "And what

have you three been up to?" he asked, having a quick look at his pocket watch.

"We've just had dinner with Agapantha's parents," Prue said.

"How lovely." The door shut behind them and Craftsman Primrose stopped and looked at them all curiously for a moment. "I was hoping to catch you all, as a matter of fact. I received an interesting note this week. It was anonymous."

Prue could practically feel the warmth of Agapantha's guilty red cheeks beside her. Edwin shuffled his paws.

"You three haven't been in the forest when I expressly warned you not to after the incident with Sollentude and the trap, have you?"

They didn't say anything.

"Of course not," he said narrowing his eyes a little. He headed for the secret door to the pneumerator, then stopped and turned back to them. They paused on the steps.

"But, if it was, I would certainly like you all to know that it's likely one of the more formidable-looking guards that Master Woolstenbury has deployed. There's rather a lot of valuable qwortzite being held at the factorium at the moment, you see. However, the note is being taken seriously, and I am personally making sure it's thoroughly investigated."

The three of them remained silent.

"Like I say, if it was you, which it wasn't, I would tell you that security is paramount at this time. Fear not, you'll be perfectly safe to take part in the catching of the spirit lights this evening, so have fun." Craftsman Primrose flipped back the mouse painting and opened the door. "Oh, and I'm pleased to report that all is ahead of schedule for the blood moon, and I can't say more, but Master Woolstenbury has confirmed that Sahwen celebrations should go ahead as planned."

*

That evening the releasing and catching of the spirit lights was much quieter. Most apprentices were being drafted in for last-minute work on the hundred; so it was only the newest apprentices, Liddy, Lavender, Queen Adelaide, Abel and a few flying personifates from the messenger tower who made their way to the lawn. Prue, Agapantha and

Edwin couldn't help but glance nervously at the forest edge as they walked.

They released the previous lights, which flitted away and disappeared like blown candles into the night.

"I'm pleased to have met you, Prue Haywood," said Luella, sitting on Prue's shoulder.

"I'm pleased to have met you too, Edith Scamp."

"It's a funny thing ... how paths cross, so many ifs and buts and chance throws of the dice. I guess what I'm saying is I feel ... very lucky ... if luck is a thing."

Prue gently stroked the pigeon's head.

The lights began appearing. Luella took flight, and everyone started leaping around the great lawn catching the new lights.

After a while, Prue sat down to catch her breath while the others continued jumping with their nets. She pulled her cloak around her. It would be winter soon. In the dusk, the treeline looked like skeleton fingers reaching for the sky. The shadows of the forest were impenetrably black. Prue was glad she was nowhere near the forest edge.

Then, Luella suddenly dived into the grass close

by. For a moment, Prue thought she was trying out some new aerial manoeuvre, but she didn't rise again – the grass was still. Then fear gripped her stomach.

Prue ran over. "Luella! Are you all right?" she called. Her eyes found Luella's bright shape in the grass, still as the night air. "Luella?" Prue said, panic making her voice high-pitched. She frantically looked around. "Ag, come quickly!" Prue scooped Luella up in her hands and said breathlessly, "Luella, wake up. Are you all right?"

Agapantha joined her.

"Ag, maybe she's sleeping?"

"Prue, personifates don't sleep."

What was wrong? She slowly turned Luella over, but her body was intact. "I just modified her wing. Did I do something wrong?"

Agapantha rested her arm on Prue's. "I think it was just her time. She's being showing signs that her qwortzite was failing for a while."

"But I just fixed her," Prue whispered.

Agapantha put a hand on Prue's arm. "Some things can't be fixed."

Prue felt the pain in her heart blaze again – it

was like what Francis had told her with the hoppity wrench back at the farm.

Edwin leapt nearby. "You two won't win at this rate! … What's the matter?" He joined the girls.

A tear glittered on Prue's cheek. "It's Luella. She's gone."

*

Craftsman Primrose asked Master Woolstenbury if Edwin could paint the picture for the gallery of Lost Personifates.

When it was finished, Prue, Edwin and Agapantha took it across to the Hall to hang it. The plaque read:

> *Luella Harvest-Moon*
> *Messenger*
> *Capax Infiniti*

"You've done a great job, Ed," said Prue.

"Thanks."

"But there's something lacking about the plaque – she was so much more than a messenger."

"Perhaps her frequency will be picked up again?" said Edwin.

"But she wouldn't remember us," said Prue. She thought for a moment then took out a pencil from her bag. Beside Luella she wrote *Edith Scamp* and beside Messenger she wrote *friend*.

Through the open door, Prue caught sight of Cora walking along the corridor. Anger was churning in Prue. After what had happened to Luella, she needed to make progress more than ever.

"Wait here," Prue said.

Edwin called after her. "What are you doing?"

"I want my journal back."

Prue stormed over to Cora. "Hey, what have you done with my journal?"

Cora put her hands on her hips. "What are you talking about?"

"I know it was you who took it. Hand it over."

Agapantha and Edwin joined Prue.

"Look, I don't know what this is about, but if you're missing something, perhaps you should look a bit closer to home. I mean, what do you really know about your little furry friend? He could have been a thief in his first life."

"Steady on, Cora," said Agapantha.

"You shouldn't even be hanging out with these two, Agapantha. They will never be like us."

"Like what, exactly?" said Prue, taking a step closer.

"You know perfectly well what I mean. Like the people who *should* be here." She flicked her hair and strode onwards, down the corridor.

Prue bit the edge of her tongue to contain her anger.

"She's something else," said Agapantha.

"I'm not sure she has your journal, Prue. She seemed surprised by your accusation," said Edwin.

"Surprised that she'd been caught, more like," Prue scowled.

Chapter 26

SAHWEN

Prue surveyed the five outfits Cora had discarded on her bed, all of varying glitter and shine. Cora had finally chosen a sparkly silver fitted dress with feathered shoulders. She eyed the other girls' dresses. "Hmm, a good idea to go plain: my mother says one's dress should always reflect one's personality." Then she floated out of the room.

Prue was wearing a red dress that she'd bought in town the previous weekend. Although Agapantha had said she'd pay, Prue insisted she use her own money as she didn't want any jibes from Cora about not being able to afford one. Agapantha had chosen a similar dress in green.

"If dresses reflect personalities, hers would be made of mouse traps," said Prue. She and Agapantha laughed.

"It's a shame craftsmen don't wear green, Ag. It suits you so well."

"I think you'll be a craftsmen before me!"

"Don't be daft." Then Prue had a sudden realization and looked down at her feet. "Err, I don't have any shoes?"

Agapantha shrugged. "Well, the dresses are long, and I personally feel pretty comfortable in my boots."

Knowing that Agapantha must've had shoes and was just being kind, Prue smiled. "Me too. I wonder if there will be dancing?" She twirled and made herself dizzy, then flopped down on her bed. She felt something under her head. Sitting up, she pulled the pillow back.

It was her journal!

"Ag, look what's turned up! I think someone had a guilty conscience, don't you?"

"At least you got it back," said Agapantha "But what if she's told Sollentude about all your notes on memory?"

"I'd probably know it by now," said Prue. "I guess I'll just have to wait and see." She stood up and hooked Agapantha's arm. "Let's forget about strange things in the wood, memory machines, and Cora Duval just for one night and have fun."

Everyone gathered in the hallway of the house. Lavender wore a purple puffy skirted dress, and Prue thought how nice it was to see her out of an apron. Liddy had opted for trousers and a lilac shirt. They smiled at the girls as they came down the stairs. Edwin was waiting at the bottom, wearing his electric blue bow tie and waistcoat made for him by Bard's Precision Tailouring.

"Very dashing!" Prue remarked.

"Likewise! Loving the boots, girls!"

The apprentices made their way to the pneumerator. It seemed strange, all the apprentices sitting in the red leather seats in fancy outfits rather than in their Guild uniforms. When they stepped out of the transport hut, they stood in awe – the factorium looked spectacular. Thousands of fairy lights streamed the length of the walls and drooped between chimneys, coloured lights lit up the fountain, and huge pumpkins carved with animal shapes lit the path from the hut to the main factorium building.

"Wow, it looks magical," Prue said.

"Look, even the messenger tower is sparkling," said Agapantha, pointing.

"And the trees!" Edwin sprang forward. "I can't wait to see inside!"

As they neared, sweet music filled the air. A choir of personifates and people sang together outside the factorium. Their harmonies were wonderful, with tenor and soprano melodies entwining in a sonic dance.

Prue thought how lovely it was to see the personifates enjoying such a magical evening together, and she pictured Luella perched with the choir singing her heart out. Her chest burned at the thought that she would never get to see her again. Biting her lip, she tried to focus on the beauty of the sound and not on the consuming blackness that came on when she thought of how much she'd lost.

"They're amazing. Mum says I sound like a strangled cat when I sing," said Prue.

"Oh!" said Agapantha.

"No, it's fine, she's completely right!" Prue

laughed, pulling herself away from the dark thoughts.

Inside was filled with more glittering lights trailing the iron balustrades of every level and crisscrossing high above. They reflected on the glass ceiling, making it look like a galaxy of gleaming stars. Long rectangular tables filled the central atrium, with crisp white tablecloths and flickering silver candles. They were laden with pumpkin soup, wholesome loaves, roasted corn, peas and pumpkin pie.

All the craftsman and masters wore suits and black bow ties and dresses, and Prue had to look twice at some before she realized who they were. Some of the personifates had dressed up too, although they mainly just accessorized with the odd tie or silk scarf. She caught sight of Phineas in a bow tie with flashing pink lights, sitting beside Craftsman Primrose who smiled at them from the other side where he was talking with Master White.

"Come on, let's sit together," said Prue.

"Now I really wish I could eat!" said Edwin.

The bread was still warm, and they dipped it into the steaming orange-coloured soup.

Prue licked the butter from her lips. "Mmm,

sorry, Ed, but this food is so good!"

"It's all right; I'm imagining every mouthful."

"Maybe they could find a way of personifates being able to taste without eating?" Agapantha looked thoughtful, then took a bite of corn.

"There's an idea," Prue said, switching to pumpkin pie with a large dollop of cream. "Perhaps some sort of smell detector to activate simulated flavour."

"Whoever reaches craftsman first *needs* to make it their first priority!" Edwin laughed.

After they'd eaten, there was more singing outside, and the tempo was faster and jauntier. People began getting up and going out to dance. Prue hadn't danced since the North Owlcot fete two years ago.

"Come on, let's join them!" Prue said, pushing the memory away before she thought about Francis again.

Edwin needed no persuasion, but it took some dragging to get Agapantha to her feet.

The music changed and a soloist replaced the choir.

"That singing is amazing! Let's see who it is," said Prue.

They hurried outside. To their amazement, Cora

stood at the front of the choir, singing her heart out.

"Goodness, I hate to admit it, but she's pretty good!" said Prue. "Look how happy she looks." Every line of her looked relaxed and at home, like a different person; Prue realized this must be Cora's real passion.

They got pulled into a stream of people and personifates dancing in a loop around the glittering box hedges. When Prue couldn't dance another step, she made her way to the fountain and sat on the edge, running her hands in the cool stream of water. Agapantha was dancing happily with some of the first-year apprentices – her shyness seemed to have been washed away by the lights for a while.

Edwin jumped up beside Prue. "I'm glad to see you happy."

"It's funny, isn't it?"

"What?"

"How music helps you both forget and remember."

Edwin tilted his head. "I think I know what you mean."

"Oh, I'm sorry, I don't mean to be insensitive about your first life!"

Edwin laughed. "It's all right."

Craftsman Primrose came out of the factorium and joined them. "Ah, I'm glad to catch you both alone. I've been meaning to speak to you on a matter of some importance, but it requires your absolute trust and discretion." He surveyed the crowd.

"Of course," said Prue.

"You were both at the Inventors Parade a while back?"

"Yes."

"And you saw the incident?"

Prue frowned. "The leopard personifate?"

"Yes. I wanted to ask you how you really felt about it? I mean, Rights for Personifates is one thing, but to actually attack the float of the Guild with the Governor in it is something else."

Prue glanced at Edwin. "Well, it was a bit extreme, but," she took a breath, "I kind of thought the personifate had a point."

"I agree," said Edwin.

Craftsman Primrose put a hand to his chin.

"Please don't misunderstand us, Craftsman Primrose. What the Guild is doing is marvellous, but perhaps the Sovereign Chancellery and the Governor just need to consider the feelings of the personifates a little more," said Prue.

"Indeed. I suspected you would both feel the same as me. I would have spoken to you both about this sooner, but I had to be sure of your position on the matter, and I've seen you share similar opinions to me, Frances, with your Rights for Personifates badge. There is much going on beneath the surface." He paused and looked around, then continued, "The one hundred personifates is an unprecedented act of treating personifates almost like factory machines to be produced and exploited. And things will only get worse. The ASL is growing stronger by the week. I think it's time to empower the personifates. If we on the inside can't do it, who will stand up for them? I want you to meet me at the factorium entrance at day-break. But this must be top-secret. I could be arrested. Do I have your trust?"

Prue had trusted Craftsman Primrose from the first moment she'd met him.

They both nodded. "Then I will see you bright and early before the others stir. Now, enjoy the rest of the party. You have a very important day tomorrow."

After he left, Prue and Edwin stared at each other.

"What in Medlock was that all about?" said Prue.

Chapter 27

PRIMROSE'S PLAN

When Prue crept to the window and peeled back the curtain, it was the ghostly half-light of daybreak. A thin layer of ice coated the rooftops like cold dust beneath a cloudy sky.

Hurriedly, she pulled on three layers of clothing and two pairs of socks, then turned the door handle as quietly as possible.

Edwin was pacing in the hallway. "I was about to tap in case you didn't wake."

They hurried silently down the stairs to the pneumerator, and pulled the lever up to bring it their way. Once inside they sat opposite each other, both deep in thought, tentative but curious.

"What do you think he means by empowering the personifates?" asked Edwin as the pod shot towards the factorium.

Prue leaned in. "Maybe there's a secret meeting of Rights for Personifates? Perhaps there's a classified meeting place and an initiation."

Edwin shrugged. "I guess we'll find out soon enough."

They stepped from the transport hut on to the frozen lawns of the factorium. The grass crunched like fine shards of glass beneath their feet, and Prue's breath chugged in steamy clouds before her.

"Look, he's at the forest edge," said Prue, spotting Craftsman Primrose.

They hurried towards him.

"I'm so glad you both came. Come along." He turned towards the forest.

"Craftsman Primrose, what about the guard?" said Prue, peering into the forest nervously.

"It poses us no threat whatsoever, trust me."

Prue was too intrigued to let her apprehension get to her. She stepped after him alongside Edwin.

"You are both very talented young apprentices."

"Thank you," said Prue.

"I took a chance on both of you which I believe was right. Now I will continue what I began to tell you yesterday evening. Then I must ask something of you."

Edwin glanced up at Prue.

Craftsman Primrose walked onwards. "The personifates are owned by the Sovereign Chancellery."

"Owned? I've never really thought of it like that," Prue said.

"The Governor sees it as a business. The personifate programme is paid for and commissioned by the Governor of Medlock using the money of the citizens. The personifates are citizens too. Wouldn't you agree?"

"Yes," said Edwin wholeheartedly. "We contribute to society as much as anyone in their first life."

"I agree," said Prue.

They trudged on through the frozen landscape of the forest, branches snapping like brittle bones beneath their feet.

"Then who do you think should be in charge of the lives of personifates – Master Hannah Woolstenbury and Governor Henri

Watson-Wentworth, or the personifates themselves?"

Prue thought he was right. Why shouldn't they have more freedom? Wasn't that what she was trying to do with her memory machine?

"But I suppose we have been given chances," said Edwin. "Look at me; you took me on as the first apprentice personifate."

"Indeed, so you, of all personifates, have had a taste of the possibilities."

A glimpse of the rising sun appeared between the clouds and shone between the tree trunks, casting bands of light on the forest floor.

"Have you tried talking to the Governor or Master Woolstenbury about these concerns? Perhaps Master White?" suggested Edwin.

"Come now, I had you both down as bigger thinkers. Especially you, Apprentice Haywood. Your memory research is groundbreaking."

Prue paused. How did he know about her research? Then it hit her. "You took my journal?"

Craftsman Primrose stopped walking and smiled. "Let's say, *borrowed*. I'd suspected you were working on something for a while with all your questions on memory."

"Master Woolstenbury doesn't know about it, does she?" she said, panicked.

"Of course not. But it did confirm for me that the three of us could work on some great projects together. We have a chance to really change things for the better."

They carried on walking; they were deep into the forest now.

Prue's mind felt as though it had suddenly become a whirlpool. Did Craftsman Primrose know she wasn't Frances? "Where are we going?" Prue asked.

"I'm going to show you the first project we'll be working on together. It's not far now."

The trees thinned, and large crooked shapes loomed beyond.

"Is that a village?" Prue asked.

"It was, long ago, but nobody has lived here in many years."

They stepped from the treeline and looked below. A dozen or so ivy-strangled buildings huddled together, most barely standing, with crumbling brickwork and tumbledown roofs. A few were more intact and had been reinforced and repaired. An old well was in the centre and there were clusters of broken carts and machinery littering the moss-covered cobblestones.

"It's taken a while to make it into a workable environment, but as long as it serves its purpose."

"Purpose?" said Edwin.

"Come along, I can't wait to show you." Craftsman Primrose grinned.

An eerie silence clung to the village as they walked towards the largest building.

"I think it was the old village hall," Craftsman Primrose said. He unlocked the door and pushed it open.

Prue's leg muscles turned to liquid at the sight inside, as though she had fallen headfirst into a nightmare.

"This, my friends, is my army of stag-men. One-hundred of them, to be precise."

Even perfectly stock-still, the bodies looked terrifying. They were all of the exact same personifate body – it was the antlered creature that had attacked them in the forest. Edwin glanced at Prue. She suddenly recalled that he had said the creature in the forest had looked like something from the Ancient Mercia books. Prue remembered her very first weekend at the Guild, and how enthusiastic Craftsman Primrose was about Ancient Mercian myths at the library.

"Don't look so afraid, they are merely shells, waiting to be inhabited. Come along inside."

Primrose walked about the stag-men proudly. "It's been quite a task getting these ready for the blood moon, especially with all the extra work at the Guild."

"Why are they so terrible looking? Human-like bodies and skull-like faces, and why the huge antlers?" Prue said, trying to keep her voice calm.

"They may seem a little fearsome, but we need them to be. The Guild won't just hand power over to us." Craftsman Primrose patted one proudly as he passed it. "Don't look so worried, Prue. Imagine if we were in control of all of Medlock and the Guild, every available technology at our fingertips. We can find a way to bring back memory. You want rights for personifates? This is the only way to get them."

"You're planning to bring these back too on the blood moon?" said Edwin. He kept flashing looks at Prue and mouthed, *He's mad!* Prue mouthed, *I know.*

Craftsman Primrose paced back towards them. "Not too, but *instead*. Qwortzite is enormously expensive and rare, so there will only be enough for one set of a hundred. Luckily I've secured the code for the vault."

Prue thought of his relationship with Master White. Was that how he knew the code?

"And what will you do with the stag-men?" Prue said, trying to keep her voice steady.

"We will harness the army together when the blood moon rises. All the most esteemed and powerful members of the Sovereign Chancellery will be at the factorium that evening. The Guild plans to start harnessing at ten p.m., but we will start sooner, at sundown. By the time they realize the qwortzite has gone, we will be finished, and they will have no option but to surrender power to the personifates. Then I take over as Governor and head of the new Guild, and you both become instant masters of a new personifate-empowered guild. You'll have all the resources to fulfil your research and unlock the memories."

"Right," said Prue, "so, you just need us to help harness the stag-men so that you can grant the personifates more freedom. Except, in order to grant more freedom, you need to create an army that will imprint on you, so you will actually be in charge." She paused. "It doesn't sound that free for them."

Craftsman Primrose's eyes were wide. "All for the greater good. Don't we all do extreme things for something bigger than ourselves sometimes ... Prudence?"

Edwin looked at her. Craftsman Primrose knew her real name!

"I was aware from early on that you weren't Frances, when I saw you write the letter home on the train, and it didn't take long to guess at your motivations in coming here once I did some investigating to find out about the real Francis. But I saw your technical skills at work on your parents' farm, and I knew you had talent anyway. Then when I heard about the name service you were providing the personifates, and the remarkable invention you've created – it's an astonishing breakthrough! I knew you would understand the plight of personifates. Imagine what we'll achieve. Remember, if you assist me, I will help you develop your machine and find a way to your brother."

"Isn't bringing back all these stag-men on one night a little ambitious for just three of us?" she said, trying desperately to hold her nerve.

"We won't need all the ridiculous ceremony that Woolstenbury insists on, and besides, there will be four of us."

Prue frowned. "Four?" Then it came to her, "Master White." Of course; they were in it together.

Craftsman Primrose shook his head. "Oh dear, no, she is quite tied to the ways of the Guild."

The door creaked open.

Finblewick stepped inside. "We could do this on our own, Charles."

"We've discussed this. Apprentices Haywood and Snow-Moon are necessary for the plan to succeed; our timing during the blood moon will be crucial."

"How long have you been planning this?" asked Edwin.

"Ever since I came here. I've had one goal and that is to liberate the personifates and lead a revolution against the Guild and the Chancellery."

Prue felt so horrified she wanted to run, but it was as though her panic rooted her to the spot. She understood the cause, but this was all too extreme.

"On the blood moon you will come here before sundown. The Guild will be busy, and no one will miss two novice apprentices so early in proceedings."

"Well, it seems like you've rather thought all this through. There's lots to prepare for, so perhaps if Edwin and I get back; we wouldn't want anyone to miss us and become suspicious, and of course we won't be saying a word to anyone – no, not a thing – will we, Edwin?"

Edwin shook his head emphatically. Finblewick observed them with narrow beady eyes.

"Good. I'm so pleased to have you on board," said Craftsman Primrose.

They both turned to leave.

"One last thing," Craftsman Primrose called.

Prue turned to face him again, a cold trickle of sweat running down her back.

"I know you wouldn't, but as security, the stag-man you met in the forest before..."

"Yes?"

"It's rather a wild one, that spirit. After its rogue actions, I had to remind it that it's completely under my command, although I rather have enjoyed the ripple of unease it's set among Medlock with its sneaking around. I've instructed it to take a little trip north to Haywood Farm where it will wait. One signal from me and I'm afraid it might take action."

Prue's heart stopped beating. That creature was heading to her farm!

"I want to do this with your cooperation, Prue; it's so much easier for everyone that way. But you do understand that I need a little insurance, just in case. Of course, the stag-man is simply watching, but things could be quite different." He held up a small device. "Some technology I've been developing to carry long-range signals. A swift turn of the crank will power it up and send a frequency to the stag-man on your farm. It will know what to do."

Fear and hopelessness swelled inside of Prue.

"Oh, don't look so alarmed, Prudence. They are quite safe, until I give the word. But I'm sure you understand I need to ensure your cooperation."

Prue nodded. "Are you sure that going about this by force is the way? Isn't harnessing ghosts into these machines to get what you want going against everything you are trying to achieve?" she said, hoping that there just might be a glimmer of hope to dissuade him.

"Hannah Woolstenbury and the Governor have prevented research like yours on memory for many years. Think about it – isn't it in their interest to keep things as they are? A people without history have no ties, no bonds to bring them together, they are no threat. The force we have to use is a sacrifice for the greater good. In every battle there are casualties."

"Battle?" said Edwin.

"No one is going to give us anything if we ask nicely, Edwin. You're a second lifer. You of all people should understand. Together we awaken the stag-men at the blood moon, but you won't need to play any part in the fighting – I wouldn't ask that of you."

Prue just couldn't understand. She looked at Craftsman Primrose, who had always seemed so calm and approachable. Nothing on the outside had reflected what was going on inside.

She glanced at Edwin. "If we help, will you promise me you'll make it your priority to find a way to bring back my brother?"

Craftsman Primrose put a hand to his chest. "Cross my heart."

"Then I'll help."

"Me too," said Edwin.

Craftsman Primrose gave a single nod of approval. "Good. Don't breathe a word to anyone."

Prue agreed, hoping that the lie didn't show in her eyes.

Craftsman Primrose escorted them back through the forest to the transport hut. "Return to the house and await my instruction."

When they were back at the house, Prue checked that the parlour was empty, then she and Edwin went inside and closed the door.

Prue sat on the sofa, taking deep breaths. "I can't believe this is happening. I just can't,"

"Your poor parents, Prue," Edwin said, pacing back and forth.

"He won't hesitate to set that creature on them. What are we going to do?"

Prue kicked herself for coming to the Guild at all, for leaving the farm and putting everything at risk. She longed for that feeling of normal, of not having a worry in the world. Like it had been when Francis was alive.

She shook her head sadly. "What choice do we

have but to make Craftsman Primrose think we are going along with it? But we need our own plan, and quick. I just don't understand how he created the stag-man we saw in the forest with only the masters having access to the qwor—" suddenly Prue straightened up. "Of course! Edwin, he was behind the dead personifate jackalope! He stole her qwortzite to make the first stag-man as a test run!"

"He killed the jackalope ... but how could he use qwortzite that had lost its frequency?"

Prue stood still for a moment, her mind whirling. "It must be possible to reuse qwortzite. Perhaps that's why he chose to kill a personifate not far into its second life?"

Edwin cocked his head, considering the idea. "Of course!"

"Well, we know how he created the first one, but that doesn't help us stop him creating another hundred." She looked at Edwin. "We'd better get thinking."

Chapter 28

PRUE'S PLAN

The clock was ticking, and Prue and Edwin had been wracking their brains, looking for an answer that was growing more elusive with every hour. They were in one of the mechanical labs working on adding the last feathers to the winged personifates of the hundred.

"You've both been exceptionally quiet since Sahwen. What are you up to?" Agapantha said suspiciously.

"Nothing," they both said quickly.

Agapantha tapped her hook tool on the table. "Well, secrets are nothing new around here and something's going on, you're both acting really strangely."

"Absolutely not, there is nothing going on whatsoever," Prue declared, finding it hard to keep her voice hushed in her urgency.

"By which you mean there absolutely is something going on," Agapantha said.

Prue looked back down at her book. It was so close to the blood moon. She had snuck away with Edwin at every opportunity, trying to work something out, and they were still getting nowhere.

"How much will they want us to do on the blood moon?" Agapantha asked. "I'm not sure I could harness a ghost on my own."

"I don't think they'll expect that of new apprentices. Maybe some of the older apprentices like Larkin and Sira. We're just there in a supportive role," said Edwin.

"Good, because I'd likely be so nervous that I'd reverse the signal and blast them straight back to where they came from," said Agapantha.

Prue looked up. "What did you say?"

Agapantha's cheeks flushed red, "Oh, I wouldn't really do that. I'd honestly be very careful if I had the chance."

"I know, but what you said about reversing the signal – is that possible?"

"Mathematically it is – you could break the loop. The signal, even though it's harnessed within the qwortzite, is a continuous movement from this world to the spirit world. If the loop was interrupted, the qwortzite would lose the frequency for ever, and let's face it, it would be near on impossible to pick it up again."

Prue and Edwin looked at each other aghast.

"Did I say something wrong?" Agapantha whispered.

"Ag, you're a genius of few words, but what you say is mighty powerful." Prue smiled. She whispered something to Edwin who nodded in agreement, then she wrote a note on a piece of paper and passed it across to Agapantha, looking around carefully to make sure they weren't being watched.

Meet in the memory lab at lunch.
Make sure no one sees you or follows,
especially the craftsmen and masters.

*

Later, in the memory lab, Prue, Edwin and Agapantha sat away from the door so that no one could listen in from the hallway. Prue quietly explained everything that had happened to an aghast Agapantha.

"You're completely stuck," said Agapantha, eyes wide. "If you tell anyone, he'll send a signal to the stag-man to attack your parents. But if you go along with him, you're half responsible for bringing down the Governor and overthrowing the Imperial Personifate Guild."

"Yes, something like that," said Prue, her heart rate quickening at the mere thought of it all.

"Your poor parents," said Agapantha.

Prue nodded. "What you said in the library earlier gave me an idea, but we can't risk getting it wrong. And I'm going to need your help, both with the machine, and on the night. Ag, do you think you could create something that would interrupt the signal?"

She thought for a moment. "We could use one of the GODAR machines and connect it to each stag-man."

"But I'm not sure we'd be able to do them one

at a time without them, you know, killing people," said Edwin.

"So, we'll need to transmit the signal to interrupt the loops of the stag-men, then focus it at the same time," Prue suggested,

"We could use a parabolic reflector to target an area!" said Agapantha.

"Brilliant. But I need you to do it all, because Edwin and I need to pretend to be going along with Craftsman Primrose. When he awakens the stag-men, they will march on the factorium and take it by force. As they emerge from the forest, you'll need to be ready to transmit the signal. But we must make sure the plan stays between the three of us. No one in the Guild can find out what's going on or we risk Craftsman Primrose hearing about it."

They fell quiet.

"This machine could kill dozens of personifates at the flick of a switch," Edwin said quietly.

Prue nodded. "We *have* to get this right."

"How about using the messenger tower? Agapantha could sneak away when all the craftsman and masters are busy at the pre-harnessing gathering. It's the perfect place to transmit a signal

347

from," said Edwin.

"We don't want to risk hitting the Guild personifates," said Agapantha. "Including you."

"They will all be helping at the factorium. As long as we focus the signal correctly with the parabolic reflector," said Prue. "Meanwhile, Edwin and I will go ahead with Craftsman Primrose's plan. We take, or break, his transmitter, so he can't contact the stag-man on my farm. When the stag-men army is taken down, Craftsman Primrose will be powerless, and the masters can capture him. Then we send help to my parents and take care of the last stag-man."

"What was that?" said Edwin.

"You mean, how do we take care of the stag-man?" Prue asked.

"No, I get that, I just thought I heard rustling."

A box creaked nearby.

Prue put her fingers to her lips and they crept towards one of the boxes. Just as they reached it, the flaps burst open.

"Surprise!"

Prue's stomach lurched.

Cora stepped out of the box and brushed herself

down. "What interesting schemes of fantasy you all seem to be concocting! Honestly, you should learn to be more careful with your correspondence: throwing that note in the library bin was pretty obvious."

Prue stepped towards her. "Please don't say anything, Cora – you don't know what you're messing with. Craftsman Primrose is dangerous, and people's lives are at stake."

"Dangerous? Craftsman Primrose?" Cora stifled a giggle.

"I know he doesn't seem like it, but he is. He's a personifate rights fanatic, and he's got Prue's parents hostage," said Edwin.

"Craftsman Primrose wouldn't harm a fly. You're making up lies about a craftsman just to amuse yourself and your friends in your little fantasy. Perhaps I'll tell Craftsman Primrose what you waste your time doing. Stag-men, ha! I think you might have actually wanted me to find that note, just so you could have an audience for your games."

"Cora, it's all true, I swear," Prue pleaded.

"It is, Cora. What possible reason would Prue and Edwin have to make up something this huge?" said Agapantha.

"Honestly, you three really need to get a life." With a flick of her hair she left the room.

There was a tense silence in the room before Edwin asked, "Do you think Cora will say anything?"

"Well, there's nothing we can do about whatever she thinks." Prue sighed. "Let's focus on reconfiguring the machine to transmit the reversal signal."

*

Later, Agapantha managed to sneak into one of the labs and take one of the many GODAR machines gathered ready for the harnessing.

"Strictly speaking, it's not theft, just borrowing. And this one was in the spares box, so I'm sure they won't miss it immediately."

Prue nodded. "Good work. We've found an old parabolic reflector in one of the boxes. It's a bit dented. Edwin, do you think you can fix it?"

"I'll do my best," he said.

Prue pointed to a page in her journal. "I've sketched out the area and made a few calculations for range. Ag, if you could check them over."

It was dark by the time they'd finished.

"Let's go over the plan. We hide the equipment in here until the last minute because we don't want the messengers in the tower getting suspicious. At nine-thirty p.m., when all the personifates, craftsman, masters and members of the Sovereign Chancellery are gathered in the atrium pre-harnessing, Ag slips away to get the equipment from the memory lab. Then Ag exits the room by the fire escape. You'll need a big back pack, maybe one of the garden sacks and rope to haul it down."

"Yes, that should work." Ag nodded.

Prue noticed that Agapantha looked pale and clammy just thinking about the ladder.

"You can do it," Prue said, putting a hand on her arm. "Then Ag takes the equipment around to the tower for nine forty-five. Craftsman Primrose aims for his army to arrive at ten, so it should be time enough to set the equipment up ready for the arrival of the stag-men."

"What could possibly go wrong?" said Edwin.

"Cora," both Prue and Agapantha said together.

"If she doesn't believe us, she won't say anything," said Edwin.

"Let's hope you're right," said Prue.

By the time they'd got back to the house they'd missed tea. Thankfully, Lavender had set some aside for them.

"Do you mind if I take mine up? I've got some work to finish," Prue asked.

"That's fine, dear," said Lavender. "My, you are working hard!"

"I'm going to speak to Cora," Prue whispered to Agapantha and Edwin.

Upstairs, Cora was lying on her bed looking at the ceiling.

Prue laid on her own and did the same. "We're not making it up," she said.

It was silent for several minutes before Cora huffed and turned to her. Her eyes narrowed. "It *is* a pretty ridiculous story."

"None of us want anything bad to happen to the Guild – it's all of our futures, right?" Prue thought about what she'd heard Cora's parents say at the Grand Principalia. "Right?" she said softly.

"But stag-men? Craftsman Primrose plotting to overthrow Master Woolstenbury and the governor?"

"I know how ridiculous it sounds, and I know you don't think much of me. But believe me, I wish I weren't here, either, knowing what's about to happen."

"Well, I don't have a choice but to be here, Frances. It's expected. You have no idea what's it's like being told what to do from the moment you were born, to act in the way that's expected of your position in society, to achieve the best grades, attend endless boring dinners with members of the Sovereign Chancellery to secure your future."

Prue didn't. She had so much freedom on the farm. "I'm sure your parents want the best for you, they've just forgotten to listen on the way."

Cora stared at her. Her face seemed to have lost its hardened mask.

"We really are telling the truth, Cora. I wouldn't make up stories about something so important. Perhaps if you help us, when it's all over your parents will see that you can think for yourself and will give you a choice? Maybe you'll have the strength to tell them what you really want."

Cora sighed. "Maybe farm girls aren't all stupid after all."

"Thank you for believing us."

Cora huffed and turned away. "I said maybe."

Chapter 29

BLOOD MOON

Snow arrived with a portent chill on the morning of the blood moon. Fitful sleep left Prue edgy and nervous. She knew she needed to be focused, so she put on her warmest clothes and decided to take a walk in the park at the end of Sovereign Row to clear her mind for the day ahead.

All was quiet and an expectant calm hung in the air. She headed across the white-carpeted grass, treading fresh tracks. There wasn't a breath of wind, and snow rested delicately on branches and leaves. The wintry air somehow made her thoughts sharp and the impending reality all too clear. Her dreams of finding a way to Francis had become buried like the white-blanketed hills, and not only that, by the end of the day she risked losing what was left of her family.

She decided to head back and at least have a good breakfast, then saw Edwin in the snow a short distance away. She waved, and he jumped through the white towards her.

"Hey. Are you all right?" he asked.

She nodded. "Never better. How about you, Jack Swift?"

He smiled. "Just thought I'd take a walk and clear my thoughts. It's strange, you calling me that, but I kind of like it. It makes me feel more like a first-lifer and forget that I might only have nine years left."

"Don't say that. Things change, inventions move on. What if there's a way to extend your second life, and we just haven't found it yet? Maybe we can find a way to move your frequency into newly mined qwortzite."

"You never see a problem you can't fix, do you?"

She shrugged and looked at him. For a moment, she let herself imagine the boy he was in his first life; perhaps chestnut hair, green eyes, the same warm side-smile he had as a personifate.

"The masters are worried the cloud cover might weaken the harnessing potential this evening if it gets any worse," said Edwin.

"Let's hope it does and the whole thing gets called off."

*

At the factorium, late adjustments were being made to the hundred for the rest of the day with a flurry of last-minute paperwork. After an early tea, Prue, Edwin and Agapantha met in the memory lab. Edwin had sketched a map of the area and Prue added notes and arrows.

"When the stag-men march on the field towards the factorium and they are all within range, don't wait. Transmit the signal no matter what. Is that clear?" said Prue.

Agapantha nodded.

"Everyone will be gathered in the atrium, so like we said before, you'll have to take the fire escape, or you'll be seen. Are you sure you'll be all right, Ag?"

Agapantha nodded and went to the window. "I'll just imagine I'm a lizard or something." She giggled nervously.

"We should probably get going," said Prue.

Dusk was upon them and the factorium lights glowed orange in the grey-blue of the descending evening. Agapantha walked with them to the forest edge and the three of them stood together for a moment, facing the wood. A break in the clouds to the south revealed a russet sliver of moon, peeping above the forest. Fine snowflakes began drifting like breath from the sky above.

"The blood moon," said Prue. "It's beautiful."

"When this is all over, I'm going to paint this scene," said Edwin.

Agapantha looked across at them both. "You'd better get going."

They hugged quickly. Prue's stomach twisted painfully and she swallowed hard. Then, without looking back, Prue and Edwin dashed into the trees.

As they made their way in the direction of the abandoned village, they barely spoke. They paused when they reached the crumbling buildings. Golden light flickered inside, casting ominous jagged shadows from the stag-men antlers on to the windows.

When they opened the door, Craftsman Primrose looked up. He was wearing his tweed suit and matching waistcoat, just like when Prue had first seen him on the farm.

He glanced at his pocket watch. "Precisely on time. We're almost ready to go."

Prue saw what appeared to be a small transmitter attached to the pocket watch. Probably the one he'd created to communicate with the stag-man on the farm.

"Finblewick will be along shortly. I suggest for quickness' sake, you two work on a harnessing while Finblewick and I will work on another. When you make a connection, you will call me straight over. I need to be the first thing they see, so that they imprint on me and are within my control."

They nodded.

"The blood moon has risen, and we need to make a start."

In the middle of the room was a box filled with iridescent qwortzite.

"Won't the Guild realize it's missing?" said Prue.

"Not until they begin. As long as they stick to their planned schedule, they won't be opening the safe until ten o'clock." Primrose led them over to one of the stag-men. "You can watch me do the first one, then you can do your own. The chest cavity opens like so. They've been designed for speed of harnessing."

Craftsman Primrose worked swiftly with the GODAR machine. He spoke as he adjusted the dials. "Your journal was very interesting, Prue. I noted your observations on the emotion portion of the signal with fascination. The more extreme the saw tooth signal, I believe the more heightened the emotion will be. So, we will select those with the most extreme patterns, and then we will have an army to reckon with!"

Craftsman Primrose had soon isolated a wildspark signal and wired the qwortzite into place. He stood facing the stag-man. The hollow red eyes lit like a struck match, its great jaw opened.

"Where am I?" said the voice of what Prue guessed to be someone about the age of her father.

"There is someone trying to enslave you and your brothers and sisters, and you need to kill them in order to stay alive in this world."

It flexed its clawed hands.

"I am your master. Await my command," Craftsman Primrose ordered.

An icy snake slithered the length of Prue's spine.

The door opened, letting in a flutter of snowflakes. "All is going ahead at the factorium according to schedule," said Finblewick.

"I feel sick," Prue whispered to Edwin. "I can't believe what we are about to do."

"Think of your parents. Just as soon as this part is over, we'll be able to help them."

Prue nodded. "Did you see the transmitter attached to his watch chain? I need to get it somehow."

Edwin frowned. "We'll find a way. Just focus on not looking suspicious."

Prue put her bag down beside one of the stagmen. She couldn't think of them as second lifers. They weren't like the Guild personifates, made with care and kindness; these were made to look fierce, to be powerful and domineering. They were fighting machines.

"Come on, let's make a start," said Edwin.

Soon they'd picked up a jumble of frequencies. Edwin turned the dials and although he took longer than Craftsman Primrose, he eventually managed to isolate a wildspark signal. Prue called Craftsman Primrose over, who had already awoken another three in the time they'd harnessed one. She carefully connected the wiring and the eyes ignited.

"Where am I?" This one was a female, young, perhaps in her twenties.

Primrose repeated the words he had said to the previous stag-man, then left them to finish up while he went to harness another.

Sweat beaded on Prue's brow. "The transmitter was so close. I could almost grab it."

"I saw it, but you can't risk it," Edwin whispered. "We'll leave it towards the end, when there's less chance he'll realize it's gone. Then I'll take it while he is focusing on getting the last one to imprint. Come on. Let's get this done."

The next stag-man awoke speaking another language. "I think we've done something wrong?" Prue said.

"No, just carry on; it happens from time to time. It'll just follow the others."

They harnessed two more young females, then an older man. They were getting quicker every time. Prue checked her watch. It was seven o'clock. By eight they only had another dozen to go.

It was Prue's turn to isolate the frequency. They danced across the screen and she turned the dials, until one remained. She called out to Craftsman Primrose as they fixed the final wire into place. The piercing eyes ignited.

"Where am I? What's happening?"

The ground suddenly crumbled beneath Prue's feet. She couldn't believe what she was hearing. It couldn't be true! She swallowed hard and reached for the table to steady herself.

Utterly helpless, Prue watched as Primrose said the words to the stag-man then turned to them. "Hurry along, now. Not many left to go." Then he joined Finblewick who had just harnessed another.

Prue stared at the stag-man before her in disbelief. "No, please, no," she gasped.

"Prue? Are you all right?" Edwin said, but his voice had become distant.

She tried to focus. Surely she'd misheard? "Can you hear me?" she whispered, grasping the stag-man by the face, her voice shaking.

"Yes. Where am I?"

"Say it again."

"Where am I?"

In panic, Prue looked over at Craftsman Primrose, but he was busy with another stag-man.

"Prue, you're scaring me," said Edwin.

"I recognize that voice," Prue said breathlessly.

"What? But that's…"

"A chance in a million," Prue said.

"Are you sure? It might just be someone who sounds similar."

Prue grappled with her bag, where the adapted name-finding GODAR was buried at the bottom. "I need to find out."

Her heart pounded like a locomotive, as she attached the wire. She kept glancing at Primrose and Finblewick, but they were both busy wiring. With shaking hands, she turned the dial, separating the history data. She enclosed the face of the stag-man in her hands and whispered, "Say your name."

There was a pause, then it opened its mouth.

It looked around and swayed slightly.

"I'm Francis, Francis Haywood."

Chapter 30

STAG-MEN ARMY

Prue tried to stop it, but a cascade of tears ran down her cheek.

Edwin's mouth was locked open in shock.

"Everything all right down there?" Craftsman Primrose called.

"Yes, we're just finishing this one and we'll move on to the next. Only one more to go," Edwin called.

Prue was still grasping the face of the stag-man.

"Prue!" Edwin said in an urgent whisper.

"It's me – Prue. Francis, can you remember me?"

"Prue, we need to move on to the next stag-man – Craftsman Primrose will realize something's wrong." He scurried up to sit on the shoulder of the stag-man and prised Prue's hands from its face. "Come on."

The burn of grief rose in her chest again as she forced herself to move to the next stag-man. "What do we do, Edwin?"

"I don't know," he said urgently, "but we've got to pretend like nothing's happened."

Craftsman Primrose and Finblewick had harnessed their last soldier and Craftsman Primrose joined them. He looked at his pocket watch. "Nine-fifteen. Perfect. Almost time to march." He began repeating his speech to the final stag-man.

Prue looked back at the stag-man that was Francis and willed him to turn and look at her. "Francis, it's me, please!" she breathed. He remained staring forward. What had they done? Prue glanced at Edwin on the table beside Craftsman Primrose.

Then Edwin jumped down and hurried her to the back of the building while Primrose and Finblewick were occupied. Panic was escalating inside of Prue. She followed him, and Edwin scampered up to sit on her shoulder, thrusting something into her pocket on the way.

"I got the transmitter," he whispered.

"Oh, thank you. I almost forgot, with Francis and…" she looked at him with tear-dashed eyes. "I can't send my brother back," she said in a desperate hushed voice.

"But what can we do?"

"I don't know, but we have to find a way to stop Agapantha." She stared at him with tear dashed eyes. "I can't lose him again. I can't."

*

The factorium atrium was rapidly filling with people and personifates. The kitchen personifates were walking around with trays of drinks and canapes, and there was a merry atmosphere of expectation. Spirit lights hung from the iron rails, and soft music was being played by a string quartet with a fox, two cats and Phineas on the cello.

Agapantha was waiting for the right time to sneak away.

Governor Watson-Wentworth stood close by in an emerald velvet suit with waistcoat and large gold buttons, along with with some fine-looking members of the Sovereign Chancellery.

"Ah, good to see you, Apprentice Young," said Master White, appearing from behind her. "Sorry – I would've been here earlier, but I was looking for Craftsman Primrose. You haven't seen him, have you?"

"Yes, he was talking with Apprentice Haywood. I saw him over there not so long ago," said Agapantha in a rush, crossing her fingers behind her back.

"Oh, I can't see him. Never mind. It's ever so busy in here. I'll be glad to get started, to tell you the truth. It's certainly been a frantic introduction to the Guild for you. I hope you're not regretting being here!"

"Not at all," said Agapantha. She glanced at the clock: Nine twenty-five. Almost time.

"Right, I'd better mingle. See you at ten in the labs," said Master White, disappearing into the crowd.

Agapantha was about to move, when a bell rang out and silence fell. She tried to edge back through the crowd, but she was penned in on all sides.

Governor Watson-Wentworth addressed the room. "Masters, craftsman and esteemed members of the Sovereign Chancellery. We all come together to celebrate this landmark day in the production of personifates. When I set Master Woolstenbury the task, I wasn't sure it could be done, but as always, when Master Woolstenbury sets her mind to things, she finds a way."

Master Woolstenbury smiled politely beside him, but she was clearly unimpressed with the whole spectacle the Governor had insisted on.

"Now, we have a no-expenses-spared blood moon firework display to enjoy, just to start the evening off with a bang. And don't you worry – we've printed a story in the *Medlock News* that today is the Medlock & Co Chaos Production's big anniversary celebration." He winked theatrically. "Come along. I'd like everyone to gather outside."

Agapantha's heart began racing; everyone was going to be looking out the front in the direction of the messenger tower, where she needed to be. But there was no time to worry; she'd have to cross that bridge when she came to it. She slipped quietly up the stairs at the side of the atrium as everyone made their way to the front steps, then ran along the corridor to the memory lab and gathered the equipment.

She opened the window, inhaled several deep breaths, then lowered the bag of equipment on a rope. With shaking legs, she climbed down the fire escape ladder, then snatched up the bag of equipment and ran around the back of the factorium, stopping at the front-west corner of the building to check if the coast was clear. There were people everywhere! If she ran now, she'd be seen for sure. What could she do?

Then, operatic singing, as crystalline as ice, rang through the air. Cora was standing near the fountain, singing the anthem of Medlock at the top of her voice.

Every head swung in her direction and people flocked towards her. Cora glanced in her direction and winked.

Agapantha blinked. Cora was helping her! She looked at her watch – nine-thirty.

Without thinking, she dashed towards the tower.

*

The stag-men filed out of the abandoned village and into the night, marching in a uniform beat, feet crunching and pounding the snow of the forgotten streets.

Prue and Edwin told Craftsman Primrose they would follow at the back to make sure that the stag-men stayed in line. Prue hardly took her eyes from Francis. She sidled as close to him as she could and whispered, "It's going to be all right, I'll get you home, we'll fix this." But he just stared blankly ahead. It felt a punch to her very heart. As they left the building, Prue glanced at her watch: nine thirty.

Primrose ordered the stag-men into ten rows of ten. They were a terrifying sight, standing in the deserted streets, their imposing machine bodies and antlers bathed in the eerie reddish-orange light of the blood moon.

Primrose addressed them. "I am your master and you are here with one purpose: to take the Guild for our own. Without me you are slaves to a system which values only those in their first lives. Those at the Guild bring spirits into this world in order to do their bidding, to serve and exist for the good of those in their first life. You are in your second life, you are the power. They are nothing like you. On my command – forward!"

The stag-men marched, legs and arms in time. Prue glanced at Edwin and they followed.

"Give it a minute," she said. "As soon as we're among the dense trees we'll be able to break away more easily – Primrose will be leading, so hopefully he'll be too busy looking forward to notice. If we head southwest, we should hit the back of the factorium and be able to get to the tower before they make it through the forest. If we can run fast enough." She prayed that they could.

Edwin nodded.

After a minute of trudging along, they hung back. Then, with a nod of agreement, they sped away from the group.

Brambles scratched and tore at Prue's clothes as she ran, her throat stinging from gasping the cold air. She kept her eyes focused on Edwin leaping in front. She could still hear the stealthy rhythm of the stag-men's footsteps in the distance. Somewhere above the trees, lights erupted in the night sky, making Prue flinch.

"It's just fireworks. Must be part of the events," Edwin called.

She tried to push thoughts of Francis stuck in

that terrible body out of her mind. She'd find a way to get him out and into something else. She had to – she couldn't lose him again. But they had to reach the tower before it was too late.

The trees opened up and they were suddenly in the vegetable patch behind the factorium. They sped onwards.

*

Agapantha connected the machinery and angled the transmitter. Cora was still singing alongside the fireworks, which were reaching a dramatic crescendo.

She prayed that she had got the calculations right and that it would work. She took her notepad from her jacket pocket and double checked them, just in case.

As the final fireworks exploded, she glanced out of the window, even though the height of the tower made her head swim. But this was too important to let that get in the way.

Then she dropped her notebook to the floor – at the forest edge, an orderly group of great antler headed figures emerged, almost as though the forest itself had come to life and the trees had broken free from their roots to march on the factorium. They trudged forward, unseen, as the crowd whooped at the last of the fireworks. Agapantha stared in horror. There were so many of them.

She snapped herself out of it, then furiously finished checking the dials and readings, just as the last of the stag-men filtered on to the great lawn.

Ten orderly lines of stag-men stood on the white lawn of the factorium with Craftsman Primrose at the front.

Like a ripple fading in a lake, the crowd below fell silent as they saw what was before them.

*

As they rounded the west side of the factorium, the burn in Prue's legs made her want to collapse, but somehow she forced them to keep going.

The fireworks had stopped. The crowd was silent in shock. She heard the voice of Primrose boom across the field.

"Ladies and Gentlemen, now that we have your

374

undivided attention, it is time for a new order of events to unfold."

"Quick, Ed, you're faster!" Prue panted.

Edwin bounded towards the messenger tower.

Up above, Agapantha's hand wavered. She glanced quickly at her watch. Prue had said nine forty-five, hadn't she? She moved her finger down towards the button.

"Stop!" Edwin called, as he flew into the room.

Agapantha whipped her head around.

"Edwin?"

"It's Francis, Prue's brother – we accidentally harnessed him!"

"What?" Agapantha said, aghast.

"He's one of the stag-men!"

"Were we too late?" Prue said desperately as she ran into the room and fell to her knees at the top of the staircase, her voice hoarse from the cold and her legs unable to take another step.

"No, they're still there," said Edwin.

Prue crawled to the window. She had no idea which of the stag-men was Francis.

The three of them watched from the tower as Master Woolstenbury walked confidently to stand before Primrose.

"Surrender in peace, or my army will advance and rip apart anyone in their way," said Primrose.

"Charles, what exactly is going on? What are you trying to achieve?" Master Woolstenbury sounded shocked, but her voice remained forceful.

"We are here to take the Guild for our own, and the Sovereign Chancellery with it. You've made every decision for personifates for eighteen years; it's time to redress the balance."

"Charles, you know very well that I can't just hand over the Guild to you. Come and talk, we can sort things out. Whatever you have become so aggrieved about can be addressed."

He shook his head. "I tried to talk, eight years ago."

"Eight years ago? What do you mean?"

"Don't you remember? You told me I showed such promise. It turns out you were right."

Master Woolstenbury took a step backwards. She put her hand to her mouth. "It can't be?"

The rest of the masters joined Master Woolstenbury, and a line of personifates formed to the sides of them: Zareen, the guard bear personifates, a winged wolf and Gisella the golden eagle.

"Charles? What's going on?" said Master White.

"Amelia, this is your final chance. You and the masters need to surrender the Guild. I don't want to harm you unless I have to." He raised an arm and the first line of the stag-men took a step forward.

Master White looked at Master Woolstenbury.

"We can't let you take the Guild," Master Woolstenbury said firmly.

"In a way, I was hoping you'd say that." Craftsman Primrose let his arm fall; the stag-men began their advance. Master Woolstenbury nodded to Zareen and the lynx personifate surged forwards, followed by the other personifates in line.

"The rest of you get back inside the factorium!" Master Woolstenbury shouted to the crowd behind.

Zareen reached the first stag-man and leapt for it, but it caught her around the throat and threw her to the ground. She cried out and scrambled backwards. The black bear and Master Sollentude both ran towards the same stag-man, Sollentude brandishing a spade as a makeshift weapon. The winged wolf took flight with the eagle and they soared above, then pitched into a dive attacking from above, claws bared, but the antlers were impossible to get through, and the eagle took a nasty tear to her chest. The bear reared on its hind legs and brought the weight of its body on to one of the stag-men, knocking it back, but it kicked the bear away like a puppy. Sollentude ducked, dived and lurched with the spade as one tried to grab him. It swiped and just caught him, so a strip of red appeared on his face.

Prue looked on in horror as the dark figures collided on the moonlit lawn. The Guild personifates and masters were no match for the stag-men. What sort of life was this for her brother? Brought back to be a killer? And what was her brother's second life to be, in this machine? She remembered her mother's warning with horror: he had become the monster her mother had feared. And what would become of her parents if Primrose got his way? She took the transmitter from her bag and carefully checked the switch was still down. She looked back at the stag-men.

And in that moment, she realized what she had to do.

"Agapantha, get down there and make sure

every one of the Guild personifates return to the factorium – now!"

She nodded and ran downstairs.

"Ed, help me make sure the parabolic reflector is angled to get all of the stag-men."

She watched from the window as Agapantha emerged from the tower below.

"Agapantha! Stay back!" yelled Master White, as soon as she caught sight of Agapantha running towards her. Prue could barely make out their hurried conversation in the darkness. Then Master White stepped back and called out, "Personifates, stand down! Get back to the factorium, that's an order!"

Master Woolstenbury was further away with Zareen, facing one of the stag-men and Charles Primrose. She stared at Master White, confused, a suspicious frown on her brow.

"It's no good, the personifates must retreat!" Master White called to her. "Trust me, please!"

The bear, winged wolf and eagle obeyed.

"Ed, is it ready?" Prue asked desperately.

"Yes, but Zareen is in range."

Master Woolstenbury gave Zareen the signal to

fall back. Zareen waivered, then ran. As she did, the stag-man grabbed Master Woolstenbury by the throat.

Prue looked at the stag-men. Francis was there somewhere. Tears streamed down her cheeks. "I'm sorry, Francis. I'm so sorry." Her finger hovered over the button and, for a terrible moment, she didn't know whether she could do it.

Then she felt a paw on her knee. Edwin nodded at her.

She closed her eyes.

Chapter 31

CHARLES PRIMROSE

Francis smiled at Prue, even though he was so weak that he could barely breathe.

"Hey ... be brave... Everything will be all right." *He spoke in starts when he was having trouble breathing. Prue couldn't speak for fear she'd start sobbing and then she wouldn't be able to stop.*

"Thought it might be a good moment ... to tell Mum about ... whose fault the scar really was."

She glanced at his brown eyes, the scar, his brow beaded with sweat.

He winked. "Kidding, Sis."

"You better be." She smiled.

"And that time you … made me go on to the roof."

"That was you!"

"Was it?" he said with a wry smile. "Take care of that hoppity wrench … won't you?"

Prue, Dad and Mum took it in turns to stave off the fever with cold flannels and sleep. The doctor said nothing could be done, but Prue hoped with every fibre of her body until that very last moment that she was wrong.

It happened during the night. Mum and Dad were asleep, Mum in the chair and Dad with his head resting on Mum's leg. Prue was lying on the bed beside her brother when the silence she feared most in the world fell.

*

Prue pressed the button.

There was a sonic whoosh of air, as the pulse radiated towards the stag-men.

Prue forced her eyes open. Like dominoes, the stag-men fell, from one line to the next. As each dropped, it stabbed her heart, like watching Francis die all over again, the pain hot and fierce as lava.

As the last line fell, Prue looked for Primrose, but couldn't see him. Had he run? She rushed from the window, down the stairs and from the tower towards the fallen stag-men. She nudged the bodies, checking their spirits were gone, until she saw why Primrose had seemingly disappeared.

He too had collapsed with the blast.

She crouched beside him. "Craftsman Primrose?"

He wasn't moving. What had happened?

A few metres away, Master Woolstenbury was pushing herself up from where the stag-man had dropped her. She stared at Primrose.

Edwin and Agapantha rushed over.

"What's the matter with him?" Edwin said.

Master Woolstenbury signalled to Master Sollentude. "Check these creatures have really all gone."

Master White stumbled over to them, her face pallid. "Charles?" she said.

"Help me roll him on to his side," said Master Woolstenbury. Prue and Agapantha helped her, then Master Woolstenbury carefully lifted his clothing. "Get me a spirit lamp!"

Edwin ran to fetch one and Master Woolstenbury

examined Craftsman Primrose. A faint line ran down his side.

Prue could hardly believe it. "He was a personifate!"

"It certainly seems so," said Master Woolstenbury, glancing at her.

"What?" said Edwin aghast.

Master White fell to her knees beside the empty shell of Charles Primrose and put a shaking hand to the side seam. "What in all of Medlock?" she said, her voice barely audible. A tear reflected like a moonlit stream on her cheek.

"Wait," Prue said, looking around. "Where's Finblewick?"

"Finblewick? Perhaps you four better come inside and explain exactly what's been happening," said Master Woolstenbury.

"Is everything all right now, Master Woolstenbury?" Governor Watson-Wentworth called from the factorium door. "I was about to step in, of course."

"Thank you, Governor, it's all under control. I suggest everyone returns to the atrium and I'll send for some warm drinks ... and perhaps a dash of rum," she added under her breath. She turned to the three of them. "I will arrange a search for Finblewick and do what I can to appease the Governor, then I expect you all in my office in fifteen minutes." She strode back towards the factorium.

Master White remained staring in disbelief at the body of Charles Primrose. "He was a personifate?"

Prue nodded, still barely able to comprehend it herself. But her mind was also on her parents. "Master White, I'm sorry, I know this must be awful for you, but it's not over. There is still one stag-man left. Primrose sent it to my farm. It was why we couldn't say anything to you; he was going to attack them if he received a signal from this." She held up the transmitter. "We managed to steal it from Primrose, but the stag-man is still there. I need to get to my parents as soon as possible."

She looked at her in disbelief, then nodded. "Of course. We should talk to Master Woolstenbury."

"Please, I can't wait – I need to leave now."

"It's quite out of the question; I can't possibly let you face one of them alone. We can catch the early morning Gigantrak and…"

Prue shook her head emphatically. "I need to get there tonight. What if it decides to attack them regardless?"

"And how do you propose to get there?"

"The night Gigantrak maybe, I don't know!"

Agapantha stepped forward. "It's too late to catch the Gigantrak. But I have an idea that requires your help, Master White." Agapantha looked at Prue and Edwin. "Do you remember we had that conversation with Craftsman Primrose in the library about transferring spirits between bodies, and he said the Guild had tried it before?"

Master White frowned. "What are you getting at, Apprentice Young?"

"Craftsman Shad has a very impressive flying lion in the design studio. It could get to Prue's farm in no time."

"Could we still harness some qwortzite under the moon?" Prue said eagerly.

"The only available qwortzite is in those fallen machines. We'd need to test it before reharnessing, and there wouldn't be time. I'm afraid the only possibility at this moment is to send someone who's already here, and that's quite out of the question."

Silence fell for a moment, then Edwin said boldly, "I could do it."

"Oh no, we'd be breaking at least seven Sovereign Chancellery rules," said Master White.

"I think we may have broken quite a few already this evening, Master White," Agapantha said quietly.

Master White fixed Edwin with her stare. "And there's the chance of things going wrong in the procedure, the risk of losing the frequency altogether, let alone what it may do to your psyche to move bodies. You may not realize how much your mind and body are intrinsically linked now."

"But it has been done successfully before? Without losing the second life memories?" said Edwin.

"There were some developments around thirteen years ago when we were experimenting with transferring qwortzite. It's not the same as harnessing a new wildspark – the frequency is already retained in the qwortzite – therefore the second life memory isn't broken and should remain. Indeed, the Guild managed to change a few personifates and keep their memories intact, but I *must* reiterate that there is still the risk of momentarily disrupting the signal. The research wasn't extensive because Master Woolstenbury realized the stress of having new bodies was too difficult, so the Chancellor and the Guild decided to stop the practice."

"But it did work for those few you tried," Edwin said keenly.

Master White nodded reluctantly.

Prue looked at Edwin. She couldn't believe he would be willing to do this for her and her family. Her heart was tugged by hope, yet also torn at the thought of any risk to Edwin. "You can't do it," she said.

"Prue, I've never been surer. If I could remember my family, I would do this for them, but I can't. You are my family now, and I want to do this. And if something goes wrong, then I will have lived two lives and I'll be the luckiest ghost in the world."

The lawns of the factorium felt frozen in time.

Then Edwin coughed. "Come on, Prue, who am I kidding? I have the chance to become a flying lion! Of course I want to do it!"

Prue and Agapantha exchanged a look and smiled.

"If you're absolutely sure, Edwin?"

"I'm certain."

"Hold on, I haven't agreed yet! And why are you calling Frances *Prue*?" said Master White.

"Oh, we can explain that later," said Prue. "Please, Master White, they are the only family I have left."

"We did just save the Guild, and the Governor," said Agapantha.

Master White looked to the sky and breathed out loudly through her mouth.

"She may be shy, but when she speaks, she always makes the most sense," said Edwin.

*

Master White opened up the inner mechanics of the great winged lion. She scanned the wires and connections. Everything looked intact apart from the missing qwortzite. All the instruments she needed had been laid out neatly beside her. She checked the diagrams again.

Edwin waited quietly on the table. Prue glanced over at him. "Are you certain about this?"

"If you ask me again, I just might bite you in two

when I'm a lion."

She laughed, but it was a nervous laugh.

"Think of your parents, Prue," he said. "There's a personifate out there, *outside Medlock*, terrorizing people. What will that mean for personifates, if that's how the outside world will come to understand who we are? I need to stop him."

She nodded. "But what if..."

Edwin shook his head. "No *what ifs*. *What ifs* are going to get in the way."

"If you could please lay on your side," said Master White.

Edwin lay down.

"I'm opening the mechanical seam." She carefully parted the fur and found the join. She proceeded to set up the wires she needed. Soon she said, "When I remove these connectors, you won't be able to talk any more."

She carefully undid all the connectors and then it was as though the lights suddenly went from Edwin's eyes.

Prue was utterly motionless as she watched Master White, her stomach muscles clenched tight.

Inside Edwin's stoat machine, the qwortzite

glowed iridescent with every colour imaginable and something that seemed to go beyond into another spectrum, lustrous and shimmering. It was still the most beautiful thing Prue had ever seen.

As though handling a delicate snowflake made of the finest glass, Master White removed the qwortzite.

Edwin's limbs were limp, the stoat body just a piece of machinery. Prue bit hard on her lip as Master White carried the qwortzite in the palm of her hands. "It needs the warmth of life to transition."

The winged lion was ready.

"Frances," she glanced up, "or should I say, Prue, can you hand me the micro solder, please, and Agapantha find a mirror just in case he…"

"What?" said Prue, passing her the micro solder.

"In case he loses his second-life memories and imprints again. Agapantha, hold the mirror to its face ready."

Prue and Agapantha exchanged a panicked look.

With a quick fizz of light, Master White connected the first one. She worked deftly, without speaking a word until they were all bridged. She began adjusting the next set of connectors, then carefully she closed the seal and smoothed the fur down. Finally, she stood back. "I'm done."

They stood watching the great animal. Nothing moved. There was no sign of life. Prue felt the swell of tears in the corner of her eyes.

"Give it a moment," said Master White.

"Look!" said Agapantha, pointing to the lion's eyes.

There was a tiny flicker. They all stared in amazement as the eyes slowly opened. It was like watching someone slowly awake from a confusing dream. The lion stared at it's mirror reflection, it's eyes growing wider.

"Edwin, is that you?" said Master White.

The lion's mouth parted a little. "He … hello," he said. "I feel … strange."

There was no denying that it was the voice of a young boy.

"Edwin, it's us; can you see?"

He looked at them and blinked. A frown on his brow.

"Can he remember?" Agapantha said quietly.

Prue rushed to him and peered into his eyes. "It's Prue, you remember, don't you? And Agapantha and Master White." Her voice rose with her heartbeat.

"My body feels so different," he said.

"But can you remember us?"

Then the start of a smile formed. "Hello, Frances." He winked.

"Hello, Jack Swift!" she said and threw her arms around him.

"Jack Swift? Why is everyone changing names?" said Master White.

"I'll explain that later too," said Agapantha.

"Do you think you can stand up yet?" Master White said.

"I'll give it a try."

The huge winged lion rolled from its side. He sprang up on his forepaws to sitting, then powerful back legs bought him to standing. He swayed and stumbled for a moment. "It's all right, I'm just getting a feel for it. Gosh, I'm huge!" Edwin said. He looked at his stoat body on the table nearby. "Wow, was I really that small? And look at the three of you down there all teeny too!"

There was a sudden whoosh of air as the lion's two great wings extended and a great clatter as books and equipment were knocked to the floor.

"Careful!" Master White said.

"Sorry! I'm not used to wings!"

Prue thought it was strange having a huge beast before you and feeling no fear. It was so beautiful – golden white shimmering fur and great feathered wings, and even more unexpected that it spoke with the voice of a boy.

"How do you feel about flying?" Prue said.

Edwin the winged lion smiled. "I can't wait."

Chapter 32

FLIGHT OF A LION

They opened the great window and cold air rushed into the room, fluttering loose paper. There was a small iron-work platform outside the window.

"Edwin, I'll need to get on your back," said Master White.

"There's only room for one," said Prue. "It's best if I go; you don't know the way to the farm, and you and Agapantha would be best explaining everything to Master Woolstenbury."

Master White sighed and nodded. "I suppose it would be best if it was the smallest of us – who knows how much added weight he can bear and still stay in flight?"

Edwin fully extended his wings and beat them once. His body rose easily from the floor before landing again.

"Do you think we'll fit through this window? I feel pretty huge," said Edwin.

"Give it a go!" said Prue.

He put his forepaws on the ledge and climbed out on to the platform. The others hurried to watch as Edwin stood on the platform edge. Falling from this distance would certainly break bones and probably result in lost life. The others watched soundlessly. Edwin tipped forwards. As he dropped, he spread his enormous wings and began gliding down, then his body tumbled head over feet. They all cried out.

"Wings, Ed!" Prue shrieked.

He managed to beat them in huge swathes of power, righting himself and landing clumsily on to the path below.

"Spend a few minutes practising!" Prue called.

She watched him beat his wings and take off again. He flew to the trees, went around in a circle then landed back on the platform.

"Ready?" Edwin asked.

"Always," said Prue, although she felt sick with both the nerves of what her parents could be facing at that moment, and the fact she was about to trust a newborn flying lion machine with her own life. She edged herself out of the window on to the platform.

"Be careful," Master White called.

"You can do it!" said Agapantha.

Prue climbed up on to Edwin's back and held tight to his mane. The synthetic hair was warm, like fur gloves around her hands, his body wide and sturdy. Edwin took a couple of quick steps, flapped his wings, and they began rising up and up above the huge lawn.

"Good job, Ed. Now, head northwards!"

Edwin banked left a bit too sharply, and Prue tensed and yelped.

"Sorry! I'm still getting used to these," Edwin called.

"If you could learn quickly, it would be much appreciated!" Prue cried.

The cold evening air rushed over Prue as everything below became smaller. She looked to her left at the great factorium of the Guild, the illuminated windows now tiny golden lights. What was still left of the crowd below pointed and called out. The burnished copper moon shone high above the forest, tinging the snow-covered grounds with amber. As her gaze moved across the lawn, her breath caught, remembering the stag-men. They were still in neat fallen lines below, and one of them had been Francis.

"I'm so sorry," she said quietly, doing her best to put a wall up to all the emotions she'd felt when she'd pushed the button.

As they rose higher, Medlock was in full view, even more magnificent at night than the day she'd viewed it from the chimney top. Snow-covered domes and spires looked like a man-made mountain range against the night. The lights appeared as though a giant hand had scattered diamonds across the city.

"Wow, look at that!" she called.

"Cool, huh! But there's just one thing," Edwin called. "Everything beyond Medlock looks pretty black to me, and I don't know the way to your farm!"

He was right. It would be hard to navigate by night.

A deep horn sounded in the far distance.

"The evening Gigantrak!" Prue called.

Just outside of Medlock, pale-grey smoke rose in the night sky and fast-moving dots of light travelled swiftly across the landscape. "That Gigantrak goes north to Batterthwaite. Follow it!"

They flew across sweeping fields and glimmering lakes and kept the Gigantrak in sight all the way. It was swift, but Edwin managed to just keep it in sight.

A couple of times Edwin faltered, his wings unexpectedly missing a beat.

"Are you all right?" Prue called.

"I think so – it's as though all of a sudden my mind is confused, and I feel like I'm back in my stoat body. I'll be fine, I just have to focus."

After a couple of hours of increasingly laboured flying, they had reached Batterthwaite. "The next village is Staplefield. Follow the river!" said Prue.

"How are we going to find a stag-man in the dark?" said Edwin. "And what are we going to do when we find it?"

"Well, I don't think we'll be able to reason with it," said Prue.

"Lucky I'm in the body of a lion, then!"

As they flew over North Owlcot, the shape of the landscape in the moonlight was so familiar to Prue.

"Land on the hill over there, behind the trees," she called. "Let's find the stag-man before it sees us."

They looked down on the farm in the valley below. She saw the lights on in her parent's room, and felt relief that everything seemed all right. They were in there, she was sure. But the creature was somewhere down there too. She scanned the moonlit fields for any unfamiliar shape. Her heart missed a beat in a brief moment of mistaking a scarebot for the stag-man.

"Can you see anything?" Edwin whispered.

She shook her head.

"Where would you hide in waiting if you were one of them?" he said.

"Somewhere close enough to act, but far away enough to hide. Where you can see, but not be seen." It was suddenly clear: the place where she and Francis hid on so many occasions.

"Haywood's Oak!" She pointed at the single-standing tree in one of the fields close to the farm. There was nothing there. Then she saw it: a tall shape behind the tree. Antlers, sharp and fierce, tinged with the yellow-orange of the blood moon. It was the stag-man.

"There it is. Now what do we do?" said Edwin. His voice was determined, but Prue felt the quiver in his muscles.

"We need to be quick. I can't quite see, but I'd guess its attention is on the farm. Maybe we should fly in from behind and take it by surprise?"

"Let's do it," he said.

She nodded, but nerves tangled like tree vines in her stomach.

They took flight again, circled back a little, then flew directly towards the oak. When they were almost upon it, the stag-man must have heard the beat of Edwin's wings because it looked up. Edwin and Prue cried out, an instinctive, fierce battle cry. There was a moment of confusion as they landed and Edwin bounded forwards, towards it. But it quickly recovered and began running away towards the house. It was incredibly fast, and as Edwin chased after it, it became clear they weren't going to catch it.

"Jump off, then I'll be quicker," Edwin called.

Without thinking, Prue took a great leap, tumbling and crashing into the barley field. She jumped to her feet and scrambled to the top of the nearest bale. More lights came on in the farmhouse.

Edwin had caught up with the stag-man who had stopped and turned back. They stood face to face, only a few metres from each other, eyes locked.

Mrs and Mr Haywood emerged from the house. "What's going on out here?" Mrs Haywood called. But Prue's parents froze in their tracks as they saw the stag-man and great winged lion.

"It's over. Primrose is dead and so are the rest of the stag-men," said Edwin.

"Who are you?" it hissed.

"I believe we've already met, actually. You attacked us in the forest."

The stag-man tilted his skull-like head. "Where is the master?"

"Your master is gone. He's dead."

The stag-man let out a coarse rasping noise.

"Give yourself up and we'll see you're looked after," Prue called.

The stag-man glanced in her direction.

"Prue! Is that you?" Mr Haywood called.

"Gone?" said the stag-man.

Edwin nodded.

"Then no more waiting." The stag-man reared back, then leapt. Edwin ducked, but sharp claws swiped across his face and Prue cried out for him. He was just a boy in his first life and then a stoat in his second, thought Prue; he doesn't know how to fight.

"Kill those in our way," the stag-man said, almost robotically, stalking around Edwin.

"Stay back," Edwin called, his voice plainly that of a scared young boy.

The stag-man flew at him again and slashed across his face. Edwin's head lurched to the side. He staggered.

"No!" Prue cried.

"Kill," the stag-man sneered.

Edwin bounded at him, but the stag-man darted to the side.

Then, with brutal intent, it put its head down and hurtled towards him, its vicious antlers blade sharp.

Prue yelped.

Edwin managed to leap out of the way, and the stag-man tumbled, but it was soon on its feet again, readying for its next move.

She had to do something. "Hey, think you're clever? Catch me!" She jumped from the haystack and started running.

"Prue! What are you doing?" Edwin called.

The stag-man turned on its heels and sped after her.

"Prue!" he yelled.

Her parents shouted too, but all Prue could hear was her desperate breaths and the thumping feet of the stag-man moments away. She darted left and right but it was gaining with every step.

The stag-man sprang for Prue, its arms reaching out, claws inches from her. She cried out.

Edwin hurtled after them, his mighty paws crashing across the field. With an almighty leap, Edwin bounded on top of the stag-man, bringing it crashing violently down. "You don't touch her!" he spat. With that he grabbed the stag-man between great powerful jaws and bolted it from side to side as fast as he could, until the stag-man's body suddenly lost all resistance and became limp in his mouth. He dropped it to the floor.

Prue lay panting. "Is it gone?"

"I think I shook it enough to dislodge the wildspark from its qwortzite." Edwin pushed it with his paw. The stag-man was just a body – an empty machine now. "Prue, it could've killed you! What were you thinking, taunting it like that!" said Edwin.

"I was thinking that there was probably no way you'd let it." She smiled.

"Yet another risky plan," said Edwin, flopping to the ground. "I rather hope our friendship quietens down a bit. You're exhausting."

"What in all the haystacks is going on here!" said Mr Haywood, rushing to them.

"Mum! Dad!" called Prue.

She ran towards them and was engulfed in their arms.

"What in the blazes!" Mrs Haywood said.

"It's fine! The lion's a friend, that thing … not so much. But it's gone now. It's all right; the lion is a personifate second lifer – just a boy really. He's my friend…" She thought for a moment on the best way to introduce him. "This is Jack Swift."

"Pleased to meet you." Edwin smiled shyly.

Mrs Haywood was staring at him, her mouth wide open.

"Mum, he's my friend. And he just saved all of us."

Mrs Haywood nodded.

"Well, this is not the night I was expecting!" said Mr Haywood. "Let's get inside. Explanations are more palatable over a cocoa with cookies."

Soon they were sitting in the farmhouse kitchen drinking steaming cocoa and eating oat biscuits, although Edwin had to sit outside with his head poking through the kitchen window as he was too large to fit through the front door. Prue told the story of what had brought them to that moment.

"You know I love you, Prue, but it'll take me time to get used to all this change," Mrs Haywood said, glancing across at Edwin.

"I can't believe that thing was prowling in our fields! I told you I thought I heard something strange the other day," said Mr Haywood, nudging Mrs Haywood.

"I'm just glad you're all right," said Mrs Haywood. "Both of you." She nodded at Edwin.

"Sometimes, you've just got to do the next brave thing," said Prue, but really she was thinking of what she'd had to do to Francis back at the Guild. She didn't think she'd ever be able to tell her parents.

Edwin looked at her. "Prue is one of the bravest people I know."

"Well, it's incredibly late. You both need to rest after all this travel and excitement!" said Mrs Haywood.

She took Prue upstairs and Mr Haywood insisted on making Edwin a bed in the hay shed by piling blankets all around.

Mrs Haywood kissed her on the head. "I'm sorry, about everything. About what happened to Francis, about not saying goodbye when you visited, about—"

"Mum, Francis wasn't your fault."

Mrs Haywood closed her eyes. "I still miss him so much."

"We all do," Prue said. They hugged and cried in silence for a while.

Eventually, Mrs Haywood pulled Prue's blanket over her.

"Like I say, all this change and technology, it might take me a while."

"I'm sorry. I know you hoped I would take over the farm, with Francis gone and everything."

"We only ever want what makes you happy, Prue. Always know that."

Prue closed her eyes and let the events of the day roll through her mind until deep and restful sleep engulfed her in its warm arms.

Chapter 33

NEW BEGINNINGS

Snow had fallen more heavily in the early part of the morning, completely covering the body of the stag-man so that only a large white antlered mound remained.

Prue dressed hurriedly and ran down to find Edwin in the shed.

"Ed, are you all right?"

He nodded, although Prue sensed something in him was reluctant.

"Are you injured?" she asked.

"I don't think so."

Prue sat beside him. "I've just realized that we no

longer have a mentor. Are we even part of the Guild any more?"

"Of course … I'm certain we are."

But Prue wasn't so sure. "Are you really feeling all right?"

"I feel a little strange. But that's only natural … after the night we had, right?"

Prue didn't like the way he faltered in his words. It reminded her of Luella.

"Are you ready to go back?" he said.

Prue nodded. "I still have so many questions about Craftsman Primrose and what happened. If I'm thrown out of the Guild, I'd like to go knowing the whole truth. But are you well enough to fly?"

He nodded.

After a quick breakfast, they said goodbye to Mr and Mrs Haywood and set off back to the Guild.

They flew high over perfect, snow-blanketed hills and frozen lakes, avoiding flying directly over towns and houses where possible; there would be enough of an uproar in Medlock, let alone creating one in the countryside.

On a couple of occasions, Edwin's wings faltered again, and they dipped, making Prue cling tightly to his mane.

"I'm sorry!" he called. "This body is … different."

Prue softly patted his head. "You're doing brilliantly." But she had a terrible feeling that he was failing in his new body, and she sensed he knew it too. "Thank you for everything, Jack Swift," she whispered.

He didn't talk much for the rest of the journey. Prue felt he needed all his concentration to fly. Rising panic was building in her that if he was in this new body much longer it would all go terribly wrong. It had been bad enough being so close to Francis again and then losing him for a second time. She couldn't bear the thought of anything happening to Edwin too.

After a couple of hours, to her relief, the great thrum of the city came into view with smoke rising from chimneys, piercing spires, domes and rooftops one on top of another as far as the eye could see. They saw the great square from above and navigated from there to the Guild house. They drew some attention from below with people looking and pointing, having not seen a personifate quite as magnificent before.

Edwin dropped Prue off in the street outside the Guild house.

"I'll fly to the factorium and update Master White. You tell Agapantha and the others," he said.

"I'd rather go with you," she protested.

"Agapantha will be worried. You should see her. I'll be fine."

"You need to get back into your old body as soon as possible," she blurted.

He paused, looking deep into her eyes and nodded. "I know. See you soon." And with that, he took flight.

Prue watched him grow smaller in the distance, her heart tight. She took a breath and let herself into the house. She found Lavender, Liddy, Queen Adelaide, Abel from the gardens, and some of the other apprentices in the dining room. A hush came over the room. Lavender rushed over and embraced her.

"Oh, my dear. Thank goodness you're all right."

Liddy hugged her next. "What a business! I can't believe you've survived without a scratch."

Cora glanced up from her lunch. "Oh great, you're back," she said flatly.

"Nice to see you too, Cora," said Prue. And meant it.

"Where's the little one?"

"He's needed to see Master White right away," Prue said, a lump in her throat.

Agapantha ran into the room, "You're back!" she cried, in the loudest voice Prue had ever heard her use. Agapantha instantly turned a shade of scarlet as everyone stared.

"Now, where were we with the snow plans?" Liddy said.

Agapantha pulled Prue into the parlour. "Are you all right, Prue? Is Edwin all right?"

Prue smiled. "He's fine." She crossed her fingers tightly at her side. "And I am too." She had so many mixed emotions: the weight of responsibility in pressing the button, the constant pain in her chest over Francis, relief that the stag-men were gone, worry for Edwin, and she didn't even know where to start when she thought about Craftsman Primrose. He'd been a ghost all along. No wonder he felt so strongly about personifate rights. But she still had so many questions.

Lavender popped her head around the door. "I'm

so glad you're safe. You can update us on the details later, but Master Woolstenbury sent a note over asking if you would visit her at the factorium the moment you return."

Prue glanced at Agapantha.

"It'll be fine, I'm sure," Agapantha said.

*

The factorium looked magnificent, as though frozen in time. It seemed like the previous evening hadn't happened; the stag-men bodies had been removed, and a fresh layer of snow had reset time.

Prue looked around, but Edwin was nowhere to be seen, so she trudged through the snow to the factorium and went straight to Master Woolstenbury's office. She took a long breath, then knocked.

"Come in."

Prue opened the door and Master Woolstenbury was sitting at her desk waiting for her. She entered nervously.

"Take a seat, Prudence."

Prue winced at hearing her true name.

"Yes, word has got back to me." Master Woolstenbury raised an eyebrow.

Prue sat down. The leather on the seat creaked.

"Apprentice Snow-Moon informed Master White that your parents were quite safe and the last stag-man has been dealt with."

Prue nodded, relief flooding through her that Edwin had returned safely.

"Good."

There was an awkward silence as Master Woolstenbury observed her with steel eyes. A wood-pigeon cooed outside.

The knot in Prue's stomach twisted.

"I wanted to personally thank you for what you did for the Guild, and for me."

Prue frowned; she wasn't expecting a thank you after all the rules she had broken.

"Things have become clear through the night – the Sovereign Chancellery guards caught up with Finblewick, who was waiting on the forest edge and was missed by the blast. He filled in the missing pieces."

Prue sat forward.

"You understand that Governor Watson-Wentworth

wants to keep the whole incident as quiet as possible. Such things would only be fuel for the ASL and RfP."

Relief rapidly turned to disappointment. Could it be that Master Woolstenbury wasn't going to tell her anything about Charles Primrose?

"But I feel that those in the Guild need a truthful overview, and you at least deserve the full details."

Master Woolstenbury stood and picked up a painting that was propped against the side of the wall. She brought it to her desk and turned it around for Prue to see. Prue frowned; it was a painting of the intelligent-looking hare from the Hall of Lost Personifates. She remembered its name – Carl something – a technician.

"I don't understand," Prue said.

"About eight years ago, a hare personifate called Carl Cold-Moon was found in a similar situation to the jackalope personifate who was brutally killed not long after you arrived at the Guild. We put Carl's untimely death down to a wild animal attack too. Everyone was mortified – not only for the brutal loss of a second life too early, but he was well known among the craftsman and a friend to me. You see, he showed such technical promise and was an absolute talent for precision design."

"I'm not sure I'm following you, Master Woolstenbury."

"Does it help if I tell you that Carl is a variant of Charles?"

There was a strange moment where all the mixed-up jigsaw pieces in Prue's mind began to organize themselves.

"Craftsman Primrose?" she said breathlessly. It wasn't Charles Primrose's first time in a personifate body!

"Indeed. I wanted Carl to be an apprentice, but the Governor then wouldn't allow it. It appears Carl harboured a grudge that grew. He confided in Finblewick, a fairly new personifate who had rather an experimental body built at a time when we allowed the apprentices to have more autonomy in their designs. Finblewick begrudged his appearance and Carl formed a friendship with him, knowing he needed an ally for his plans.

"Carl used his incredible aptitude and skill to craft a human personifate body in secret. Then when it was ready, eight years ago, he enlisted Finblewick to help, with the promise of a new body.

But he needed Finblewick to stay as he was for the time being. Whether he used his original qwortzite or found a way to transfer his wildspark signal from one piece to another is unclear. He then planted his old hare personifate body to look like a wild animal attack and faked his death. He knew that in human form he could achieve anything he wanted to. But his ambitions seem to have exceeded him."

Prue was astonished. It all made sense now.

Master Woolstenbury put the painting back against the wall and sat back down opposite Prue.

"I'm sorry for not seeing what was going on under my own nose and not protecting you from danger. The Sovereign Chancellery and their ridiculous demands for one hundred personifates rather blinded us to bigger matters."

There was another moment of uncomfortable silence before Master Woolstenbury continued.

"I also wanted to show you something, something I wish I'd shown you before." She turned a picture on her desk around. "This is my daughter, Ferne."

A girl around Prue's age smiled back at her.

"She died when she was only twelve."

"Oh, I'm sorry," said Prue. It was terrible for a

parent to lose a child. She'd not wish to see anyone go through what her parents had endured.

"It was a long time ago, but as you know, a wound is left in your heart that never heals. No matter how inventively we look to fill it. I searched for years; it was what drove me to succeed. I was always interested in what happens beyond, from a young age, but after Ferne, and when I was so close to discovering qwortzite and the connection, I became obsessed with finding her and bringing her back."

Prue swallowed. She knew exactly what she meant.

"I never found her, Prue. And no good can come of trying to make it happen. As you may have guessed, I have confiscated your adapted GODAR machine."

Cora must have told her. She would certainly be told to leave now.

"What we do at the Guild … it's complicated, and not just scientifically, but morally. You understand that, don't you? Your invention presents a real danger to all personifates too."

She nodded, even though she didn't really understand.

"Perhaps we're all still finding our feet and learning. I hope we can all grow from this ghastly experience." Master Woolstenbury clasped her hands together. "Taking all this into consideration and the fact you find yourself without a mentor, I'm afraid it leaves both you and me in an unusual situation. One I believe I have an answer to. I wonder if you would accept an offer of transferring your apprenticeship to a new mentor?"

Prue's eyes lit up. Despite having to let go of Francis and her mission to bring him back, she found she wanted to stay at the Guild more than anything. Right now she would have taken anyone as a mentor, even Sollentude. "I'd like that very much!"

"Good. Then I shall expect to see you after the winter break. You will report directly to me."

"To … you?"

"I haven't taken on an apprentice in years. I feel it may be time for a change. I plan to speak to Apprentice Snow-Moon too. There's never been a more important time to ensure the success of a personifate apprentice."

Prue beamed. "Thank you!"

"Of course, you understand that remaining

here is on the strict condition that you give up your memory plans and all related machinery?"

Prue nodded.

Master Woolstenbury put her hands together. "Good. Now, I've called a meeting in the atrium in an hour to bring everyone together. I will see you then."

*

Prue felt like the past day had been a dream. As she walked back through the atrium, she half expected Craftsman Primrose to appear. Despite his crazed plan, she found she missed him. After all, without him she would never have been here.

Abel had put some star-shaped blue and pink flowers in a vase close to the entrance. She took a couple then glanced at the corridor which led to the Hall of Lost Personifates.

Inside it was utterly silent. Not a cold silence, but peaceful. She passed a gap where the painting of the storm-grey hare with intelligent eyes had been, and thought about the second day at the Guild, when Craftsman Primrose had brought them here. The plaque remained below the empty space.

Carl Cold-Moon
Technician
Capax Infiniti

"Holding the infinite," she said quietly. What and who had Craftsman Primrose been in his first life? It was probable that she'd never know. She wondered if Master Woolstenbury would return the painting to the room.

She moved further down the hall to where Edwin's painting of Luella rested, carefully laid the flowers on the floor below, then put her fingertips to the pigeon's chest. "Thank you for being a friend. Maybe you're somewhere with Francis now, looking out for each other. I think you'd get on brilliantly." She smiled at the thought.

She regarded it for a minute longer, thinking of everything that had happened, how a few moon-cycles had felt like a lifetime. Then she took something from her pocket and left the room.

The door gently clicked shut behind her.

Back in the Hall of Lost Personifates, tucked inside the frame of Luella Harvest-Moon's painting, was the picture of Francis grinning and leaning against a mechanimal plough horse.

*

As Prue walked back through the atrium, she suddenly caught sight of something moving in the white through the window. She ran outside.

Two beady eyes blinked in the snow, then Edwin bounded towards her.

"You're you again!" she cried. Relief, warm and soothing, coursed through her.

"Master White returned me to my real body straight away. It was fun being a flying lion for a while, but she thought that a quick transferral back would be the least risk to my wildspark signal."

"It's good to have you back. I mean, how would you be able to sit on my shoulder as a flying lion?"

"You've not been thrown out of the Guild, then?"

"Not yet!" Prue tapped her shoulder. "Hop up for a moment, Jack Swift, if it's not invading your personal space?"

Edwin scampered up to sit on her shoulder and they took a walk along the path. Abel was in the distance by the gates, shoveling away.

"Are you really all right?" Prue asked. "This week has been pretty overwhelming."

He nodded. "More to the point, are *you* all right? What happened with your brother, what you had to do... I mean, Prue, that must've been a terrible choice. I can't even imagine how you did it."

"I'm glad I've got you to talk to about it. You're the only one who saw Francis; if you hadn't witnessed it, I would have thought I'd imagined it."

"I'm glad too."

"In truth, I still don't know what to make of it all. I can't help but think that Charles Primrose had a point, even if he chose a rather extreme way to try and tackle it."

Edwin looked at her. "I feel the same."

"But I know that it was right to let go of Francis, that I have to move on, find my own way."

Prue trudged along the path. It was just like the first day she'd arrived at the factorium, yet her world had changed so much. "Is there a part of you that would want to be back inside a human body, if you had the chance?"

Edwin was quiet for a moment. "It was a bit confusing changing bodies back then, but given the chance to be the first-lifer boy me? Yes, I think I would take it."

Prue wondered again what he would have looked like in his first life. How he might have died. She wondered what it would feel like not to know.

"Master Woolstenbury has taken my adapted GODAR, so there will be no more name discovery for now."

"That doesn't surprise me. At least I got to find out my real name first."

"And she had some news for us," said Prue. She paused and turned back to face the factorium. She glanced at Edwin. "She's taking us on as apprentices!"

Edwin laughed. "What? Are you serious?"

"She's going to tell you herself, but, yes!"

"That, I didn't expect!"

Agapantha appeared from the nearby transport hut. She waved and jumped through the snow towards them. "Ed!" She picked him up and hugged him, then grabbed Prue and pulled her in too. "What did Master Woolstenbury say?"

"Well, we've not been thrown out of the Guild. And it seems we have ourselves a new mentor."

"Craftsman Shad? Oh, is it Master Tinubu? She'll be brilliant… No wait – it's not Sollentude, is it?" Agapantha grimaced.

"It's Master Woolstenbury."

Her mouth opened wide. "No way! Wow!"

"On the condition that I let go of my plans to bring back memory."

"Are you all right about that? What with Francis and everything."

Prue nodded. Even though it still compressed her throat to think about it, the moment she'd decided to press the button, she'd known it had to be that way.

More apprentices began emerging from the transport hut.

"Come on," said Prue, tapping her shoulder for Edwin to jump back up and hooking Agapantha's arm. "We'd better get to this meeting."

Subdued light filtered through the snow-specked glass ceiling, high above the central atrium. Below was packed with members of the Guild, and every personifate who worked there – Prue spotted Phineas and Zareen chatting together. They looked across and smiled. Edwin nudged Prue and gestured to Thackery the thunderbird personifate who was perched on an iron railing not far away, talking with Queen Adelaide.

"It wouldn't surprise me if I was royalty too," Thackery said. "Did I mention I was the fastest in the messenger tower?" He ruffled his feathers.

"Four times," Queen Adelaide said snootily.

The three apprentices stood in the spot they had been in the first morning at the Guild. Soon Master Woolstenbury appeared and silence fell. She recounted the events, leaving some of the details out that she'd given Prue. She impressed how pulling together and solidarity would be vital in the coming times and how the events must stay within their walls. Zareen appeared and passed a note to Master Woolstenbury. She read it quickly then spoke.

"Governor Watson-Wentworth thanks you all for your discretion in this incident. He would also like me to iterate that he knows about the use of the unlicensed personifate and he's agreed to overlook it, just this once."

"Just this once? After we prevented the downfall of the Guild and his Sovereign Chancellery?" Prue whispered to Edwin. He shook his head.

"Now, I would like to personally thank the people without whom the events of yesterday could have had dire consequences for all of us. Apprentices Haywood, Snow-Moon and Young."

Heads turned in their direction. Prue could almost feel the warmth of Agapantha's burning cheeks beside her.

"These three apprentices showed great initiative and courage against a terrible foe. And we thank them for their service to the Guild." Master Woolstenbury started clapping and everyone joined in.

"It was more luck than judgement," Cora whispered from behind. "And I don't care if you saved the Guild, you three are still weird." She shook her head.

"If that's what we are, I'm pretty proud of it," said Prue.

*

The snow continued to fall for the following week and Master Woolstenbury declared the winter break early. The great lawns in front of the factorium became everyone's favourite place for sledging and snow fights.

"My parents' letter said the snow is so deep that all the mechanicarts between Batterthwaite and North Owlcot are out of action, so I'm going to stay here for Yule. What are you all doing?" said Prue.

Agapantha was scribbling calculations on a notepad. "Mine are off on some jaunt to New Mercia – I think word is out about the stag-men, and they're keen to find out more about the ancient myths and customs. They think they might hold the key to transferring frequency across qwortzite in a sustainable way. So, I'm staying here," she said.

"Well, this is my home, so I'm staying put," said Edwin.

Something flew through the air close by – Abel was launching snowballs with a spade.

"Excellent!" said Edwin, leaping and gathering a handful of snow to launch back.

Lavender emerged from the factorium with Phineas bearing a tray full of steaming cups of cocoa and spicy gingerbread.

"Brilliant, I'm ravenous!" said Agapantha running towards them.

Prue stood for a moment and watched her friends.

"Francis, you can't launch a snowball from a

hoppity wrench!"

"An adapted hoppity wrench, Prudence Haywood."

"Let's see then." She folded her arms.

"I've added the super hop. Just clip the arms back like so, place the snowball here, then release the restrainer, and..."

The snowball hurtled through the air and smacked Prue in the chest.

"Hey!" she laughed, grabbing great handfuls of snow.

"Ed, Ag!" she called. "Wait for me!"

Prue's mum was wrong when she'd said time flowed like the river and there's not a thing you can do about it. Yes, time flowed, but you could swim in different parts of the river if you wanted, you could swing over it, even change its course if you really wanted to.

Things hadn't worked out as she'd planned. Prue had come to the Guild looking for Francis and it wasn't at all what she had expected. She understood that some things couldn't be fixed, but she *could* make a difference. Time was ever-moving and so was the world around her. She didn't know what that meant for first and second lifers, and the rights of the personifates, but she was certain that whatever that future was, she was going to put herself right at the heart of finding the best way.

And she would have two extraordinary friends beside her.

Acknowledgements

This story blossomed from seed to fully realized world faster than the Gigantrak racing to Medlock, and I couldn't have done it without two incredible people. For me they are the best in the business and both deserving of a ruby jacket. The guidance from my lovely agent, Kate Shaw, set me on track at an early stage – she really is a one-in-a-million (and I'm never letting go!). My editor, Linas Alsenas, is a gem of a human and also someone I adore working with – a story wizard of the very highest level. This book really wouldn't be what it is without you, and I hope I get to work with you on many, many more stories! My heartfelt and endless thanks to you both.

The whole team at Scholastic are simply wonderful, and a huge thank you to every shining cog in the wheel there, especially Tanya Harris-Brown, Eishar Brar, Harriet Dunlea, Peter Matthews, Jenna Mackintosh, and when it comes to book design, Scholastic's Jamie Gregory is without doubt a complete master. His stunning eye for what works and attention to detail utterly wows me, and I couldn't have hoped for a better design. George Ermos, the cover illustrator, is also a marvel, injecting his creative magic into creating a scene that exceeds my hopes and dreams.

Continued thanks to the many booksellers, book bloggers, educators, librarians, reviewers, and fellow writers out there, championing stories with your hearts and souls. You are utter marvels. A special shout out to the teachers who have used *Brightstorm* so creatively – your support is so appreciated, and I hope *Wildspark* gives you a world to run with too! Thanks to my friends and family for continued support while writing this, especially Darren, Meg, Sammy, Poppy, Mum, James, Lorraine, Jen, Sinéad, Lucy, Ness, the Golden Egg crew and Kate Gieler of my patron of reading school – you rock, Glebies!

Lastly, and of course most importantly, I'm looking at you, the reader, holding this book in your hands right now. Thank you for running away to Medlock with Prue (you rebel!). Now go and dream big. Invent the incredible.

Vashti Hardy is the author of *Brightstorm*, the Bookseller Association's Children's Book of the Season (Spring 2018). An active member of the Golden Egg Academy, she lives near Brighton with her family.

Follow Vashti on Twitter **@vashti_hardy**